# NEVER A FUGITIVE

# BOOKS BY JAN THOMPSON

## Romantic Suspense/Thrillers

**Protector Sweethearts** (6 Books)

JanThompson.com/protector

**Defender Sweethearts** (6 Books)

JanThompson.com/defender

**Binary Hackers** (4 Books)

JanThompson.com/binary

## City/Coastal/Beach Romance

**Seaside Chapel** (7 Books)

JanThompson.com/seaside

**Savannah Sweethearts** (12 Books)

JanThompson.com/savannah

**Vacation Sweethearts** (8 Books)

JanThompson.com/vacation

JanThompson.com/books

# NEVER A FUGITIVE

## DEFENDER SWEETHEARTS
### BOOK 3

## JAN THOMPSON

Never a Fugitive (Defender Sweethearts Book 3)

Author Website: JanThompson.com
Book News: JanThompson.com/newsletter

Published by Georgia Press LLC

eBook Cover Design: Lynnette Bonner
Paperback Cover Design: Lynnette Bonner and Rocking Book Covers

eBook ISBN: 978-1-944188-88-7
Paperback ISBN: 978-1-944188-89-4

*To my Lord and Savior, Jesus Christ, who died on the cross to save me from my sins and rose again from the grave to give me eternal life in heaven.*

*For God so loved the world that He gave His only begotten Son, that whoever believes in Him should not perish but have everlasting life.*
*—John 3:16*

# READ A FREE EBOOK IN THE SAME STORY WORLD

Set in Georgia, South Carolina, and Tennessee, this clean and wholesome Christian romance tells the story of art gallery archivist Sheryl Breckenridge and world-famous sculptor Winton Pace. Read this ebook for free!

*Time for Me* (A Vacation Sweethearts Prequel)
JanThompson.com/time-free

## ABOUT DEFENDER SWEETHEARTS
### CHRISTIAN ROMANTIC SUSPENSE NOVELS

Defender Sweethearts is a sister series to the Protector Sweethearts Christian romantic suspense collection. While the heroes in Protector Sweethearts search for lost treasures and lost people, the Defender Sweethearts novels focus on protecting the helpless and hopeless.

- Book 1: *Never a Traitor*
- Book 2: *Never a Hostage*
- Book 3: *Never a Fugitive*
- Book 4: *Always a Maverick*
- Book 5: *Always a Champion*
- Book 6: *Always a Guardian*

For more information about Defender Sweethearts:
JanThompson.com/defender

# ABOUT NEVER A FUGITIVE
## DEFENDER SWEETHEARTS BOOK 3

*A grieving brother.*
*A former mistress.*
*A stash of stolen secrets.*

A grieving accountant seeking justice for his murdered

brother finds himself on the run with a senator's former mistress who knows too many secrets.

## Starting his own investigation...

After his brother is killed by a car bomb, Armin Dhillon quits his job to conduct his own investigation into the murder. His efforts lead him to a former senator's ex-mistress who is now a devout Christian trying to leave her past behind. Only her sordid past won't let her go, and neither will Armin, who thinks she has the answer that will bring closure for his family.

## Stuck together for better or for worse...

Kelsey Murphy wants to start over with a new life in Christ, but her old career keeps telling her that she's unworthy and must pay some sort of penance. The FBI finds her and asks for her help to take down some money-laundering criminals related to the former senator. Thrown together for a common cause, Armin and Kelsey find that they have no choice but look out for each other.

## Solutions are nowhere to be found...

Thrown together, Armin and Kelsey find that they like each other's company. All around them, mirages appear. Things are not what they seem to be. Friends may not be friends. Enemies may not be enemies. But they all have the same goal: to get to the stash of seventeen billion dollars worth of cryptocurrencies. Will they be able to wade through the fog of misinformation to get to the truth? The winners take all, or do they?

*Never a Fugitive* is Book 3 in *USA Today* bestselling author Jan Thompson's Defender Sweethearts Christian romantic suspense collection, a sister series to Protector Sweethearts. While the heroes in Protector Sweethearts search for lost treasures and lost people, the Defender Sweethearts novels focus on protecting the helpless and hopeless. The main characters in Defender Sweethearts come from the supporting cast in Protector Sweethearts.

*Never a Fugitive* (Defender Sweethearts Book 3)
JanThompson.com/traitor

Defender Sweethearts
JanThompson.com/defender

For Book News from Jan Thompson:
JanThompson.com/newsletter

# NEVER A FUGITIVE

# CHAPTER ONE

Kelsey Murphy crouched down in the narrow space between the kitchen sink and the small bathroom of the camper van. She resisted looking behind her, where the only thing separating her and the sounds of gunshots in the dark campground outside was an old bedsheet taped over a broken back window.

The other windows had blinds, but the left back window above the full-sized mattress had been shattered hours ago, when Kelsey backed into some protruding rods at a construction site when she was driving FBI Special Agent Ruby Tanaka to the emergency room after their meeting with an informant went awry.

They were ten minutes from the Savannah Memorial Hospital ER, and it was faster for Kelsey to drive Tanaka there than to call 911 and wait for an ambulance. Besides, Tanaka only broke her arm—even though that was awfully painful—and she was still able to walk on her own two feet.

Still, Kelsey couldn't remember how they'd made it to the Savannah Memorial Hospital ER without getting into a serious wreck on the road.

While she was waiting for Tanaka at the hospital, another FBI agent came to see her and told her to drive away to a particular campground and wait.

Here she was, waiting. Waiting for what?

Thinking back, Kelsey had asked the FBI agent for credentials, but how was she to know whether his badge was real? However, there was no time to ask any questions. Kelsey did as instructed, and ended up at this campground between Savannah and Richmond, just as night fell over Georgia.

Kelsey barely sat down to eat a dinner of cheese and crackers when she heard the first popping noise. That made her drop down to the floor, the crackers falling out of the box and onto her head and all around the floor of the camper van.

A second and then a third popping sound made her scream a little, and she reached for the bathroom door and rushed inside. She shut the door tightly, locked it, and sat down on the closed toilet seat cover.

She covered her ears.

*Help me help me help me...*

Minutes later, the gunfire ceased outside. Now Kelsey began to doubt herself. Were they really gunshots? They couldn't possibly be. After all, former Senator Felix Braun-Dean's ex-wife, Roxanne, usually hired former military henchmen who'd use silencers— just as Agent Tanaka had.

Speaking of whom, Kelsey wondered how Tanaka was doing at the ER. The FBI agent had protected Kelsey with her life in the last twenty-four hours as they fled from Roxanne Braun-Dean, who seemed set on vengeance. Kelsey's testimony had put Roxanne behind bars, but allowed her husband to be out on bail.

Roxanne was still under investigation by both the FBI and the Secret Service for money laundering and illegal arms sales to foreign operatives. In a nutshell, Roxanne had used her husband's position in the Senate Committee on Armed Services to build her multi-billion-dollar empire on the dark web.

*Pop! Pop! Pop!*

Kelsey checked the bathroom door. Locked. Maybe this was bad news because she had imprisoned herself in this small bathroom.

She wished she had her Glock with her, but she'd left her purse on the... Where had she left her purse?

She couldn't remember. Inside her purse was a burner phone she could use to call Tanaka.

Perhaps she should call her friend, Nicholas Bay, who'd rather be known as The Stylist—although he'd made an exception for Kelsey, whom he had said could call him anything, including boyfriend, if she wanted. Over and over, Kelsey had told him that she only considered him a friend, and if anything, a big brother, but no more than that.

Still, Nicholas had been a great help to her since the Braun-Deans were arrested. In fact, Nicholas had filled in the blanks and answered all her questions about the former senator's dealings. Also, he didn't judge her past profession, and treated her as a friend.

After all, Nicholas owned the vehicle. He had let her use it for free after he upgraded to a more expensive recreational vehicle for himself. He had let her borrow this camper van because she didn't have a place of her own in Georgia, or a job to earn enough income to rent an apartment yet.

To call Nicholas, Kelsey had to leave the bathroom to find her cell phone. She was debating with herself on whether to do that when she felt the floor shifting beneath her feet.

*What...?*

The camper van was clearly moving. She could hear the engine now.

How had she not heard it before?

She placed a palm over her chest, where her heart thumped wildly against her rib cage.

Calm down.

Logically, she shouldn't fear. FBI agents should be all over the campground, right? After all, she had paid her taxes...

*I have to get out of here.*

She zipped up her thigh-length jacket, made sure the shoelace on her boots were tied up. She couldn't put on gloves because then she couldn't hold her Glock properly.

She unlocked the bathroom door and peeked out. No one stopped her. From what she could tell, it was a lone driver, who had the build of a man—even though he could have been an athletic woman. In any case, he was wearing a baseball cap and a leather jacket, and his gloveless hands gripped the steering wheel.

The van picked up speed, and Kelsey fell back against the bathroom door.

She looked back to see if she could jump out of the broken back window. The bedsheet was fluttering in the wind. The van must be going at least thirty or forty miles per hour. It might be too fast for her to jump out without injuring or killing herself.

Well, if she died, she'd go to heaven to meet her

Lord and Savior, Jesus Christ, so it wouldn't be a total loss.

Not yet, though. She had to stop Roxanne, who had no qualms about shooting at a federal agent or disabling her own husband. More people would be hurt if she wasn't stopped.

But first, she had to deal with the driver who had carjacked the camper van. If anything happened to the vehicle, how was she going to explain it to Nicholas?

Kelsey spotted her purse on the floor, surrounded by crackers and a tray of cheese. It must have fallen with her earlier.

Slowly she crawled toward her concealed carry crossbody purse. She knew her Glock had a full clip of ammunition, and she had four more clips in her purse.

She yanked the purse toward her, put it over her shoulder, and pulled out her loaded Glock. Since Glocks had no safety, she hadn't put a bullet in the chamber. Her trembling hand reached for the slide, when the van came to a screeching halt at a stop sign.

Falling forward, Kelsey nearly lost her Glock.

Kelsey regained her balance as the driver put on the blinker to turn right.

*Hmm... A carjacker who obeyed traffic laws.*

The van itself was was about twenty-three feet from end to end, so standing in the center of it put Kelsey about ten or eleven feet away from the carjacker. At this distance she could shoot the carjacker easily, but then would it cause a wreck if the driver lost control of the van?

Kelsey racked the slide, and shuffled her feet slowly toward the front of the camper van, bending down slightly to prevent the driver from seeing her through the rearview mirror. She pressed her hips against the edge of the kitchen counter for support.

She held the Glock in both hands and pointed at the driver.

"Stop the van!" she yelled.

He ignored her.

"Stop the van or I'll—"

The man slammed on the brakes. He unbuckled his safety belt and leapt off the seat and came toward her. "You'll what, Zuriel?"

Zuriel?

She hadn't used that name in over a year since she'd been rescued, having been held hostage with Felix Braun-Dean. In fact, that had been the last time she'd seen him in person.

Since her escape, Kelsey decided she would call him Braun-Dean from now on. It would save her from remembering the days when she'd called him "sweet Felix" and he'd call her "my lovely Zuriel."

Zuriel wasn't a secret name. Anyone could have

read it in the news following the former senator's arrest.

The Glock shook in Kelsey's hand. It was too late for her to change her mind. "Who sent you?"

"You know who." He made it sound like it was a friendly gathering he'd be driving her to.

No way would he confess so quickly.

"No, I don't know who."

The man moved a finger.

"Don't move!" Kelsey yelled. The entire time, she wasn't sure if she could follow through with the Glock. Nicholas had told her that if she couldn't handle the consequences, she shouldn't be pointing the handgun at anyone.

Too late now.

"She sent me to scare you, but I think we can have a little fun before I drop you off." The man smiled.

She? Roxanne Braun-Dean?

Why should she believe him? Yes, it was true that Roxanne had been coming after her because she believed that Kelsey kept cryptocurrency belonging to her husband. Well, if Kelsey had, then why was she still poor, living at campsites?

Even though Roxanne might have wanted to scare her, she wouldn't have sent someone like this traffic-law-abiding carjacker. She'd have sent a professional. And she could have also sent an assassin. However, she hadn't so far because she needed Kelsey to be alive to tell her where the billion dollars worth of Bitcoin was stashed away.

How was Kelsey supposed to know?

Still, not talking was her only ticket to staying alive.

This carjacker declared who he worked for. Was he telling the truth? Would a criminal tell the truth? Maybe, maybe not.

The man stepped forward. "I locked all the doors."

He was bigger than she was, though Kelsey believed she could take him down. The self-defense training that Nicholas had put her through could help.

Then again, fleeing should have been her Plan A instead of B. What was she thinking?

Kelsey stepped back in the narrow passage between the stove and dining table, between the kitchen sink counter and the bathroom. She knew that the bed at the back of the van would impede her movement toward the door. She'd have to hop on it to open the latch on the door.

The man stepped forward, like they were two in a tango—albeit in slow motion with the handgun between them.

There wasn't much space between her and the man. He was still inching slowly toward the nozzle of her Glock, and countering that, she was stepping back.

The Glock shook in Kelsey's hands.

"Nervous? You might miss a shot." No snarl. Just a statement of facts.

If she turned around and made a mad dash for the back window, he'd tackle her from the back, and it would be the end of her.

*If I died here, would anyone know? I can't die at thirty-four.*

Tears welled in her eyes.

*Wait. I texted Armin, didn't I?*

What good was that? Armin Dhillon was still in Chicago the last time she had talked to him two days ago. In fact, he hadn't replied to her text at three this afternoon to tell him that the FBI had sent her to wait at this campground. She had taken a photo of the piece of paper with the address scribbled on it that the FBI agent had given to her at SMH and sent it over to Armin.

So now two people besides the FBI agent knew where she was.

Her Glock was still pointed at the carjacker.

"We don't have all day, but I work by the quarter hour—just like my lawyer." He grinned. "Let's play nice and be done with this. I have another job to go to."

"Who sent you?" Kelsey asked again. She wanted clarity so that she could justify shooting him.

Nicholas had taught her to look for body mass

when firing, but she couldn't make herself do it. What if the carjacker suffered internal bleeding? What if he died? Kelsey was no murderer.

So she shot him in the shoulder, exactly where she'd aimed.

The man yelled in pain. Expletives exploded from his mouth.

*Oh dear. I think I made a mistake.*

He reached into his jacket—

And Kelsey shot him again—this time on his thigh. Actually she had aimed for his other arm, but missed this time because the Glock shook wildly.

"Do you see this? I can't control my trigger finger." Kelsey was blanking out. "You need to...need to...uh... You need to back away."

The man growled and lunged toward her, dragging a leg and an arm. His undamaged hand reached into his jacket again a second time—

Kelsey didn't miss her third try as she shot the handgun out of the carjacker's hand. The handgun went flying.

The man fell back, hit his head on the dining table, and dropped to the ground. He was bleeding from his limbs, but his mouth was still working. He yelled and screamed.

"Look, mister. I don't want to hurt you." Kelsey sprinted toward the back of the camper van, leapt up on the mattress, and reached for the back door handle—

It was stuck.

She jiggled it. It made no difference.

"Told you I locked all the doors." The man laughed. He hissed in pain.

Kelsey wasn't sure which part of the shoulder she'd shot, but she could do it again if she needed to, although rehabilitation on his shoulder might be unpleasant.

She shoved her Glock into her jacket pocket, and yanked the flapping bedsheet off the windows. A gust of January wind slapped her face. There was no snow in most winters in Georgia, but the biting air was chilly. She was a Florida girl, so this was plenty cold to her.

The window was small. It had been modified from the original utility van window into this small porthole, almost, but she could potentially climb out of the van through it.

The carjacker was still screaming and cussing at her.

She didn't know what to do. Her mind went blank, and all she could see was the darkness outside the window. The road was deserted, and there were no street lights in this rural part of Georgia.

Without thinking further on the matter, she

started to climb out of the window. She dared not look behind her as she wiggled, barely fitting. She could feel her palm and hands gashing on the broken glass.

Her thick winter jacket snagged at her hip, and next thing she knew, she was stuck.

*Oh no.*

A strong force pulled at her legs still inside the camper van, preventing her from getting out of the window. Her boots kicked at the mattress and at the assailant, who was cussing at her a mile a minute.

*Didn't I shoot his arms? How could he still pull my legs?*

Outside the van, bright lights came at her. Headlights of a truck or SUV of some sort.

"Help! Help!"

The high headlights shone in her eyes, but she couldn't see anyone. She squinted and screamed as the carjacker pulled her legs, and he was now gripping her hips to try to yank her back into the van. But his strength waned, and pretty soon, she didn't feel pressure on her legs anymore.

She realized then that the carjacker had told her the truth, that he was only messing with her. That meant that he had no intention of killing her or even incapacitating her. The carjacker could have located his handgun that Kelsey had shot out of his hand, but he hadn't shot at her while she was dangling there in the window, like a target at the gun range.

Had Roxanne really given him instructions to keep Kelsey alive? Then again, Roxanne was an enigma. Kelsey believed that she had no problem hurting Kelsey and making her pay for being one of the women that her sleazy husband had bedded.

Just not today.

*God, thank You for having forgiven me of my past. If I die now, I know I die forgiven.*

The carjacker's grip on her legs was subsiding. Kelsey guessed that his bleeding shoulder was causing him problems.

Her arms flailed in the air as she dangled in the van window, her stomach as the fulcrum with her shoulders and arms on one side and her legs and hips inside the van.

All around her, the night was dark on this rural road, save for the vehicle coming toward her, two front headlights drawing closer and larger.

She squinted in the glare.

Pain seared through her palms as she waved frantically in the air. "Help me!"

Maybe she should've just killed the carjacker instead of trying to escape through the back window that she had barely fitted through. Too late for regrets.

She closed her eyes, bowed her head, and prayed, trying very hard to think of what to say to God.

*Oh Heavenly Father...*

Before she could form the words, she heard a gunshot. It sounded like it was coming from inside the van. Or maybe her brain was imagining things. After all, she hadn't slept in two days.

She slumped over the window, still stuck. She kept her eyes closed tightly.

*Lift me up to heaven, Lord.*

She heard tires screech to a stop and vehicle doors slam.

"Kelsey!"

*Hear that? The angels are calling my name...*

She heard a click, and felt the back door open—like someone was opening it—with her hanging there, still stuck in the window, swinging slowly. Swinging...

*Swing low, sweet chariot...*

"Kelsey!" It was a male voice in her ear.

She felt strong hands on her arms.

"Kelsey, it's me!"

# CHAPTER TWO

K elsey opened her eyes.

Standing in front of her, wearing a leather jacket and a beanie hat, was none other than the pen pal she had been texting and chatting with for the last year, since he'd contacted her about his brother's murder three years ago.

Armin Dhillon, the guy that Kelsey was starting to have a crush on.

"I'm sorry we're late." His phone flashlight was bright. "You okay?"

"Do I look okay to you?"

"Sorry, wrong question."

Kelsey ignored him. "The carjacker is in the van!" She pointed with her bloody hand.

"Your hand is bleeding!" Armin looked around. "Where are the paramedics?"

"Got him!" A second male voice came out of the van. He sounded like Private Investigator Earl Young from Hu Knows, Inc. Kelsey guessed that he must've entered the van door when her eyes were closed.

Kelsey felt relieved that Armin hadn't come alone.

"He's badly hurt," Earl shouted. "Looks like he's shot in the chest."

*Where?*

Kelsey didn't remember shooting the carjacker in the chest.

"Is it self-inflicted?" Kelsey asked but nobody answered her.

"Are the paramedics on the way?" Earl yelled from inside the van. "This dude is bleeding a lot."

Kelsey began to shake. She worried that she might have shot an artery in the carjacker's leg, but then again, he'd pulled out a gun on her—after she'd done the same to him.

But who had fired the fourth shot?

Armin held her shoulders. "Let's get you out of this window."

He pulled Kelsey's shoulders, but she didn't move. "How did you get stuck?"

"Bad decisions," Kelsey said as she heard emergency sirens in the distance. She saw flashing lights coming nearer to her.

"I'm sure you have your reasons." He sounded non-judgmental.

A firetruck pulled up in the left lane directly beside the van. Its extendable light bars flashed on, bathing the entire scene in very bright lights that made Kelsey squint.

An ambulance screeched to a stop behind the firetruck. Its sirens cut off.

Doors slammed, voices rose, boots crossed the asphalt in the cold Georgian night. Emergency medical technicians and firefighters surrounded Kelsey. They told Armin to step back.

"Whose SUV is this?" One of the firefighters pointed to Earl's SUV.

Earl raised his hand. "Mine. You want me to move it?"

"Yes, sir."

Earl climbed into his SUV and rolled it to the shoulder of the road to give the rescue team more room to work on freeing Kelsey.

When the SUV cleared away from the road, Kelsey could see that police vehicles had also arrived. Officers redirected what little night traffic there was away from the intersection, and a police car pulled up to block the road from new traffic.

This was a somewhat rural road, yes, but it led to the edge of Savannah, a tourist city that was busy around the clock. That meant it wasn't too far away from the reach of the Savannah Chatham Metropolitan Police.

The firefighters set up scene lights all around the van. Now Kelsey could see the rows of trees on both sides of the road.

EMT approached Kelsey and asked her questions.

She stretched out both hands in the air. Her watch and bracelet were still there.

On her left wrist was a diamond-studded watch, a gift from Paige, the twenty-six-year-old daughter of Braun-Dean and also his campaign manager in his last failed senate seat bid. Word was, Braun-Dean had wanted to give Kelsey the watch himself, but didn't want his constituents to know about their affair. Ironically, their after-hour dalliances had been an open secret at Braun-Dean's campaign headquarters. In any case, Braun-Dean worked it out with his daughter as the proxy.

On her right wrist was a stretch bracelet made of gemstones. She couldn't identify all of them, but she thought the purple ones were amethyst and the green ones were jadeite. There were a couple of tiger's eye too. All in all, the bracelet was crude and the color scheme was hodgepodge, but it had been a gift from

Braun-Dean's younger adopted daughter, Carmelita. She'd made it when she had been ten years old, kept it for ten years, and then gave it to Kelsey as a sign of their friendship. Kelsey had kept it for three years and hadn't lost it, so she wasn't about to lose it now.

At one point in the last three years, Braun-Dean had borrowed the bracelet for one day, and hadn't told her why until he returned it. It had been a strange conversation between them just before they left for their last stay in Miami, the city by the Atlantic Ocean.

"Promise me you'll wear it at all times," Braun-Dean begged her.

At first, Kelsey thought that she was simply sentimental.

"Some day when I'm gone, will you visit me in the Braun-Dean mausoleum and sing me 'The Twelve Days of Christmas'? That's our song now."

"Are you drunk again?" Kelsey remembered asking.

"I'm as sober as the sun is in the sky." He didn't slur his words though.

"You're drunk."

"Promise me." He held her hand to his chest. "I'm older than you, Zuriel. I will die sooner than you will—especially with this liver problem I now have. I just want to know that you will come to see me. You can bring Carmelita, if you want, but nobody else."

In spite of Braun-Dean's issues, he did love his adopted daughter more than his other offspring, Paige. He had no other children, and he couldn't get Kelsey pregnant.

Carmelita had been Braun-Dean's favorite daughter of the two, mainly because he'd been convinced that Paige wasn't his. As such, he'd poured all his resources on the adopted daughter instead. Carmelita had the best. She'd driven to Princeton in a Ferrari, partied it up for six years—because she'd changed her major five times and then some—all with Braun-Dean's blessings and at his expense. Sometimes, Kelsey wondered whether Carmelita wasn't Braun-Dean's real daughter by the way he had lavished such luxuries on her.

Eventually Carmelita graduated with a degree in economics. As a graduation gift, Braun-Dean gifted her over ten million dollars worth of bitcoin. She proceeded to spend all of it in two years. But Braun-Dean wouldn't give her more.

That was when the father-daughter rift had widened. By then, Kelsey had moved on from their Braun-Dean family drama.

"Okay, okay. I promise. I'll bring Carmelita and no one else." If it made Braun-Dean feel better to think that at least someone would visit his grave long after he was gone, then who was Kelsey to rain on his parade?

The memory faded as quickly as it had come.

She closed her eyes. There were a million things she didn't want to think about, but sometimes they surfaced in her life when she least expected it.

"Pain anywhere?" The EMT asked again.

"Oh sorry. My mind wandered. Ah, no pain except on my palms. Got cut on glass, I believe." Kelsey was thankful her winter coat was thick enough to prevent the glass in the window from cutting her stomach.

She thought that the EMT would bandage her hands while she was hanging out the van window. They didn't. Instead, they climbed into the van to save the carjacker while the firefighters assessed Kelsey's situation.

Kelsey watched the EMT team running as they pushed the stretcher carrying the carjacker toward the ambulance. He wasn't moving at all. The ambulance sped away.

What in the world? Kelsey hadn't killed the carjacker, had she?

The police would question Kelsey soon about the three bullets she pumped into him in self defense. She could have killed him with one shot to the heart, but she had never killed anyone in her life, and this was not the time to start a new career.

Now, waiting to be rescued, she couldn't imagine

all those things that had gone through her mind while she'd been with the carjacker.

*What on earth was I thinking?*

Three bullets to his limbs shouldn't have killed him unless Kelsey had nicked arteries and he bled out. However, he had been strong enough to pull her legs—for a while anyway.

Earl Young stood nearby and spoke with a police officer who had approached the crime scene.

All Kelsey could hear was "critical condition" and her mind went numb. What were they talking about? Was she a criminal now?

*Wait a minute.*

She had fired only three shots, but while she was hanging in the window, she had heard a fourth shot. It had been when Earl's SUV pulled up. She wasn't sure she had heard or seen any other vehicles.

The moonless night was getting colder, and Kelsey started to shiver. She closed her eyes, waiting for the firefighters to free her. To distract herself from her present predicament, her mind raced back to the events of the afternoon and evening.

Why had the second FBI agent at the hospital told her to drive to this particular campground to wait? Was he even a real agent? Why hadn't he provided security for her? He'd told her to go to the campground alone, and she'd obeyed because he had FBI credentials.

Kelsey had many questions to ask Agent Tanaka when she came out of the hospital.

"What's your name?" a firefighter asked her.

"Kelsey Murphy."

"Miss Kelsey, how did you get stuck?"

"I—uh... I panicked, I think?" Kelsey chided herself for trying to climb out of the van through a broken window. She must've been either desperate or unthinking or both. Thankfully, her insulated winter jacket was thick and had a secret feature: it was Kevlar-lined. For that, she had to thank The Stylist, whom she would contact as soon as she could.

"We've seen worse."

Kelsey nodded. She felt like she was in some comedy caper or something. Truth be told, her life had been more tragic than comedic.

A tragicomedy.

"To be honest, I don't know why I tried to climb out the window. Forgot that the manufacturer had modified the back windows and made them smaller for privacy since that's where the camper bed is. I feel stupid now."

When all this was over, she might consider looking for a remote spot in Wyoming or Alaska or somewhere, and retire in peace and quiet for the rest of her life.

"No problem. We're going to get you out of here." The firefighters pushed the door back so that Kelsey's legs could rest on the mattress at the back of the camper van.

"Thank you." Kelsey still faced away from the van, so she couldn't see what they were doing.

One thing was clear to her. She had to live. Had to fight back. Had to regain her freedom.

"We need to remove your purse." A firefighter pointed to her crossbody bag that was hanging out of the window.

"Whatever you need to do."

"We may have to cut the strap."

"No problem." Kelsey turned to Armin. "Could you hold my purse for me?"

"Sure." Armin stepped forward, just as a police officer approached the van. Inside the van, the paramedics said something to the officer about gunshot wounds and collapsed lungs.

"Who fired shots in the camper van?" The police officer came around and stood in front of Kelsey in the window.

"I did, but only three shots," Kelsey said. "The carjacker was coming at me."

She decided not to mention the fourth shot because she wasn't sure she'd heard it at all. In fact, she might not have heard any of the other supposed gunshots outside the van back at the campground.

"Do you still have the weapon?" the police officer asked.

Kelsey nodded. "In my right jacket pocket, but I can't reach it."

"May I get it for her?" Armin lifted up a hand. He was wearing leather gloves.

"No, sir. You may not. It's evidence. The fewer people touching it, the better." The police officer shook his head, then turned to Kelsey. "Normally, we'd let one of our female officers retrieve it for us, but you need to go to the hospital right away to have those bleeding hands looked at. So if you give me permission, I will retrieve the weapon out of your pocket."

"What if I just give you my entire jacket?" Kelsey asked the officer. Then she had an idea. "Or how about we ask the firefighters to cut away the part of my jacket that has the pocket with my Glock in it?"

"That will work, if you don't mind," the police officer replied. "I'd rather we get the Glock out of your jacket so the firefighters can work safely."

The police officer turned to the Incident Commander overseeing the firefighters. "Captain, what do you think?"

The captain agreed to the idea.

"It has a Kevlar lining," Kelsey added, just in case.

No one asked her why she needed such a protective layer nor did they look shocked that she had extra padding in her jacket. She had come prepared for a gunfight, though being stuck in a camper van window wasn't what she had in mind.

"No problem. We have scissors." The firefighter captain said something to his lieutenant.

The latter promptly produced a pair of trauma shears with blunt tips, which he used to cut through the Kevlar in Kelsey's winter jacket. Feathers flew out from the goose down jacket.

In the bright beam of the firefighter's helmet light, Kelsey could see the various layers in her once expensive jacket, a gift from Nicholas for her safety.

Nicholas was even more paranoid than Kelsey.

Which meant she had to call Nicholas as soon as possible.

"I have a spare winter jacket in my carryon if you want, but it doesn't have a fancy Kevlar lining," Armin said.

"Thank you. I'll borrow it until I can get it replaced." Turning to the officer, Kelsey said, "My driver's license and concealed carry permit are in my crossbody purse."

Usually, Kelsey would return the Glock to her purse, but this time, she hadn't. Which went to show that she wasn't her usual self in her great panic to escape from the carjacker.

Armin handed the entire purse to the police officer, who then opened it with gloved hands, and retrieved Kelsey's driver's license and handgun permit. He returned the purse to Armin before he walked away with a giant piece of Kelsey's jacket.

At this juncture, there was no point panicking or freaking out. Kelsey wasn't sure about every decision she had made in the camper van, how she reacted the way she had, and why she ended up stuck in the window of this camper van.

Now she wasn't certain if she had been genuinely in fear of her life, whether it had made sense for her to shoot at the carjacker. She made a mental note to ask Tanaka for advice later.

For now, she thanked God that help had arrived.

The firefighters used a spreader to widen the window. Kelsey could breathe better, and she knew she was almost free. Then they cut the steel away, and lifted her out of the door.

The paramedics escorted her away from the van, now in the hands of the SCMPD.

Kelsey sat on a stretcher as the paramedics checked her vitals. She was still shaking slightly. She wasn't sure if she was shivering because it was wintertime or whether it was because the gravity of her situation had finally affected her emotionally.

The EMT asked her to remove her watch and bracelet before they bandaged both hands. The watch came off easily, but the bracelet snagged on her cuts and she hissed in pain.

Armin was right there to take the two items from her. He put them in her crossbody bag.

The EMT told Kelsey to go to the hospital to get the pieces of glass removed from her palms. Her injuries were not life-threatening and didn't require an ambulance ride.

Kelsey felt relieved.

"Thank You, Jesus," she whispered.

Armin was saying something to her, but Kelsey wasn't paying attention. Maybe he thought that chatting would keep her spirits up. At this point, Kelsey was plain old tired of the events of the day—and night.

Then again, hearing Armin's voice—no matter what he was saying—reminded her of the many times they'd talked on the phone. He had been her emotional support person for the last two months since they'd met online due to his investigations into his brother's murder three years ago.

Thing was, Kelsey knew very little about Arun's death in Conyers, but Arun had a side job working for Braun-Dean as his go-to cryptocurrency guru, up until the day before his family van exploded in his driveway, killing him.

It had been a month now since Kelsey and Armin started to connect the dots, when FBI Agent Tanaka called Kelsey to participate in a sting to track down a mysterious witness who could put Braun-Dean away for life.

Roxanne Braun-Dean hid well. Even while sitting in jail, it seemed that she hadn't missed a beat. Her goons and minions fanned out, doing her bidding. No one could pin anything on her.

"Why are you here, Armin?" Kelsey whispered in the wind.

Armin didn't hear her. He was talking to Earl now. Earl handed him the SUV keys. Kelsey assumed that Armin was going to get her his jacket from the vehicle.

Kelsey had never expected to see Armin in real life. Otherwise she wouldn't have shared all her private concerns with him. It seemed easier for her to chat without inhibition when she was online, as though she was confessing anonymously. However, in real life, she'd rather not talk about her personal problems.

And now she felt ashamed to see Armin. Ashamed of her past, her previous career, her inability to move forward in life, everything. If only she had a less color-ful, less eventful past, perhaps she and Armin could have dated. Now they could only be friends. After all, who would date the former mistress of a former senator with criminal connections?

In Kelsey's unsaved past, she had chosen to live with Braun-Dean as a means to have food and shelter without having to work for it other than in the former senator's bed. Looking back, she was ashamed of it.

All that had changed since she trusted Jesus Christ as her Savior, but those memories of her past still stained her emotionally. She was thankful to God that her church friends and people like Earl and his wife, Sienna, and Armin hadn't written her off as an untouchable. If they had, they hadn't said it aloud to her face.

Most of all, she knew that Jesus had accepted her into His family. In her heart, she believed that Jesus had said the same thing to her as He had to the adulterous woman in John 8:3-11, a passage that her now friend Pilar Santiago had shared with her back in Florida.

*Then the scribes and Pharisees brought to Him a woman caught in adultery. And when they had set her in the midst, they said to Him, "Teacher, this woman was caught in adultery, in the very act. Now Moses, in the law, commanded us that such should be stoned. But what do You say?" This they said, testing Him, that they might have something of which to accuse Him. But Jesus stooped down and wrote on the ground with His finger, as though He did not hear.*

*So when they continued asking Him, He raised Himself up and said to them, "He who is without sin among you, let him throw a stone at her first." And again He stooped down and wrote on the ground. Then those who heard it, being convicted by their conscience, went out one by one, beginning with the oldest even to the last. And Jesus was left alone, and the woman standing in the midst. When Jesus had raised Himself up and saw no one but the woman, He said to her, "Woman, where are those accusers of yours? Has no one condemned you?"*

*She said, "No one, Lord."*

*And Jesus said to her, "Neither do I condemn you; go and sin no more."*

Tears fell from Kelsey's eyes as she recalled the passage that she felt was meant for her. Five words resonated with her.

*Go and sin no more.*

Earl must've noticed that Kelsey was crying, though he probably had no idea that she wasn't crying because of the trauma of being carjacked. He handed a couple of sheets of wadded-up napkins to Kelsey. "It's clean."

"You sure?"

"Yeah. We bought hamburgers on the way here, and I asked for extra napkins." Earl pointed. "Those are the extras."

"I called 911 for you," Earl said. "You're welcome."

"Thank you, Earl." Kelsey blew her nose.

"Sienna said your pineapple upside-down cupcakes were delicious and she's been craving them," Earl added.

Kelsey knew that Earl wasn't making light of her situation. He was probably only trying to take her mind off the drama she was in, although this was a terrible time to talk about baking cupcakes. Kelsey resolved to stop baking because she had been eating way too many desserts. If she were ten pounds lighter, would she have been able to make it through the window?

Probably not. They had modified the windows, and they were way too small. Only a little kid could have gone through it. She had underestimated the window dimensions, and learned a painful lesson from it.

"If your wife wants me to, I can show her how I make them," Kelsey said. "Then she'll always have cupcakes."

Just like that, her mind was on cupcakes and not carjackers. "How's Sienna doing, by the way? When's the baby due?"

"It's already two days late. If I get a call from her right now, I'm out of here," Earl said.

"How long are you going to be gone?" Kelsey asked.

"I'm taking three months of paternity leave."

"Good for you."

"You won't be on your own. Deshon Kernaghan from our Atlanta branch is filling in for me at the HQ, so he will be taking over this case. He's arriving tomorrow morning—I mean this coming morning, when the sun rises sometime."

"Thank you."

"Originally, I asked Cade Sumter. You worked with him in Miami."

Kelsey didn't want to remember that part of her life, but Earl had brought it up. "I was with Pilar mostly. But I've met Mr. Sumter. Now I know him as Pilar's husband."

"Cade and Pilar would come up here together to help you, but Helen assigned them to another case overseas, and they decided to go for it."

Overseas? Kelsey knew that Hu Knows had clients from all over the world. She wondered if she might be able to travel if she worked for the private investigative firm. However, she'd rather travel for vacation than for work. Right now she couldn't go anywhere.

"Anyway, are you ready for fatherhood?" Kelsey changed the subject.

"Since Sienna and I believe that life begins at conception, we're already parents."

"Yes." A new Christian, Kelsey was still learning

about her newfound belief from biblical perspectives. "I hope that both mom and baby will be healthy."

Perhaps she should say, "I pray that..." However, she was also still learning how to pray.

In her heart, she asked God to give Sienna a safe delivery. Was that a prayer?

"Thank you. We're packed for the hospital." Earl seemed excited.

Kelsey had nothing more to say to him, and was glad when Armin returned from the SUV with a jacket, just as the EMT finished with Kelsey. Nothing serious, but she had to go to the ER to get the glass splinters removed from her palms.

"You still doing okay?" Armin asked.

Kelsey wanted to say something like, "Nice to meet you in person, finally. You're better looking than on the phone." But she didn't. She simply nodded.

Kelsey had questions of her own. Why would Roxanne come after her now when she was already in jail? Wouldn't such a thing jeopardize her future plans for an early release?

Felix Braun-Dean and his ex-wife's business associates and enemies far and near all wanted a piece of her. Her three-year association with them had caused her endless woes.

*Please, Lord, let all this be over.*

"Your fifteen-minute fame, Kelsey." Earl laughed.

"I don't need it. I just want to go home." But where was home? She had been homeless for months, living incognito at campgrounds.

She was tired of running away. But this was the only way she knew to stay alive.

"You're surprisingly calm," Armin said to her.

"I just look calm. Inside, my heart is beating a mile a minute," Kelsey said. "Nonetheless, God is good, no matter what happens to me."

She had left her old life a year ago, and had no wish to relive it. However, repercussions from the past had followed her to Georgia, where she had tried to start over.

Still, she refused to cry.

The police officer returned. "We'll meet you in the ER. Let's have the doctor take care of those hands first."

Kelsey nodded. Armin and Earl helped her to her feet and walked her to the SUV they'd come in.

"Why don't you and Armin sit in the back? That way if you have to take cover, you can just duck." Earl climbed in on the driver's side.

*Take cover?*

"W-what do you mean?" Kelsey's eyes widened.

"I'm just kidding. Got your attention, didn't I?" Earl checked his GPS. "SMH is twenty minutes away.

After they make sure you're fine, I'll take you both to the Hu Knows office."

"You're not dropping us off at some hotel to clean up?" Armin asked.

"Agent Tanaka sent me a message, asking if she could meet Kelsey there."

"Why?" Kelsey asked. "Doesn't she have an office of her own?"

Earl shrugged. "Ask her when she shows up."

"Didn't you usually meet outside her office?" Armin buckled Kelsey in so that she didn't have to use her bandaged hands. Then he busied himself with his phone as Earl pulled away from the crime scene.

"In the camper van she rented for me. But that's been impounded." Kelsey leaned back. Her trembling hands were on her lap. She did not feel safe yet. No, she wouldn't be safe until Roxanne Braun-Dean stopped chasing her.

When would that be?

# CHAPTER THREE

Armin Dhillon glanced at the sleeping beauty on the other side of his backpack in the backseat of Earl's SUV. She slept quietly, didn't snore, and didn't twitch. She looked like a princess, and Armin wanted to protect her with his life.

Not!

Even as she slept, Kelsey's face didn't look at ease. She looked exhausted, like a person on the ropes with nowhere to go but down. Her fists were clenched around the safety belt.

Thinking back at what just happened to her, Armin felt pity, but happy that she'd made it out alive. The same could not be said about his brother, Arun, who hadn't survived the car bomb three years ago in Atlanta.

After three years of paying Hu Knows to look into the case, and conducting investigations of his own, Armin was no closer to finding justice for his brother. There would be no closure for the family, especially for their mother, who was still grieving in Mumbai.

Kelsey stirred a bit. "Where are we going?"

She fell back asleep before anyone could answer her.

Private Investigator Earl Young chuckled in the driver's seat. He seemed calm. Everyone was, in spite of what had just happened. At least nobody died in the camper van, especially Kelsey.

Watching her sleep—or nap, or whatever this was —wearing his jacket, two sizes too big for her, made Armin feel like he was prying into her personal space.

Well, this wasn't her house. This was Earl's vehicle, and they were on business. People dozed off in cars all the time, right?

Armin couldn't help but think about how Kelsey was very different in real life compared to her online persona that exuded confidence in spite of the adversities she had endured. In the months he'd known her and spoken to her in audio and on video, he'd believed that her positive outlook had carried her through her many difficulties in life.

He didn't want to accuse her of bringing those hardships on herself, including her regrettable years as Braun-Dean's live-in girlfriend before she had become a Christian. Who was he to cast the first stone? He had logs in his own eyes—indicted by Matthew 7:1-5.

*Judge not, that you be not judged. For with what judgment you judge, you will be judged; and with the measure you use, it will be measured back to you. And why do you look at the speck in your brother's eye, but do not consider the plank in your own eye? Or how can you say to your brother, "Let me remove the speck from your eye;" and look, a plank is in your own eye? Hypocrite! First remove the plank from your own eye, and then you will see clearly to remove the speck from your brother's eye.*

For example, why hadn't Armin sensed trouble when Arun had complained about his hard life? As the oldest brother among his siblings, he should have been more understanding. However, Arun had told him all that during tax time, and Armin had been too busy at his CPA firm to listen to his brother's issues.

With his brother dead, his six-figure salary as a Certified Public Accountant was meaningless to him. For a while, he was down in the dumps, until he decided to keep busy by looking into all the things

Arun had told him. After one year of dead ends, Armin began to realize that perhaps the people behind bars were not the same people who'd blown up Arun's family van with him inside.

Two years after Arun died, his fears were confirmed when Arun's widow sent him what looked like a keepsake box that Arun had left behind. After the funeral, she'd taken her baby daughter and moved home to India, and hired a moving company to pack up their house in Georgia and ship their belongings to Mumbai. It had taken her over a year to finally open all the containers, and several more months before the mystery keepsake box appeared among Arun's personal effects.

In that box were several things that made Armin cry. There were a couple of photos of the brothers together when they had been in little league baseball in elementary school. There was a signed baseball that Arun had caught at a Major League Baseball game so many years ago. There were some old skeleton keys that Armin didn't know what to do with.

Two pieces of folded paper with eight seemingly random words on them had caught Armin's attention. Arun had handwritten those words and listed them vertically. If Armin guessed it right, they were keywords that, when put together in some order, would form the recovery passphrase to recreate a hardware wallet storing retrieval information for Arun's cryptocurrency investments.

If the words were truly a recovery passphrase—itself merely a string of words—then Armin would never know because Arun hadn't left him any instructions. Still, he didn't want to throw out the piece of paper in case it became handy later on.

To one side of the box was a burner phone with the label "best friend" on it. When Armin called, Kelsey Murphy answered, not Dana Nesbitt, whom Arun had been in love with at work before he gave up on her and married a woman from Mumbai whom their parents had arranged for him.

Over the next year, Armin and Kelsey spent a lot of time on the phone because of their common connection: Arun. Kelsey seemed to know a lot about Arun's personal life, from his failed dating attempt to their mother's matchmaking skills. She also listened to Armin as he processed his own grief.

When they had first met, Kelsey was single again, having left Braun-Dean several months prior, in a strange October in Miami. She had gotten saved and was attending church with Pilar Santiago, the private investigator who had led her to Christ.

Six months after Armin contacted Kelsey, he quit his CPA job in Columbia, South Carolina, and moved to Atlanta to continue his investigation when Hu

Knows moved to a bigger building in Buckhead that had a spare desk for Armin to work at.

For the next two months, while Armin settled down in Atlanta, Kelsey was still in Miami. She had quit her minimum wage job at the grocery store because she had to go into hiding after receiving continual threats and harassment from Roxanne Braun-Dean, who couldn't let her husband go. Somehow, Kelsey decided to become an informant for the FBI and started working with Agent Tanaka to collect data against Roxanne, still sitting in jail.

Armin was still talking with Kelsey, until yesterday, when he found out what she was doing with Agent Tanaka. He flew out from Atlanta on an early morning flight to Savannah, not only to check in on Kelsey in person for the first time, but also to talk to Earl, with whom both of them had contact.

Yeah, she was still the same person on the phone, but after meeting her for the first time at the red light on the rural road, Armin began to think that she was perhaps slightly unpredictable.

To begin with, who'd try to escape from a carjacker by climbing out of a smashed window that could barely fit a high school teenager? No wonder she had cut her palms on the broken glass.

That thick winter jacket Kelsey had worn had

saved her from being shredded by broken glass, but it had also caused her to be stuck in the window.

Then again, she had come prepared. The jacket was lined with Kevlar. She also carried a loaded Glock with her. But she was alone in that camper van with the carjacker, and that bothered Armin.

Armin and Earl had arrived at the campground in time to witness a barrage of gunshots from several directions, firing at one another. Stray bullets embedded in the recreational vehicles and in tree trunks.

No police presence, no FBI presence. Only two or more opposing sides.

There was no ceasefire, and Earl almost made the decision to leave the campground, until they saw a man enter Kelsey's camper van and drive off. Earl floored the gas pedal while Armin called 911.

Armin had no idea that it was possible to drive a camper van at a hundred miles per hour, but he'd witnessed it. Running red lights would've been dangerous in the nearby city, but in this rural area in the middle of the night, there was nothing stopping the camper van from tearing down the road.

"Except he stopped at every red light," Armin said aloud.

"And stop signs," Earl added.

"That too." Kelsey lifted a finger in the air. Her eyes were still closed.

Earl drove through several historic Savannah squares, gloomy at night, until they reached East Bay Street. There were still vehicles on the road, including a trolley filled with tourists on their night tour of the city.

It started to rain lightly as Earl pulled into an underground parking garage. He parked close to Armin's rental car near the elevator.

Kelsey sighed and unbuckled. "When will this be over?"

No one could answer her.

Kelsey grabbed her purse with the cut strap, and inched out of the door. She looked worn out, like she needed to sleep.

Armin didn't know how to comfort her. Didn't know what to say to someone who had gone through so much. He got out of the vehicle and followed Kelsey and Earl into the elevator.

No one talked until they reached the Hu Knows international headquarters on the top two floors of the office building.

When the doors opened to the lobby, no one greeted them. Earl led them down a hallway, passing by several conference rooms, some with glass walls, and some without. The open doors showed Armin that each of them were tastefully decorated with high-end wood furniture and what looked like ergonomic chairs.

Earl continued walking until they reached a lounge. "This is where we eat meals if we don't leave the building or if we have to work through lunch or dinner."

Armin entered the large room. It was warm and spacious with clusters of seating areas and casual meeting spaces. "Nice."

"Helen got the design idea from Binary Systems in Atlanta, albeit on a smaller scale. For example, we don't have a kitchen and a chef."

Binary Systems was a familiar name to Armin because the things in Arun's box included two encrypted USB drives as well as a couple strange devices that Armin wasn't familiar with. He then called Hu Knows because one of their PIs, Earl, had been the last person who'd seen Arun alive. Armin ended up hiring Hu Knows by cashing out some of the bitcoin that Arun had left for him.

Then Hu Knows ended up hiring Armin to work for them in their Atlanta branch, which specialized in white collar crime.

"We used the same interior designer that RYUCP recommended," Earl added.

"RYUCP?" Armin asked.

"Ruttledge Yamada Urquhart Commercial Properties," Earl replied. "We worked with the Savannah branch, but their HQ is in Atlanta."

Kelsey said nothing. She walked to a couch, took off Armin's jacket, and sat down. She leaned back.

Armin joined her in an armchair across from the couch. He placed his backpack on the carpeted floor next to the coffee table. He might need to do some work at the coffee table.

"Unfortunately, we don't have a gym and sleep bays like Binary Systems lounges do, but we're petitioning for perks like that." Earl was still standing. "Anyone want coffee? I can brew a pot."

"No thanks," Armin said. "I've had too much today."

Kelsey stretched out on the couch with her shoes still on and pulled Armin's jacket over her like a blanket. "Wake me up when it's all over."

Just like that she was out again like a lightbulb. Seemed that she could sleep anywhere.

As for Armin, if it wasn't his bed or a plush hotel bed, if the room light was too bright or the temperature was off a little, he couldn't sleep.

If he was worried about something, he couldn't sleep either. Like right now. He checked his phone. The battery was at fifteen percent. He retrieved a charging cable from his backpack. He looked around for an electrical outlet. He couldn't find it on the floor around his armchair.

"Whatcha looking for?" Earl asked.

"Outlets to charge my phone and potentially my laptop."

"Look at Kelsey's side of the coffee table."

Armin got out of his armchair. Sure enough, facing the couch, and the once-again sleeping Kelsey, was a row of sockets. He plugged in his phone and then went back to his armchair.

The smell of brewing coffee started to fill the lounge. Armin didn't know what kind of coffee it was, and didn't care to ask. Coffee was coffee to him. He'd drink it as long as it had caffeine in it, and with milk. He sometimes liked his coffee with a lot of milk.

Before Earl could join them, his phone rang. "What? Are you serious?"

He paused, his eyes widened. "Okay. Stay put. I'll be right there. Love you, babe."

He froze for a moment, and then turned to Armin. "Sienna's water broke!"

"Go go go!" Kelsey yelled.

Armin's eyes snapped toward the couch. Wasn't she sleeping?

Kelsey was sitting up now. Clapping her hands. Her eyes were halfway closed. "Drive safely, Earl."

"Twenty minutes there." Earl looked like he was calculating something.

"Can anyone else drive her to the hospital and you can just meet her there?" Kelsey asked. "You're five minutes away from SMH, and it would take forty minutes for you two—three, actually—to get here if you have to drive all the way to Tybee and pick her up."

"Forty minutes versus twenty. You have a point." Earl called someone. "Hey Ming, is Sabine in town? Oh good. Look, Sienna's water broke. I'm at the Hu Knows office. You're three minutes from her—yes, that's what I was thinking. Okay. I'll call Sienna back and tell her I'll meet her at the hospital."

Armin wondered why Earl hadn't planned this ahead of time, but then again, who was he—a bachelor with no kids—to advise anyone?

Earl hung up his phone. "Thank God that Ming and Sabine are at home. They didn't mind that I woke them up. Ming is staying home with their kids, and Sabine is going to pick up Sienna and drive her to the hospital."

"Before you go, we should pray for safe delivery," Kelsey said.

Earl nodded, but he didn't sit down.

Armin closed his eyes and waited for someone to pray.

"Lord Jesus, it's me again," Kelsey said. "I have so

many needs, but right now, I'm not praying for myself. I'm praying for my friend, Sienna, whose water just broke and she's about to deliver her first child. Sabine is on her way to pick her up and drive her to the hospital. Earl is about to leave for the hospital. I pray for travel safety and mercies on the road at night. I pray for the logistics of this childbirth and may the child whom You have gifted the Young family be born healthy with no birth defects or delivery complications. We lift up the baby and mommy and daddy to You. In Your holy name, I pray. Amen."

The two men gave a hearty "amen" and then Earl had to run.

"Thank you for praying!" He disappeared through the door.

"Are we basically stuck here for the night until someone comes in the morning and lets us out?" Kelsey smiled.

Armin shrugged. "I've only been here twice, and it's usually during the day, so I don't know."

"I guess we could have coffee and breakfast of some sort." Kelsey checked her watch. "Oh, it's only three in the morning. Maybe I'll go back to sleep."

"I'm going to read some more news about Felix Braun-Dean," Armin said.

Kelsey barely nodded. "I don't want to hear his name."

"I'm sorry he hurt you." Armin recalled those midnight hours when Kelsey had cried. He'd stayed with her on the phone, keeping watch as she poured out her heart.

"I was a prisoner and I couldn't leave."

"I know. You told me." In those sleepless nights, Kelsey had told Armin that she deeply regretted her past life. What had started out as a novelty experiment for her as a "geisha" on American soil had turned into a nightmare for her.

"He made me believe that without him, I could not survive in the world. I only have a GED, so what could I do? Sleeping with him was my ticket out of poverty."

Armin wanted to say that she had told him that many times, but he didn't. He let her repeat herself.

"There's no shame in getting a GED. Many people don't have it, you know?" Armin countered. "Did you know that Steve Jobs didn't finish college? Without him, you wouldn't have your iPhone."

"I know you're trying to encourage me, but I meant that when I was with the senator—former senator—he abused me emotionally and physically." Kelsey drew a deep breath. "I didn't know how his ex-wife put up with him—until I met her. Now I wonder how he had put up with her all those years. She's still coming after me, even after her husband's been exposed. Do you think she's going to stop after he dies?"

She laughed. Then she cried, burying her face in Armin's jacket, clutching it tightly, as she remained in a prone position on the couch.

Armin wanted so badly to go over there, sit down next to her, and hold her in his arms instead of being substituted by his jacket, but he resisted. A man's touch might be the last thing that Kelsey needed right now. He watched her weep alone.

He prayed that God would give her a hug.

She stopped crying. "That was for myself."

"Okay." He believed her.

"I'm really free. I'm already free spiritually in Christ, but now I need to be free physically. I want to fall in love again and marry and start a family."

Armin nodded at Kelsey's declaration. He knew not to say anything else because it might dredge up unwanted memories for Kelsey. She had left that world behind after she met Jesus, and now she had a new life in Christ. Armin had to let her be, if he were to believe what the Bible said in 2 Corinthians 5:17.

> Therefore if any man be in Christ, he is a new creature: old things are passed away; behold, all things are become new.

Armin unzipped the laptop compartment on his

backpack. He placed the laptop on the coffee table and booted it up.

The battery was almost fully charged, so he didn't have to worry about that. However, he still looked for his charging cable. He usually plugged in his laptop to the power supply whenever he had it on so that his laptop would remain a hundred percent charged every time.

Just in case.

As he went around the coffee table again, he noticed that Kelsey was watching him. "Whassup?"

"Nothing." Kelsey smiled a little, then closed her eyes.

She was still facing him when he sat down, and it was distracting. Looking over the laptop screen, he could see her sleeping on the couch.

He had seen many beautiful women in his life, and had dated one or two in the past. Kelsey was attractive, with her big eyes and long eyelashes, and reminded him of his cousins in New Delhi. They were the product of a mixed marriage between an Indian father and an Italian mother. Looking at Kelsey again, Armin thought she might have Italian features like his sister-in-law, but he couldn't begin to describe what that even meant.

All he knew was that if things were different, he'd date her.

Then again, it would cause a whole lot of problems with his mother, who had been pleading with him to move home to Mumbai. Job opportunities, she'd said, but Armin knew better.

Mother's ulterior motives were open secrets in the family. She'd prided herself on successfully pairing up Arun with his wife. Arun had no problem going on blind dates. Armin didn't like the idea of having dinner with strangers.

Armin hadn't told Mother that he was already in love—but with a woman whom Mother would never approve of in a million years.

# CHAPTER FOUR

"Do you know how close that was?" FBI Special Agent Ruby Tanaka almost raised her voice in the conference room. She was standing at the end of the conference table, facing Kelsey, who sat down somewhere in the center of the table, facing the glass wall between the conference room and the hallway outside.

There were bags under Tanaka's eyes, like she hadn't slept. In fact, she was supposed to meet Kelsey in the early morning hours, but Kelsey was fast asleep in the lounge, and Armin later told her that Tanaka didn't want to wake her up. So the agent waited in the conference room the entire time.

Kelsey felt sorry for her.

Tanaka's arm was in a sling, and her elbow was

heavily bandaged. She'd had surgeries at SMH only the day before, and should be recuperating, but there she was at the Hu Knows office, berating Kelsey.

As far as Kelsey knew, Tanaka had nerve damage and broken bones in her elbow. Recovery would take time, longer than eight weeks, perhaps.

*It's my fault. All my fault.*

So today, Kelsey decided she wouldn't argue with Tanaka. Let her rant. Let her get it out of her system.

There were just the two of them in the conference room with the door closed. Surely people could hear Tanaka yelling at her, but Kelsey was more concerned about Armin hearing them. However, he'd stayed up all night to work on his laptop, and had only fallen asleep after Kelsey woke up and then fell asleep again.

Now it was almost noon in Savannah. The debriefing had started late because Tanaka had let Kelsey sleep in at the Hu Knows lounge. Perhaps Tanaka wanted to prepare her for this lambasting. Or perhaps Tanaka herself needed a few extra hours to rest from her injuries sustained because she was protecting Kelsey.

"Next time when someone tells you they're a federal agent, ask for proof," Tanaka said. "Check their credentials. Don't just believe."

"I did." Kelsey remembered. "They look legit."

"Oh. Now the crime thickens."

"I didn't know what else to do. I couldn't call you because you were in the ER."

"I'm sorry." Tanaka sat down at the table and placed her phone next to a bottled water already on the table. "I'm just frustrated is all."

"So you wouldn't have wanted me to go to the campground?" Kelsey asked.

"Not alone in a camper van that had already been spotted earlier in the day."

"Oh."

"Anyway, you're a civilian and I don't expect you to know what to do in cases like this." Tanaka sighed. "If only I wasn't injured and stuck in the ER."

Kelsey blinked a few times. "I'm glad you're alive, Agent Tanaka."

"It's because you drove me to the hospital that I'm here today and that my arm is saved." Tanaka's voice softened. "Thank you."

"No problem. I'm glad you're on the mend now."

Tanaka turned her attention back to their situation at hand. "Did you know there were active shooters all around the camper van last night?"

Kelsey nodded. "Yes, I told the police officer that I heard gunfire."

"The FBI is on the scene now with the SCMPD, but I have no new information." Tanaka tapped her phone but didn't unlock it. Maybe she was checking her notifications or time. "They might want to ask you more questions."

"Do you think it related to our case?"

"We don't know." Tanaka didn't say more. "You didn't tell anyone about the informant, did you?"

Kelsey shook her head. "Not at all."

The only way they would have known...

*No, that can't be.*

As if reading her thoughts, Tanaka shook her head. "I checked the camper van. No bugs, no tracking device."

"I trust Nicholas. He's not a bad guy. He's always been good to me. He lets me use the camper van for free, you know, as long as I need it."

"If he only ever shows you one side of him, beware."

Tanaka's warning resonated with Kelsey for two seconds before it disappeared into thin air. Kelsey had no reason not to trust Nicholas.

"Is it possible that the gunfire was chaff?" Kelsey asked.

"Why do you say that?"

"Because you told me earlier that nobody was injured."

"You think they were shooting for fun?" Tanaka grinned.

"No. I was thinking that they made a lot of noise to

hide something." Kelsey wasn't sure where she was going with that, but she had felt it easy to share her thoughts with Tanaka, even if some of the things she said didn't make sense.

"What do you think they were hiding?"

"I don't know. The campground was isolated, and there were only two or three tents with people."

"Do you think they might be trying to scare you?" Tanaka asked.

"They being Mrs. Braun-Dean's associates?"

Tanaka nodded.

Kelsey nodded.

Tanaka nodded again.

Then she laughed. "Well, you made it out alive."

"Thank You, Jesus." Kelsey closed her eyes.

"The carjacker they sent to take you somewhere, wherever that was..." Tanaka took a sip of water from the bottle.

"Yes?" Kelsey waited.

"He also scared you to the point that you shot him three times."

"I didn't want to kill him." Kelsey started to cry.

"You didn't incapacitate him. You shot his shoulder, hand, and leg, and you made him angry. He could've really hurt you, but he didn't. Why is that?"

"I don't know. Perhaps he didn't want to break any more laws than he already had?" Kelsey recalled how the carjacker had tried to adhere to traffic laws. "He didn't seem to be maniacal."

Tanaka didn't smile. "I read your statement to SCMPD. He didn't fight back as much as he should have."

"Obviously, Roxanne Braun-Dean doesn't want you dead at all."

"She just wants to torture me." At the back of Kelsey's mind, she wondered if the carjacker really worked for Mrs. Braun-Dean.

"We don't know what she wants, but it might be related to the former senator."

The last person Kelsey wanted to think about. At all. "It would be easier if someone wanted me dead. Then I wouldn't have to deal with this crazy mess."

"Don't wish for something I wouldn't," Tanaka said. "Speaking as a friend, I believe that God let you live for a reason. So you need to find out what your purpose in life is. The old you is gone. It's the new you now. What does God want the new you to do?"

Kelsey could think of a few things, but she wasn't sure about any of them. She hoped that whatever God wanted her to accomplish in life included sharing the success with someone she loved. A significant other she could spend her life with. Someone who didn't look down on her past but encouraged her to live her best life in the present. Someone stable and quiet and reliable. Someone like...

She brushed away the thought.

"...which means she hasn't gotten what she wants," Tanaka finished her sentence.

"Sorry?" Kelsey hadn't paid attention because her mind veered off somewhere else.

"I was saying that we don't know what Mrs. Braun-Dean wants. Whatever it was, as long as she doesn't have it, you'll still be alive."

"Oh. How do I know what she wants from me?" Kelsey placed both hands on the table, fingers splayed out.

"That's the billion-dollar question, isn't it?"

Tanaka's phone rang and that was the end of the meeting. Tanaka was going to leave the conference room to take the call. That meant she didn't want Kelsey to hear it.

Kelsey put her palm up. Pointed to herself and then to the door.

"I go," she mouthed as she gathered her phone from the table.

Kelsey closed the conference room door behind her so that Tanaka could have some privacy. The hallway was empty and it was odd because this was right after lunch, and she had expected the Hu Knows headquarters to be filled with people.

But no. With the exception of the front desk receptionist and the two office workers Kelsey had run into in the lounge, none of the other private investigators were around. Perhaps they were all at work out there somewhere in the field. That might explain why Hu Knows netted millions of dollars in profit each yet.

Work was the key.

Kelsey made her way back to the lounge, feeling down that she was jobless. That was a brutal way of saying "in between jobs," which she was. How did one move from a full-time mistress to a respectable member of society?

With only a GED and a lot of vices on her resume, how could she move on?

In the last year, she had gone through many jobs, from cleaning toilets in a hotel to working night shifts at fast food joints. Whatever job she could find in which she didn't have to show her face, she did.

However, Roxanne's arrest had been all over the news, and the media had no problem plastering her face everywhere. Customers at the fast food restaurants recognized her and started taking photos, calling her facial features "stunning" and "surgically enhanced."

None of it was true. Kelsey knew she had a memorable face, but it wasn't artificial. She was simply an ordinary girl. Everything she had was natural. In fact, she had her mother's face, and if Mom had been alive, she'd be devastated at what her daughter had become, what she had used her natural beauty for.

Natural beauty?

It was a curse, actually.

Kelsey wished she were smart and intelligent and wise. Then she wouldn't have ended up as the senator's mistress. Then the media wouldn't have branded her as one of the many homewreckers, and made a saint out of Roxanne, who herself had been photographed with a string of men half her age.

If Kelsey could do it all over again, she'd stay as far away as possible from the Braun-Deans. They were up to no good, and they had ruined her life.

Kelsey sat down on the same couch she had slept on this morning, and wiped tears from her eyes. "My life is so worthless."

"Says who?" A man's voice. A familiar voice. A comforting voice.

Kelsey opened her eyes.

Standing there next to the seats was Armin, a towel in one arm, and a duffel bag slung over his other shoulder. His hair was wet, and he was wearing a long sleeved tee-shirt and a pair of jeans.

"You showered," Kelsey said. "Do they provide soap and shampoo?"

"No, I brought my own. My rental car is in the

parking lot, remember?" Armin put down his duffel bag. "There's no place to hang the towel."

"Is there a dryer? Maybe you can tumble dry it."

"That's an idea." He folded the wet towel and placed it neatly on top of his duffel bag. "I'll ask the front desk in a minute."

He came over to sit down next to Kelsey. He smelled good. Fresh soap. Like springtime.

"Don't come too close," Kelsey said. "I haven't showered. My clothes are in the camper van, which the police have impounded, as we know."

"I have some spare shirts and sweatpants in my bag." He pointed. "You can use my shampoo if you want."

"And soap?"

"There's a new bar in the duffel bag. You can have it."

"Thanks." Embarrassed now, Kelsey got up. She hadn't meant that she wanted to share Armin's soap. She was merely asking him if he had any soap she could use. She didn't want to explain that now because it would make it even more awkward. She didn't want Armin to remember her past and put a label on her.

Would he, though?

She had no idea.

She started walking, but someone held her hand.

"Hey, you're not worthless," Armin said.

Kelsey had almost forgotten what she often absent-mindedly recited to herself.

"Stop telling yourself lies, Kelsey." His voice was soft and genuine. "Jesus Christ died for your sins. You are priceless in His eyes."

He let go of her hand.

Kelsey wished he had held on to her hand. She could use some physical human touch right now. She wanted to lean down and hug him, but she didn't.

"I don't even have a job right now. I feel like a nobody."

"But you know you're not. You need to separate self from salary. Life from livelihood."

"I still need a job. I'm running out of savings, and in a few months, I'll be on welfare if I don't find a job."

"That's good that you still have savings," Armin said. "Do you have a budget?"

"Lean and mean and 'don't buy anything' is my budget."

"No, that isn't. I can help you with a budget."

"I can't pay you, Mr. CPA." Kelsey meant it.

"I'll help you free of charge as a friend."

Kelsey was moved. "Thank you."

"No problem."

"I still need a job. But I can't send in my resume anywhere because I'm busy right now helping the FBI catch Roxanne, you know."

"What jobs are you looking for?" Armin asked.

"One that pays." Kelsey laughed.

"Can you do office work?"

"You mean like data entry?" Hmm. She hadn't thought of that. It would be in the office. She didn't have to show her face to the public, like a retail job required. And she didn't need a college degree to do data entry. She just needed training.

"I mean like an office manager type of work," Armin corrected her.

"That job option hasn't crossed my mind."

"When this is over and I go back to my office, let's talk." He sounded serious.

"You mean you'll give me a job?" Kelsey's eyes widened.

"No guarantees. I'll give you an *opportunity* to apply for a job at my office. Whether HR hires you or not is going to depend on your skillset, which you can learn if you choose to check out the possibilities."

Possibilities.

Every time Kelsey was with Armin, she came out more positive about her outlook in life. Even though life was still hard for her, she could see the sun slowly peeking out behind the dark clouds.

Truly, Armin was a blessing to her. She recalled the 1 Thessalonians 5:11 verse that Pastor Flores had preached on at Riverside Chapel, five minutes from this building on River Street.

*Therefore comfort each other and edify one another, just as you also are doing.*

Pastor Flores also referenced another translation of the passage, and read from New American Standard, which used the phrase "build up one another" instead of "edify one another" as found in the New King James Version of the Bible.

Either way, Armin was doing it. Not only was he building her up, he was also edifying her.

"If you want, you can take online courses that teach you how to become an office manager, for example."

"Online courses. I haven't thought of that." She really hadn't. "What a great idea. You're so good to me, Armin. I like you."

Armin stopped her. "Hold up. What happens when I tell you there's hard work ahead? Will you dislike me then?"

"I'll always like you." Kelsey blushed. She shouldn't have said that, but the cat was out of the bag.

"What about me?" A third voice interrupted their conversation.

Both of them turned to look. Agent Tanaka

strutted forward in her combat boots, one arm in her leather jacket sleeve and the other in a sling. Her free hand was carrying a phone.

"This must be Armin Dhillon." She fist-bumped him with her left hand. "Sorry my right arm is out of commission at the moment. I'm Ruby Tanaka, but you knew that."

"Yes, ma'am." Armin smiled. "Thank you for taking care of my good friend, Kelsey."

Good friend?

Kelsey's optimism dropped a notch. She supposed friends could like one another, but when she had blurted that she'd always like Armin, she meant it more than merely friendly words.

Perhaps she had been too forthcoming.

# CHAPTER FIVE

D ue to budget cuts, the FBI was unable to provide Kelsey with a temporary camper van while the old one was with the local police. Kelsey had apologized to Nicholas, but even he couldn't provide her with another vehicle.

Tanaka told Kelsey that it would be two or three days before they could return the van to her, but at least a week more if she wanted them to fix the broken back window first.

In other words, Kelsey had to find somewhere else to stay, and it had to be a safe place where she could sleep in peace and feel protected from Roxanne and her vile schemes.

After meeting Armin, Tanaka left to go back to the FBI office in downtown Savannah for a meeting where she would try to make new arrangements to keep Kelsey safe. A place to stay, food, that sort of thing.

Speaking of food, Kelsey was more worried that Tanaka hadn't eaten any breakfast or lunch, but the agent didn't care. She grabbed a power bar and a room-temperature bottled water from the Hu Knows kitchen pantry, and off she went, after telling Kelsey to stay put in the Hu Knows office.

That, Kelsey wasn't going to do.

It had turned out that the FBI agent at the hospital who told Kelsey to wait at the remote campground was a real agent. He was reprimanded and put on paid leave while they figured out what was going on.

Just that one thing didn't make Kelsey mistrust the agency.

She trusted Agent Tanaka but only her. Her elbow injury meant that she could be replaced.

She trusted PI Earl Young, but the man was over the moon because his wife had delivered safely. The new parents were happily parenting their new baby boy, a ten pounder, and would be on parental leave for a month. Whoopee!

All Kelsey had left was CPA Armin Dhillon who had told her that he'd never fired a weapon in his life, wasn't terribly athletic, and would rather spend his time reading the stock markets than a novel.

And this was her only buddy to rely on.

Unless...

Unless she contacted Nicholas.

Kelsey wasn't sure what Nicholas could do to keep her safe, but he had contacts everywhere. When Braun-Dean wanted to go off the grid for a few months for his mental health and wellness, it was Nicholas, also known as The Stylist, who'd found him a nice, exclusive hideaway in the hills of Tennessee, where not even Roxanne could find him.

Perhaps it was time to call Nicholas. After all, he'd told Kelsey that he'd help her at no charge, and had even provided her with a burner phone she could use for this very matter.

She left the lounge and found an empty conference room for privacy. She locked the door and called Nicholas.

He answered at the first ring. He was sitting in his gaming chair in his small office. "Tell me everything, love."

And so Kelsey did. There wasn't anything she had to hide anyway because Nicholas had always been on Kelsey's side. Before the senator had fired Nicholas, the latter had protected Kelsey. Everything went downhill after Nicholas left the campaign trail and another stylist took over the hair and makeup department.

Kelsey suspected that Braun-Dean had regretted

firing his best stylist who could bring out the highlights in his hair, but it was all too late.

Kelsey also felt unprotected once Nicholas was gone. The senator's irrational behavior and fits of anger grew more and more unpredictable until that crazy weekend in Miami.

Ironically, it had been the hostage situation that had freed her from the senator forever. Pilar Santiago, who worked with Hu Knows, had rescued her from the hotel and then prayed for her.

Pilar then proceeded to tell Kelsey the good news about how she could be saved and have a new life. The fact that Jesus Christ had cleansed her from the many sins in her life made Kelsey weep. She believed in Jesus Christ that day--under the hot Miami sun—and was baptized in the ocean five months later.

Ever since then, Kelsey had been telling everyone that she had accepted Jesus as her Lord and Savior, including Nicholas, whom she considered to be one of her best friends.

Even though Nicholas wasn't a Christian, he didn't look down on her for being the senator's mistress for three years. In fact, he had cheered her on when she told him about her conversion to Christianity. He had never left her side all this time. If anyone had seen the worst in the senator's private life, it was Nicholas, more than the senator's own security guards.

"So you don't want to go to a safe house?" Nicholas asked. "You'd think the FBI has a lot of those."

"A camper van is more flexible. I can go anywhere."

"Makes sense. But you need someone else to rent it for you and let you drive so it won't be traced back to you."

"Right."

"Where do you plan to go with the camper?" Nicholas asked.

"I knew you'd ask. I'll tell you later, but now I just need to go hide somewhere."

"Somewhere you don't want your friendly neighborhood federal agent to know?"

"You got it."

"What are you planning, love?"

Kelsey didn't answer him. In fact, she didn't know what she was planning. She had no idea where she was going from here. But she had to get away to somewhere she could sit down and think about all the things that had happened to her in the last three years, and how that horrible time of her life might be the reason she was in a crisis now.

"When I find out what's going on, I'll tell you," Kelsey said.

"Be sure I'm the first to know."

It was a good thing that Kelsey was talking on a

burner phone, but she was in a Hu Knows conference room, which might have ears. Or not.

Even though she trusted Agent Tanaka, she couldn't trust the people around her.

She also couldn't bank on the hypothesis that Roxanne didn't want her dead. Without knowing what Roxanne wanted from her, Kelsey couldn't just sit around and wait for the news to unfold itself. Besides, the former senator had many enemies, and his ex-wife was only one of many.

Any one of them could be after Kelsey.

For example, Braun-Dean owed people money, especially The Steward, his go-to crypto guru who had helped him amass his bitcoins. The Steward was supposed to take ten percent of every cryptocurrency sale that the senator made, but he took more than that behind Braun-Dean's back. So the latter found a new consultant to balance out The Steward and prevent him from accessing the former senator's cryptocurrency fortune.

The consultant was found dead in Puerto Rico one month after Braun-Dean was arrested and released on bail.

Therefore, there were only certain people Kelsey dared to trust.

It was time to take matters into her own hands. She prayed that she wasn't making another mistake. Being a new Christian, she felt that she didn't have enough wisdom to make every decision the right way.

One thing was for sure. Going forward, she would measure the dimension of a window before she tried to climb through it.

"Have you eaten lunch?" Nicholas asked.

On camera, he looked genuinely concerned.

"No. Why?" Kelsey asked.

"Then it's my duty as your best friend to remind you to eat three meals a day."

Best friend? Kelsey wouldn't consider Nicholas her only best friend, but she didn't want to correct him lest he stopped helping her. Maybe he considered her his best friend.

"Bet you skipped breakfast today," Nicholas said.

"I was asleep. Long night."

"When you woke up, what did you do?"

"Brushed my teeth and studied my Bible."

"And..."

"And it was time for a meeting with Agent Tanaka. Then I went back to the lounge." She didn't give him the details, including her conversation with Armin or wearing his clothes after showering. "Then I called you."

"How about we eat lunch together?"

"You mean while we chat on video?"

"Yeah. Then you can tell me about your meeting

with Tanaka. What did she have to say? What does she want you to do next?"

"Aren't you the curious cat?"

"Am I?" Nicholas laughed with her.

He made Kelsey smile. Another person who could make her smile was Armin. Speaking of him, where was he? The last time she had seen him, he was asleep in the armchair with his laptop on his lap. He didn't look uncomfortable, but Kelsey moved the laptop to the table and covered him with the jacket he had loaned her.

"So what did Tanaka tell you to do?" Nicholas asked again. "Did she say you should stay put or sacrifice yourself?"

"Sacrifice myself? Whatcha talking about?"

Nicholas didn't answer. He was looking away from the camera. "Hey, did you see the news?"

"I haven't paid attention all day. I'm treading water."

"Then I'll tell you." Nicholas drew a deep breath. "Your nemesis, the formerly infamous Senator Felix Braun-Dean, is dead."

"What? Dead? How?" Yet Kelsey felt nothing.

Absolutely nothing.

"It's in the news. I'll send you a link." Nicholas seemed gleefully calm. "He can't hurt you anymore, Kelsey. It's finally over."

"Over? Is it?"

"I know that you're concerned about Roxanne Braun-Dean."

Kelsey nodded, hoping that Nicholas had a solution.

"Do you know what she really wants?" Nicholas asked.

"Does she know herself?" Perhaps that wasn't how she should've replied to Nicholas, who had nothing but her best interest in mind. "I truly don't know beyond the usual stuff like jealousy or some such."

"We know she's a vindictive person. If she couldn't have her husband, then nobody else could—not the string of mistresses that the former senator bedded in every state he traveled to during his failed reelection campaign. The beast was addicted."

"I should've left a long time ago."

"If you had, you wouldn't have met me," Nicholas said. "I'll take care of things for you from now on. Don't worry about Mean Dean."

Only Nicholas dared to call Roxane Braun-Dean that nickname. Nobody else did, not even Kelsey.

"What do you mean?" Kelsey didn't want to guess.

"You want a peaceful life without anybody bothering you, right?"

Kelsey nodded.

"Mean Dean is bothering you."

"She scares me. If we could just sit down and talk, maybe we could both move on."

"You want to visit her at the Miami jail?"

"Is that possible? Can you find out?"

"Are you naive or do you have something planned?" Nicholas laughed.

"I have no idea what I'm doing. I'm just trying to survive." There, she said it. There was no point putting on airs and pretending like she had anything under control. In fact, control was the last thing Kelsey had.

Beeps went off on Nicholas's end of the chat video, and he disappeared for a couple of minutes.

Meanwhile, Kelsey prayed for resolution to her crisis. When she'd been carjacked, she wondered if Roxanne could have sent the carjacker. However, now that she saw how unbothered Nicholas was, she wondered if she might have been mistaken about who was behind last night's crime.

With Roxanne in jail, it might be someone else who was pulling the strings. Who? Braun-Dean had many enemies, and Kelsey had met or known about most of them because he'd tell her when nobody else wanted to listen to him.

Whenever she had listened to him, he'd deposit more gold into her bank vault. Unfortunately, the FBI had confiscated all of the gold bars as a part of their investigation into the Braun-Deans' money laundering schemes.

Hmm... Perhaps all this mess had come from their own failed business venture, and had nothing to do with Kelsey.

*Oh I wish.*

Nicholas returned, his face pale. "A couple of videos are being passed around in the media. My associates obtained a copy of them. You need to see them but it's bad news all around."

"For me?"

Nicholas nodded. "Before you view it, I need to tell you that it doesn't look good. After you view it, I need to tell you that you must get out of there."

"You mean out of Savannah?"

"Yes."

"I think we are leaving as soon as Deshon arrives," Kelsey said. "Earl called Armin earlier to say that Deshon is delayed. He missed his flight due to a late project, so he's driving out here sometime this afternoon. He should be here five hours after he leaves Atlanta."

"Deshon who?" Nicholas looked perplexed.

"He's a PI working at the Hu Knows office in Atlanta. He's replacing Earl on paternity leave."

"Do you even know this guy?"

Kelsey was surprised that Nicholas even asked

such a question. "Uh, I've never met him personally, but Earl has worked with him. After all, Helen vets every person who works at Hu Knows."

"I don't trust anyone but myself."

"I trust God."

"Good for you, but we're trying to save your life."

"God can save my life."

Nicholas paused. Drew a slow deep breath. Then smiled into the camera. "Kelsey dear, please listen to me. Don't trust anyone but me."

*Don't trust anyone but me.*

A red flag popped up in Kelsey's mind. Why would Nicholas say such a thing to her? He knew that she worked with Agent Tanaka, PI Earl, and CPA Armin. She was sure she could trust these three people.

Plus Cade and Pilar Sumter. And Helen Hu.

"What do you want me to do, Nicholas?" Kelsey fished.

"Too late!" Nicholas's eyes were on his phone. He spat out a few expletives, then apologized to Kelsey.

She brushed it off, but recalled that Nicholas had shown such a contained anger before. He'd look calm on the outside, but Kelsey could sense the powder keg about to explode inside of him. However, she had never seen him totally lose his cool in front of her.

"Too late what? Tell me, Nicholas." Kelsey

sounded helpless, but it was because she was. "Send me the video now."

"Yes, ma'am." Nicholas straightened up.

They watched the video together, and Kelsey's jaw dropped. "That can't be real."

"Does it matter? What they want is to get you arrested. They can sort out the deep fake later, but by then, you're already in their custody."

"That can't be me." Kelsey shook her head. Then stopped. "Did you say deep fake? As in the video is AI-generated?"

"That's my guess."

"How can I fight this?" Kelsey wondered who she could go to for help. Armin was in the lounge, and she knew she had to show him the video.

"You can't. I'll send a car to get you out of there." Nicholas had made the decision for her.

Something about that bothered Kelsey. Not that she didn't appreciate his gesture. However, it was bad enough that she was figuring it out as she went. It was worse if Nicholas also did the same.

"Where are you taking me?" Kelsey asked.

"To me. You'll be safe with me. Don't you agree?"

Kelsey couldn't answer him.

"I'm visiting my grandmother in Spartanburg. It will only be about four hours from you to me."

Spartanburg, South Carolina, was where Nicholas

had grown up, although he'd spent most of his teen and adult life in Atlanta, where he'd established himself as a celebrity stylist.

There was a fallout of some sort with a singer he'd dated, and he disappeared from the scene. He had emerged a few years later as an active supporter of Braun-Dean, and had become his stylist and make-up artist.

He hadn't settled down somewhere he could call home, preferring to live out of a recreational vehicle. That way he could travel all over the country.

It had been Nicholas who'd introduced the Braun-Deans to someone known as The Steward, the cryptocurrency king who'd laundered more money for the Braun-Deans than anyone else.

After the Braun-Deans were arrested, The Steward disappeared. Nicholas severed all ties with him, and closed his salon. However, he had kept in touch with Kelsey. In the last year, he had helped her with groceries and bills, all without asking for anything in return. He had dipped into his savings to hire a defense attorney for her.

He would have hired a security team to protect Kelsey if she hadn't turned him down. At that time she had started working with Agent Tanaka to round up Roxanne's associates in her money theft, so Kelsey figured that Tanaka was enough protection for her.

Still, Nicholas worried.

Such a good man.

Why wouldn't Kelsey trust him? Nicholas was such a dear. He looked younger than his forty years, perhaps due to botox and a facelift. His look alone made him a fortune on YouTube and TikTok, as he live-streamed himself solving strangers' life problems while cutting and styling their hair.

To everyone out there in the world, he was The Stylist. To Kelsey, he was Nicholas Bay, somewhat shy and reticent in front of strangers, but ultra caring toward her.

So yes, she would trust him.

"Ten minutes," Nicholas spoke into the camera. "Go gather up your stuff, go to the bathroom if you have to, and then go downstairs to the building entrance on East Bay Street. A midnight blue SUV will be parked outside. The doors will be unlocked, and the key fob in the glove compartment."

Why would Kelsey willingly go with Nicholas?

She remembered what Tanaka had told her about their purpose. There was no other choice. After all, as long as Roxanne hadn't gotten what she wanted, she'd keep Kelsey alive. That belief was her immunity ticket.

This time, if Kelsey did what Tanaka had planned, there'd be enough evidence to incarcerate Roxanne for a long time.

Then again, Kelsey couldn't assume that Roxanne was her sole enemy. Kelsey had been with Braun-Dean at meetings she shouldn't have attended, and mingled with associates who might not want their dealings with the dead senator to be known. Those unknown people working in dark shadows might be more dangerous than Roxanne.

"I'll go to see you if I can bring another person with me," Kelsey bravely said. It was risky, but she didn't feel safe going alone to Nicholas.

"Who?"

"Armin." A while back, she had informed Nicholas that she'd been in touch with Armin.

Still, Armin was a CPA, and he wasn't exactly built like a bodybuilder. In fact, he was tall and lanky, and didn't seem athletic at all. In terms of a formidable bodyguard, he wasn't one at all.

*I'll just have to protect him.*

"Arun's CPA brother." Nicholas seemed to be deep in thought. "Do you really want to involve him in this?"

"He's already in it. Then again, he might not come with us. We're waiting for Deshon from Atlanta. Armin might simply want to stick to that plan."

"Is that all he knows?"

Kelsey nodded without hesitating.

"You can never tell him everything, but you knew that."

"Yeah, I know." Kelsey assumed that when Nicholas said "everything," he meant everything about Roxanne, how he'd had a summer fling with her a few years ago when Braun-Dean had been out of town. This happened long before Kelsey had shown up on the scene.

Maybe Nicholas didn't want Kelsey to tell Armin about their past history. Kelsey had known Nicholas long before she had met the Braun-Deans. Shortly before Nicholas had dropped out of college in Missouri, they had met at the convenience store where Kelsey worked, stocking shelves while studying for her GED. They hit it off right away, and Nicholas tutored her in Math at no charge if she paid for his occasional snacks.

When Kelsey passed her GED, they became fast friends. Nicholas spent time looking for a job for her. One of the skills she had was to make people trust her, almost implicitly. She could say anything and make it sound real. She thought she could get a job in retail, but Nicholas said that he had a better sales job for her that'd pay five figures a year.

He sent her to Braun-Dean.

Looking back, she shouldn't have taken that job. It had started very simply with Kelsey working at Braun-

Dean's reelection campaign headquarters. Nicholas had arranged for the previous worker to be fired to create the vacancy for Kelsey.

Nicholas—who had lied, cheated, and stolen his way into Braun-Dean's trusted inner circle of advisors—had been instrumental in getting Kelsey a permanent position by Braun-Dean's side. Her price for that: her body.

That was then, in those dark days of her life, when she had struggled to find food to eat and a place to stay. Working night shifts at the convenience store didn't cut it. She had gone through six or seven jobs in fifteen months, had no health insurance, and no future.

Nicholas had given her an opportunity. All she had to do was—

*Go and sin no more.*

Yes, that old life was gone.

Today, Kelsey was a believer in Jesus Christ, and she trusted God to keep her life clean. Even if she never had a boyfriend again, it mattered not. Kelsey's soul had made peace with God.

Unfortunately, the ghost of Christmas past wouldn't leave her alone. Nicholas was pulling her back into a past she wanted to forget. He wasn't the only one. Tanaka wanted to put away Roxanne for good, and she had convinced Kelsey that she was the tipping point for her old boss's ex-wife.

All these meant that Kelsey had to dredge up her dirty past before she could walk into a clean future.

Kelsey's face felt hot. She felt ashamed in her heart of her horrible past. She knew God had forgiven her, but she had to bear the consequences of her sins. This would bring closure, and she could finally move on.

Nicholas cleared his throat. "All right. Go ask."

"Thank you."

"The less your new friend knows, the less we need to clean up afterwards, right?" Nicholas's eyebrows rose.

Sometimes, those blonde eyebrows rose when Nicholas was unsure about something and was looking for verification or confirmation.

A second red flag popped up in Kelsey's head.

She stared at the screen, trying to read Nicholas's face. He looked concerned, like a best friend would. Or like the former senator had, just minutes before he took out his frustrations on her with his fists. To Nicholas's credit, he had never laid a hand on her. In fact, he hardly touched her beyond a perfunctory hug whenever they ran into each other at the campaign headquarters.

If anything, Nicholas had been a very good friend.

And that was why the red flag popped up. Nicholas was too good to be true. If he had lied and stolen when he wasn't with Kelsey, why would she be an exception? Why could she trust him to always tell her the truth and to never steal from her?

"Kelsey, I'm super concerned about you," Nicholas said sweetly.

Too sweet.

She could almost hear a hissing sound.

Was Nicholas a snake in the grass?

Nicholas leaned into the camera. "If you need a companion, it's me you want, not Armin."

"He's just a friend."

"Okay. If you say so." Nicholas sat back in his chair.

Kelsey nodded, all innocent like.

She could not afford to let Nicholas doubt her. The moment he did, her agreement with Agent Tanaka would all fall apart. For now, she had to walk the tightrope between Nicholas and Tanaka. Both wanted something from her, and both made her keep their deals a secret.

Being a double agent made her tired.

*Oh so tired.*

# CHAPTER SIX

Something didn't feel right, but Armin had no time to verify. Kelsey was leaving to meet Nicholas in South Carolina, whether Armin wanted her to or not.

As soon as Kelsey had told him that she was leaving town, Armin packed quickly, shoving stuff into his duffel bag, and ran out of the lounge after Kelsey. He didn't want to be separated from Kelsey for many reasons, most of which he couldn't process in his head then and there.

There was no receptionist at the front desk, but he was sure there were cameras watching them leave the Hu Knows premises.

Down the elevator they went and then out the door into a late afternoon chill on Bay Street as

January rain pelted cars and sidewalks. They had no umbrella, but Armin had a baseball cap and Kelsey wore Armin's hooded jacket.

They said nothing to each other. Kelsey was busy looking at her burner phone where a walking map showed her where to go.

"What type of vehicle?" Armin was hoping to be useful.

"I don't know."

"You said it has arrived?"

Kelsey nodded. Still taking the lead, she walked briskly.

The only thing Armin could do was follow. The compromise had been his. He had to yield to her in order to protect her and keep her safe.

No, he didn't want to be a hero. He'd rather go home to Nashville and read a book.

However, this was a part of his new job, one that he had been instrumental in creating. In the beginning, he had wanted to go solo with his investigation into his brother's murder, but the leads had grown cold and his savings had run out.

Borrowing money from family wasn't going to be enough. His parents were aging and they needed money to retire in comfort in Mumbai.

Armin had to find new funding that wouldn't require him to go to the authorities, who had since given up on his brother's murder case, after establishing that none of Arun's criminal employers had been responsible for the car bomb that had taken his life and destroyed his family van on his driveway.

One call to Helen Hu had been all it had taken to secure a new position for himself at the white collar crime department of Hu Knows at their Atlanta branch. He was grateful that Helen had trusted him, but she had been a maverick herself and was open to new ideas, including hiring people of various professions, not just former law enforcement personnel, for her ever-expanding worldwide private investigative firm.

Sadly, six months after he moved to Atlanta, Armin still hadn't achieved his goals. However, he'd become friends with Kelsey, and that had led to the discovery of one Nicholas Bay, a person of interest in Armin's eyes.

This very person had now convinced Kelsey to leave the Hu Knows office before Deshon arrived and to tell no one of their change of plans.

Armin sighed. His feet were stuck to the sidewalk, his duffel bag slung over his shoulder. His heart felt heavy, like this was a huge mistake.

To go or not to go?

Wasn't it a bit late to ask that question?

Kelsey stopped in front of a midnight blue Toyota Highlander. "This one."

Before Armin could say anything, Kelsey was in the driver's seat. Armin climbed into the passenger seat, the duffel bag in his arms. He tossed it to the backseat and buckled up.

Kelsey placed her phone in a cupholder. She put a foot on the brakes and pressed the ignition button on the dashboard near the steering wheel.

"I've never driven this before, but it feels like a regular SUV." Kelsey inched her way into the East Bay Street traffic, stopping a few times at crosswalks to let tourists get to their destinations.

*Well, let me correct that.*

Not all people who crossed East Bay Street to get to the Savannah River were tourists. Armin was sure there were locals in the mix as well.

They were on East Bay Street for a good five minutes before Kelsey spoke again. "Sorry."

"About what?"

"Dragging you into my mess."

"You mean leaving town without letting Helen, Earl, or Deshon know?" Armin asked. "Or feeling guilty that you're hiding something from me?"

"Can you tell?" Kelsey smiled. Her eyes never left the windshield.

That smile that Armin had seen before meant that she agreed with him on his statement but that she would not offer any explanation or divulge any information.

If only they could talk amicably and transparently with each other, perhaps Kelsey might feel more comfortable sharing more about what she was up to.

Knowing what was going on would certainly make things easier for Armin.

Or would it?

The more he knew about things, the more he had to share that information with his new employer, who might very well stop Armin from continuing his quest.

Therefore, the only logical conclusion was for Armin to go with Kelsey, stay close to her, and stick to his cover story, which was only one part of his plan. Kelsey did not need to know the rest of it beyond Arun.

"We have a full tank of gas. I think we can make it to Spartanburg. If we have to stop to get more gas, then we will."

"A friend at work has the same vehicle. I think it can go over five hundred miles on a full tank of gas." He checked Kelsey's phone. "Spartanburg is less than half that distance. I think we'll make it without stopping."

Kelsey glanced over at Armin. "Thanks for coming with me. It's no fun going alone."

"You'll meet Nicholas when you arrive, so you won't be alone all the way."

"I could use some conversation in these four hours on the road. Might take longer since I'm driving."

"Don't speed," Armin blurted out the words and regretted it.

"Are you telling me what to do?" Kelsey chuckled.

"Do we need to stop for snacks on the way?" Armin changed the question.

Kelsey sighed. "We should've gotten some chips and water from the kitchen."

"I have some bottled water in my bag."

"If we don't have to stop, I'd rather not." Kelsey followed the directions toward Interstate 17, which would lead them across the Georgia-South Carolina border. "We might show up on camera at gas stations. I don't have money, and credit cards are traceable."

"I have cash," Armin said.

"Too risky. Did I mention cameras?" Kelsey changed lanes and nearly sideswiped a convertible. "Sorry."

She said it so casually that Armin almost missed the point that her mind was probably preoccupied.

"Maybe I should drive," Armin offered.

"What's that supposed to mean?" Her voice was calm.

"Nothing. I just thought that maybe I should drive."

"Oh, because you're a man or because you think you're calmer?"

"I'm not saying this or that. I offered to be your chauffeur because I think you have a lot on your mind." It was all Armin could think of to say.

Kelsey nodded. "I do have a lot on my mind, but how about we wait until the halfway point, and then you can drive the rest of the way while I navigate?"

"Okay. That's fair enough."

Then they were quiet again. Armin didn't want to speak first because he didn't want to distract Kelsey.

"Do you think I'm irrational?" Kelsey asked.

More like unpredictable. "How do you mean?"

"The rational thing to do would be to wait for Deshon to take over from Earl, and then go from there. Tanaka's at a meeting, and she's going to return to Hu Knows to find us gone as well."

When Armin didn't say anything, Kelsey continued.

"The irrational thing I've just done is to remove myself from an 'official' support team, and put all my hopes in Nicholas."

At the mention of his name, Armin realized that this vehicle had been sent by Nicholas himself. Kelsey might trust Nicholas, but Armin did not. In this state of distrust, he could not assume that Nicholas wouldn't have bugged this vehicle.

Armin recalled the story that Earl had told him about the time he'd met his wife. They were driving in Atlanta and found out that the FBI had placed a listening device in the vehicle.

Fast forward three years, would Nicholas also do the same thing? Might he also include a video camera to record them talking?

Truth be told, Armin didn't know Nicholas from Adam, and could not differentiate him from a pervert, so to speak. All Armin had known about Nicholas had come from Kelsey's perspective of the hairstylist who was also a millionaire from his cryptocurrency trading.

If Nicholas had amassed wealth, why was he still a hairstylist?

On that point alone, Armin couldn't trust him.

"I've known Nicholas for some years now," Kelsey said. "He has helped me a lot. He knows what he's doing and this is for our safety and good."

Armin decided he shouldn't speak much because everything he said might be recorded.

Kelsey opened her mouth to say some more. Armin gently tugged at her jacket sleeve. She turned her face.

Armin put a finger over his lips, and another finger on his ear.

*Let's not talk too much. Someone might be listening.*

Kelsey made an 'o' with her mouth. It looked like she understood.

"Did you realize something?" Kelsey said.

"What?"

"It only rained near the river. We're outside Savannah now and there's no rain."

"That's a good observation."

And so began their mindless conversation about the weather. Armin had to give Kelsey credit for understanding his finger signs earlier.

Vehicles seemed to be slowing down on the highway, and suddenly red tail lights were everywhere. The truck in front of them suddenly stopped.

Kelsey slammed the brakes. Her right arm swung out, and her fingers splayed out on Armin's chest, gently pushing him back in the passenger seat.

The vehicle slowed to a stop.

Kelsey retracted her arm. "Uh...um...sorry... Are you okay?"

"I'm fine. Thanks. I have my seat belt on." Poor reply. He should have stopped at "thanks" and no more.

"Ah yes. Okay." Kelsey didn't look at him. "I

don't know why I did that. I mean, the vehicles around us stopped so suddenly that I was merely reacting."

Merely? "Did you work with children a lot?"

"Children don't usually sit in the front seat. What are you trying to say?"

"I was thinking that maybe your protective instinct kicked in when the vehicles in front of us stopped too quickly."

"Are you saying I was trying to prevent you from flying through the windshield?" She laughed.

"So you care." Armin's heart felt warm and fuzzy inside.

"I shouldn't have invited you on this road trip." Kelsey frowned.

"And let me miss all the fun?"

"Fun? Wait until you see the video circulating in the media about me." She pointed to her phone. "Check my messages on the Home Screen. Nicholas sent me a few links. One of them is the news about Braun-Dean's death. See if you can find it."

Armin realized that Kelsey had nothing to hide—or at least she felt that way—because she wanted him to check her private messages with Nicholas.

He picked up her phone, which was open to Google Maps. He had the same phone, so he knew how to navigate back to the Home Screen. Very quickly, he read the messages from Nicholas. His words seemed benign.

He tapped on the video. It was the six o'clock news from this morning.

"Breaking news!" The reporter said. "Sixty-six-year-old former senator Felix Braun-Dean has been found unresponsive in a bathtub in his home. He had just posted a twenty-billion-dollar bail, and had gone home to rest and await his own trial, when this happened."

"When did this happen?" Armin asked too quickly.

The reporter had all the answers. "The coroner is figuring out the time of death as we speak."

"There's a follow-up clip," Kelsey said.

"In the next video?"

"No. Wait until the end."

Armin noticed that there were two new clips in that one video. That was to say, someone had combined the two videos into one file. Edited? Tampered?

The second news clip explained more about the situation. Not the same station, but another. Armin assumed they were Atlanta stations because the ticker tape showed metro Atlanta weather for the next day.

"We have now received confirmation that former Senator Felix Braun-Dean died around four o'clock in the morning two days ago, after which the killer had placed him into his bathtub."

Something didn't add up.

To begin with, Armin had been paying attention to the news all morning and afternoon. There was not a single news channel reporting the death of Braun-Dean. Surely news all over the country would have reported it.

"I didn't see this news anywhere else," Armin said.

"Maybe it's the Hu Knows Wi-Fi. Maybe there's a firewall that prevents us from seeing certain things on the internet."

"I don't think Helen has time to censor incoming news." Armin regretted mentioning names. He prayed that he wouldn't get Helen into danger.

"You mean Earl? He's in charge of the Savannah office now."

Armin checked his own phone. Scrolling past the market reports and general weather news, he came across a slew of headline news reporting Braun-Dean's death.

But...but... He hadn't seen any of these back at the lounge earlier.

*What is going on?*

"So the news outlets are now reporting it, right?" Kelsey asked. "Nicholas got the video clips sooner than even the news outlet."

Where had Nicholas obtained the news clip? Perhaps he had an inside connection to early bird news or something.

Regardless of his concerns, Armin knew he couldn't question Kelsey in a vehicle sent by Nicholas. He had to wait for another opportunity outside the vehicle.

"The next video is why I agreed to leave town." Kelsey went with the traffic flow on I-17.

Armin closed that video and then opened the next one, which seemed to have been recorded on a surveillance camera outside someone's house.

"Whose house?" Armin asked.

"Braun-Dean's. He has a home outside Marietta. That's the back door, facing about ten acres of wooded lot."

The video showed the back view of a woman walking out of the house, onto the porch, and then down the steps. She stopped to look at the darkness that shrouded the distance. Then she turned and walked back into the house.

It was then that Armin saw who it was.

Someone who looked like Kelsey Murphy.

On screen, the similarities were uncanny, except...

He replayed it.

The woman's right eye twitched.

As far as Armin knew, Kelsey's eyes didn't twitch,

although he couldn't be a hundred percent sure since he hadn't been with her every day for enough days to confirm it.

"When was this video recorded?" Armin asked before he spotted the timestamp on the bottom left of the screen. "Shortly before four in the morning. But it can't be you."

"Of course it can't be me. In the middle of the night two days ago, I was driving here from Miami. I was on the road for nearly eight hours, arriving in Savannah mid-morning to meet Agent Tanaka at the FBI office downtown." Kelsey's eyes were on the road.

"Did anyone see you when you left Miami?"

"I got gas at three o'clock somewhere outside Miami." Kelsey glanced at Armin. "Someone impersonated me."

"Maybe it's not even someone. Maybe it's a deep fake video that's generated by AI."

"Seriously? Why would they go to all that trouble?"

Kelsey's phone rang.

The screen showed a cartoon avatar with The Stylist written above it. Armin held the phone in front of Kelsey so she could tap the screen.

"Hey. Whassup?" Kelsey's voice was serious.

"I'm sending you a new video," Nicholas said. "This one is bad news."

"What else isn't?"

Her phone pinged.

"Tap open it for me, please," Kelsey asked Armin.

So he did.

The video showed a reporter standing outside Braun-Dean's lakeside cabin.

"We're back at Felix Braun-Dean's five-million-dollar mansion, where a tragic death happened two days ago." He walked a little bit toward the front door, where people who looked like they were from law enforcement entered and exited.

A woman stepped into the video frame.

"We're here with Chief of Police Molly Henry of the Marietta Police Department," the reporter said. "Chief Henry, may we ask you what is happening now?"

"A warrant has been issued for the arrest of Kelsey Murphy, who went by the mononym Zuriel, for the murder of Felix Braun-Dean. If anyone has any information about her whereabouts, please contact our hotline."

An arrest warrant on the same day meant that the local police department had enough evidence to potentially convict Kelsey—more than the surveillance video. What exactly did they have?

Something definitely didn't add up, but Armin

couldn't say anything in front of Nicholas, who was still on the phone.

"Now are you happy I had the foresight to get you out of there?" Nicholas seemed to be talking to Kelsey.

"Yes, big brother. You always have my best interest at heart."

"Big brother? You insult me, Kelsey." Nicholas's voice sounded hurt.

What was going on there? Armin had no idea.

"Listen, we're three hours away from you," Kelsey said. "Should I be worried we won't make it to you?"

"You mean in the sense that you're fleeing the state of Georgia?"

"Yes." Kelsey's voice turned serious.

"Don't worry about any of that. I'll take care of everything for you."

"Everything?" Kelsey asked. "What's my price?"

"We'll discuss that when I see you. I'll be waiting." He hung up without a goodbye.

"Is he always abrupt like that?" Armin asked.

Kelsey nodded. "You get used to it after a while. He doesn't waste time."

An impatient man.

Armin checked his phone. No arrest news. Nothing. He googled all the news outlets. Checked X, the social media platform formerly known as Twitter, and YouTube. Not a single piece of news about the arrest warrant for Kelsey Murphy besides the two videos that Nicholas had sent her.

Armin was beginning to think that Nicholas had fed them a false narrative, including perhaps some deep fake videos, but he couldn't be sure, and he couldn't talk to Kelsey about it in the vehicle.

"Could you forward these videos to me?" Armin asked, at the risk of putting himself on Nicholas's blacklist.

"Just do it yourself from my phone," Kelsey told him.

So he did.

The first thing Armin did upon receiving the files on his burner phone email was to forward them to Deshon.

Nicholas wasn't the only person with connections. In fact, Deshon ran the Atlanta branch for Hu Knows and was in close contact with Binary Systems, also headquartered in Atlanta. The computer security company would probably be able to analyze the videos from Nicholas and ascertain whether they were false narratives using deep fake video technology, as Armin suspected.

At this point, Armin didn't want Kelsey to know that he'd been in contact with Deshon for some months now. If she did, she might accidentally blurt out their names to Nicholas.

Seeing that she trusted Nicholas quite a bit, Armin decided that he would speak less from now on.

It was too bad because he wanted to be transparent in his conversations with Kelsey.

Perhaps some day they could once more, over a cup of coffee or perhaps dinner.

But not today.

# CHAPTER SEVEN

Past the unincorporated Coosawhatchie on Interstate 95, Armin saw the flashing blue lights first before he heard the sirens of the South Carolina Highway Patrol vehicle ordering them to pull over.

"Was I speeding?" Kelsey asked, both hands gripping the steering wheel as she eased off to the right shoulder. She put the vehicle in park in the emergency lane.

"Were you? I wasn't looking at your speedometer." Armin glanced back as the police cruiser stopped behind them.

"What do I do now?" Kelsey started shaking. She covered her face with her hands.

"Don't worry. It's a traffic stop. I'm sure they will tell us why in a minute."

"There might be a warrant for my arrest, in which case they'd treat me like a felon, right?"

Armin had no idea. He started to pray for wisdom. Wisdom? Oh, and safety. Safety first in this case.

"If the police are trying to arrest you, how did they know you're in this particular car in the first place? Didn't Nicholas borrow this car for you to use? Who else would know that you're driving it and might have tipped off the police?" Armin tried to keep his voice down, but he'd immediately blamed Nicholas. That might be a bad idea if Kelsey was partial to her friend.

"I don't know. Nicholas is trying to protect me."

*See there?*

Still, Armin couldn't help himself. "He didn't tell you to turn yourself in. That would've been the right thing to do."

"I trust his judgment."

"Never trust someone who tells you to break the law." Armin looked in the right side mirror as a uniformed officer approached the front passenger door of the High-lander. Glancing over his left shoulder, he spotted another police officer walking toward the driver's side. Apparently they had both exited the same patrol vehicle.

Didn't police officers usually drive separately?

Kelsey reached for his arm. Armin held her hand and gently squeezed it. "Don't worry."

He wanted to calm her down, and he tried not to show that he himself was terribly worried. His thoughts went everywhere. He even wondered how much it would cost to pay a good defense attorney to keep them out of jail. It was not only for himself but also for Kelsey. That would double the cost. How many bitcoins would he need to sell?

His mind flipped through a memory rolodex, trying to think of how to contact a defense attorney in South Carolina. He knew a few but they practiced in Columbia.

Well, he didn't have to pay for Kelsey's defense, but she had been out of work, and he felt that if he could help her, he would. There was no reason not to... Was there? They were only friends, not any closer than that, but he'd been attracted to her since their nightly phone calls began.

The officer tapped Armin's window with his knuckles, and Armin rolled it down.

"Please step out of the vehicle," the officer said. "Both of you."

Immediately, alarm bells rang in Armin's ears. He had lived in South Carolina for some years now, and had gotten his fair share of traffic tickets. The first thing the officer always asked him for was his license and registration.

Secondly, the officer would tell Armin why he was stopped. If this was a felony stop, then wouldn't the procedure be different? For example, wouldn't they—at a distance away by the police cruiser—have instructed him and Kelsey to exit the vehicle one person at a time with hands in the air?

So. This had to be only a traffic stop.

The officers probably didn't know that Kelsey was a suspect in the murder of Braun-Dean.

Under the officer's watchful eyes, Armin couldn't call Deshon.

"Step out now." His voice was louder now.

In the driver's seat, Kelsey started to cry.

"It's okay. Don't worry." Even as Armin said it, he felt that he should tell himself the same thing.

Kelsey unbuckled her seat belt, but was too slow in getting out, so a second officer came to her door and dragged her out. She screamed as he pulled her hair.

A third alarm bell went off in Armin's head.

Armin wanted to yell "police brutality," but then the officer next to him pushed him back, so Armin froze. He tried to remember the scene so that he could tell his lawyer about it.

Also Deshon! Armin wished that he could somehow contact Deshon, his supervisor at Hu Knows.

Both of the officers were armed, so Armin was afraid to reach for his phone in his jacket pocket.

Something was terribly wrong here. Who were these people?

"Sir, why are we pulled over?" Armin knew enough about state law to know his rights.

The officer still standing at his door ignored his question. His eyes were fierce, and there was no kindness on his face. Something was totally off, but Armin couldn't put his finger on it.

The second officer nearest Kelsey handcuffed her. She didn't resist at all, even though he didn't tell her to lie face down on the asphalt.

"Miss Murphy, there is a warrant for your arrest for the murder of Felix Braun-Dean," he finally said.

"Oh." Kelsey was back to her controlled self.

With both of them handcuffed, the two officers removed their phones and tossed them back into the Highlander. That action alone told Armin all he needed to know.

These two men were not real police officers. They were impersonators.

In that split second, Armin knew that Deshon and Tanaka had enough data in his phone GPS to find the Toyota Highlander. Armin was glad that he had left his phone turned on. The GPS tracker had been active. Deshon was five miles away, the last time he'd checked. Deshon would be able to find their vehicle by the side of the highway.

*Any time now, Deshon!*

Secondly, the officers had touched their phones with their bare fingers. That alone should provide fingerprints that the real police officers could use to find these two fake cops.

Armin would be very surprised if they were real police officers.

He decided to remain silent while he took mental notes. One of the officers strong-armed Kelsey. The officer nearest to Armin was at least a foot taller than him and built like a linebacker, so when he held his arm out to "invite" Armin to get inside the police vehicle, Armin didn't protest. He merely stared at a healed scar on the man's hand, between the thumb and his index finger, and it went all the way down to his wrist joint.

The man's uniform was tight on him, and he didn't wear a name tag. The body cam was also missing.

When Armin passed by the side of the vehicle, he noticed what seemed to be decals. Would South Carolina use "State Trooper" and logo decals? Wouldn't they have been painted on for durability?

If those weapons were real, it would be impossible for Armin and Kelsey to get away, especially since they were now handcuffed.

The passenger door had been keyed. As far as Armin knew, the South Carolina Highway Patrol was not operating on a deficit. Wouldn't they keep their patrol vehicles in good condition?

Kelsey didn't want to get into the police vehicle. "Please let me call my lawyer."

Armin waited to see what the men said to that.

Before they could reply, a black van pulled up alongside the police vehicle. The van door opened and two men appeared, holding handguns with silencers in front of them.

Armin flinched when he heard two popping sounds. The two men in police uniform went down.

Armin also dropped to the ground, outside the passenger door. The handcuffs behind his back made it hard for him to get up. He tumbled into a prone position.

Someone pulled him off the asphalt and nearly dragged him to the other side of the vehicle. He was still handcuffed.

He saw Kelsey climbing into the van. "Kelsey, no!"

Kelsey smiled. She pointed to someone in the back of the van, hidden from Armin's view. "It's Nicholas. We're fine now."

"Wait," Armin said. "They've taken our phones. Also my backpack is still in the SUV."

"No time. We have to save our lives first. Get in!" Nicholas shouted.

Against his better judgment, Armin entered the van. Sitting in the last row, Nicholas was wearing a black bucket hat and dark sunglasses. His mouth muttered some words that Armin couldn't hear.

"Will someone go back to get our phones?" Kelsey asked. "My bag is also in the car, though there's not much in it but a change of clothes and some makeup."

"Just like you to think of powdering your face." Nicholas chuckled.

"You do too. Tell me you don't have lip gloss or chapstick in your bag."

"That's not makeup."

"Whatever." Kelsey brushed him off.

"I'll get you a new burner phone if that makes you feel better," Nicholas said.

"I meant one of my phones. I still have the burner phone that Agent Tanaka gave me."

"Good girl."

Armin didn't like the way Nicholas said those words to Kelsey, but this wasn't the time to be jealous.

Right now he was worried about his own phone. Without it, Deshon couldn't follow or track them. His trail would end on the side of Highway 95.

The van door slammed shut, and the driver sped off.

Neither Armin and Kelsey were wearing seat belts. With their hands behind them, they were unable to help themselves.

"We'll remove the handcuffs as soon as we get somewhere safer than along the highway," Nicholas said. Then he laughed. "Kelsey, why are you always in trouble?"

"I'm in even more trouble now that you've shot two state troopers." Kelsey shifted in her seat to face Nicholas.

Nicholas didn't seem perturbed, and neither did he correct Kelsey.

Armin didn't recall Kelsey ever telling him that Nicholas the celebrity hairstylist was a gangster in real life.

One of two things could be true. Either the police officers were real cops, or it was a staged traffic stop with a police car from a movie studio or someplace. If this were Georgia, the entire state was open to movie productions. Armin wasn't sure about South Carolina, though.

For now, Kelsey was troubled, but Armin couldn't speak his thoughts aloud in front of Nicholas.

Armin wanted to tell her that nobody but Nicholas's people knew they were driving a borrowed Toyota Highlander. How could the police have known that Kelsey—a wanted person—was in a particular vehicle not registered to her name? It might as well have been a routine traffic stop.

However, as soon as they had been stopped, the officers had handcuffed them—without any ado, or questioning, or whatever. It was as though the officers had known that Kelsey was in that Highlander.

"Did someone follow us from Savannah and then turn us over to the police?" Kelsey asked.

*Good question.*

Someone might have reported them. Armin had thoughts of his own, but for now, he wouldn't disclose them in front of Nicholas.

Nicholas didn't directly answer Kelsey's question. Instead, he chided her. "I don't know what to do with you, love. You can't even drive four hours to see me."

*Love?*

Armin didn't like how Nicholas addressed Kelsey, but he didn't want to complain while he was inside the lion's mouth.

"Can we stop somewhere so you can remove the handcuffs from us?" Kelsey asked. "I feel better if I have my safety belt on."

"Now is not a good time," Nicholas replied. "We have to keep driving."

"What about our handcuffs?" Kelsey asked.

"We don't have the key, and my locksmith who can

pick locks is driving this van right now," Nicholas explained.

He didn't have the key. Or pretended not to have the key? Armin didn't want to stir the water to make it even muddier, but he didn't trust Nicholas. For all they knew, he might have been the mastermind behind the fake traffic stop.

Or he might be telling the truth.

"However, we have bolt cutters at the barn, and we can snip the cuffs right off your pretty wrists."

Armin didn't like how Nicholas said it to Kelsey, but she didn't seem to mind.

"All right. So climb over now and buckle me in."

And he did.

Nicolas was a skinny man, and Armin couldn't tell his height at this point. He climbed over the back rest and squiggled between Armin and Kelsey. He pulled the safety belt over Kelsey's shoulders and buckled her in. Then he turned to Armin, hesitating a bit before he reached for the seat belt on the other side of Armin.

As Nicholas adjusted the safety belt over Armin's chest, Armin smelled a whiff of men's perfume on the man's hooded wool sweater. A quick glance revealed that the zipper pull showed Louis Vuitton initials.

It was too early to judge him. Perhaps Nicholas had money to splurge on designer sweaters. Considering that Nicholas was a hairstylist to wealthy clients, he could easily have afforded such a sweater, even if it cost thousands of dollars—or they could've been gifts for a haircut well done.

But that perfume though.

It had a familiar scent of agarwood and incense.

About four months ago, Armin was working with Deshon on a white collar crime case in which they had to travel to Tokyo to meet their nouveau riche expatriate client, who had lost half of his fortune, stolen by his American investment manager. At the meeting at his penthouse overlooking the city, the client let Armin and Deshon test out a whiff of his newly-acquired Shumukh by Nabeel perfume that had an interesting combination of ylang-ylang and patchouli scent, as well as agarwood and incense.

That same smell was on Nicholas today.

Hu Knows' Tokyo client had bought a three-liter bottle of Shumukh perfume. Decorated with gold, silver, and thousands of precious stones, the large crystal bottle would set him back at least two million dollars in today's market.

Armin didn't know anyone else who bought perfume by the liter.

How could Nicholas have afforded such a lifestyle while working as a hairstylist? Maybe he had inheritance to play with. Maybe he had a sponsor.

Now, the probability was not slim that two random

people who had never met might have bought the same perfume, especially in the elite billionaire circles. But was Nicholas one of those high income earners?

Kelsey didn't remark on the perfume. Which told Armin that it wasn't anything new to her. Otherwise wouldn't she have said something to him? Something like: "That's an interesting perfume you're wearing, love."

Armin coughed. *Banish the thought.*

"So who called the police on us?" Kelsey asked as Nicholas sandwiched himself in the bucket seat, sitting shoulder to shoulder with her and Armin.

"I'm guessing Mean Dean's people did it." His answer came swiftly.

Was Mrs. Braun-Dean really behind all this? It seems that Nicholas was too quick to pin the tail on the donkey.

*Ping.*

"Someone's texting me," Kelsey said. "Phone's in my jacket pocket. Actually this is Armin's jacket because mine's all cut up."

"Which side?" Nicholas asked.

"Left side."

Armin held his breath. Nicholas was reaching into Kelsey's pocket to retrieve her phone for her.

"Who is it?" Kelsey asked. Her voice sounded like she had the utmost trust for Nicholas.

It made Armin frown.

*Jealous much?*

No, no. How could he be jealous? Weren't Kelsey and Nicholas only friends?

Still...

"Looks like Tanaka has sent you a message." Nicholas looked up. "Want me to read it?"

"Sure. She's probably mad at me because we were supposed to wait for her at the Hu Knows office, and here we are in South Carolina."

Nicholas swiped the phone. "Same PIN?"

How did Nicholas know Kelsey's personal identification number to unlock her phone? Armin looked out the window, blinking a couple of times. He reminded himself that he had nothing to do with Kelsey at this point, and even their six-month friendship was still developing. He shouldn't fuss at the poor lady who had gone through so much in the last several years.

If Nicholas wanted to help her, then great. Kelsey needed all the help she could get.

Nicholas read the text message aloud.

TANAKA

Where you at? I just got back from my meeting and you were gone. Deshon also just arrived, and we're both wondering what happened.

Armin realized that Tanaka did not mention any deaths today. Was the news a false narrative in its entirety? That was, nobody died?

"How shall I reply?" Nicholas asked, ready to tap the phone.

"I guess we should just ignore her for now." Kelsey's response seemed measured. "Since only Tanaka has this phone number, I don't expect Deshon or Earl to text me next."

Was she hiding something that Armin didn't know?

"I know who Earl is," Nicholas said. "But who is Deshon?"

"Earl was supposed to be helping us, but he's on paternity leave, so they sent Deshon from Atlanta to take over," Armin said.

"I see. He's a PI then, like Earl." Nicholas turned to Kelsey. "Isn't Tanaka enough? Why do you need a PI?"

"Actually I paid Hu Knows to help me solve my brother's murder," Armin said. "Kelsey didn't know about it until we showed up last night."

"Oh, I heard about that." Once again, Nicholas didn't engage Armin in a conversation. He primarily focused on Kelsey. "You poor thing."

Armin wasn't sure how long it would take before Nicholas became suspicious of him, but for now he prayed for his own safety as well as Kelsey's.

While Kelsey was busy chatting with Nicholas, Armin tuned them out because he didn't want to hear another sentence from Nicholas that ended with "love."

Armin stared at the moving trees beyond Interstate 95. The landscape reminded him of highways in Georgia, flanked by green forests everywhere. He hoped that it would stay this way instead of being overbuilt.

South Carolina wasn't too much colder than Georgia, so Armin didn't have a problem adjusting to Atlanta weather when he moved from South Carolina to Georgia. It had been six months since he had been in South Carolina, and he missed it some.

At the intersection near Bowman and Whetsell, the van made a left turn northwest on Interstate 26 toward Columbia, the capital city of the state—the last city Armin had worked in before he moved to Atlanta.

If the van had gone in the opposite direction, Interstate 26 would have taken them to Charleston, where Armin had often vacationed with his family. Back when Arun had been alive, the two brothers had often rented a southern plantation home for a month and invited their parents' other grandchildren plus nieces and nephews to drop in anytime during that month. It had been usually a wedding anniversary present for their parents that Mother would brag about all year long until the next vacation.

Charleston had been the place where Armin and Arun had their brotherly discussions. In the last year of Arun's life, he had lived in paranoia, an unusual turn of events for a man who was brave and fearless, who was a self-taught cryptocurrency specialist who had earned millions of dollars in the crypto market.

At first, Armin had thought that Arun's fears were unfounded. All he needed was a safe place to park his millions, and he wouldn't be worried about thieves stealing them. Right?

Nope.

As Arun shared his deep fears, Armin realized that Arun was in trouble. He had been working for former Senator Braun-Dean for less than three months before he realized that Braun-Dean had evaded taxes, laundered money overseas, and was involved in the sales of arms to enemies of the state. How could a senator—uh, former senator—do such a thing? How much of his activities had been while he'd been a senator in Congress?

Arun hadn't told Armin everything, and now Armin wished he had. Weren't they best friends? Only one year apart, middle child Arun and oldest brother Armin were closer to each other than they were to their youngest brother, Andrew, now studying at Oxford University in England.

Arun had known a lot about Mr. Braun-Dean's financial dealings and money stashes. He kept talking about cryptocurrency stashes. When Armin had pressed him about it, Arun stopped talking, lamented that he had overshared, and wept that the whole mess stressed him out.

Three years later, Mr. Braun-Dean was dead, and his ex-wife was still in jail, convicted of selling arms to enemies of the state. Did the former Mrs. Braun-Dean know anything about her husband's problems leading up to his death? Did she have anything to do with it?

Armin wished that Arun had told him more, though, because now that he was dead, the trail had gone cold.

Sadly, Arun had been angry with God for not protecting him and his family. He did not want to hear Armin mention anything related to the God that Armin worshipped. To Arun, all the gods were alike, and he wanted nothing to do with yet another deity who could not solve the world's problem with hunger and pain and suffering.

Armin had tried to share some Bible verses with Arun, but he didn't understand, not even when Armin tried to explain the Christian belief that Jesus Christ was his overcomer, as it was written in John 15:33.

*These things I have spoken to you, that in Me you may have peace. In the world you will have tribulation; but be of good cheer, I have overcome the world.*

Arun didn't believe that Jesus Christ could be his peace. None of that "Christian mumbo jumbo" for him. Armin stopped trying to explain the Bible to Arun because he wasn't listening.

Instead, Armin had prayed for his brother, for God to give him peace. He also prayed that some day Arun might become an overcomer—a victor instead of a victim. Armin prayed 1 John 5:5 back to God for his brother.

*Who is he who overcomes the world, but he who believes that Jesus is the Son of God?*

But then Arun died.

Armin had no idea whether Arun might have had a change of heart about Jesus before he passed away. Armin figured he probably wouldn't know until heaven someday. If he saw Arun in heaven, then he'd know that Arun had believed in Jesus.

Meanwhile, Arun's death filled Armin's heart with regrets—to the point that he had to take many sick days from work for his own mental health.

When the company that Arun had worked for

went to court, it became clear that Arun's death had nothing to do with that case in which Earl's wife had been a whistleblower.

If Armin's sister-in-law had not sent Armin his brother's keepsake box, Armin would never have known that Arun had done more for Braun-Dean than just help him to buy and sell bitcoin.

Even though Arun hadn't been willing to commit a crime for Braun-Dean, he had still lost his life.

Now it was up to Armin to find Arun's murderer.

A tall order, but he was willing to try. It was all he could do as the oldest brother in the family, carrying a greater responsibility. At least that was what Armin thought.

After this drama was over, Armin wanted to fly to England to visit his only surviving brother. The kid was only nineteen, a surprise to their parents, who'd thought they were done birthing kids in their late forties. There was a twenty-year age gap between Armin and Andrew, with Arun in between them.

Arun wasn't the only reason that Armin wanted to solve the case. Once he had met Kelsey, he wanted to know her, and someday he hoped to be more than just an acquaintance to her. Would that ever happen? Maybe. Maybe not.

For now, they must deal with Kelsey's arrest

warrant. If it was real, it would change the trajectory of their lives, let alone their relationship.

If the arrest warrant wasn't real, if the surveillance video was fake, if Mr. Braun-Dean was still alive... All that will make a huge difference. Perhaps the conclusion of the matter would come sooner than later.

If so, it wouldn't be long before Armin would have the opportunity to ask Kelsey out to dinner—before Nicholas beat him to it.

He closed his eyes as he heard Nicholas and Kelsey chuckle at some inside joke that Armin wasn't privy to.

*Sigh.*

As for Armin, he couldn't remember when he really laughed out loud. Certainly not after Arun had passed away. Thereafter, Armin had turned somber. Even meeting Kelsey hadn't lifted up his spirits too much yet.

He prayed that Deshon and Tanaka would look into Nicholas Bay pronto, to figure out whether he was a friend or foe. If Nicholas was the latter, Armin prayed that the duo would find a way to rescue them. If Nicholas was harmless, then he prayed that they would get closer to finding out who killed Arun and why.

Either way, he prayed that Kelsey was innocent,

and that she wasn't responsible for Arun's death. If she was, Armin would be devastated.

# CHAPTER EIGHT

K elsey had no idea how long she'd napped in the van, but when she woke up, she found herself jostling with the van as it meandered through a winding road. There were no houses or structures anywhere. It was as though they were driving through a forest.

"Where are we?" Kelsey's arms hurt behind her. She told herself to be glad they were still alive.

"Somewhere outside Spartanburg."

Spartanburg. It meant Kelsey had slept for over two hours since they had been picked up from the roadside. She glanced at Armin who was napping on the other side of Nicholas.

"Want some water?" Nicholas asked.

"Not right now." Kelsey didn't want Nicholas to feed her. "Where are we heading?"

"My new barn. You haven't seen it yet."

"Not your grandma's house?" Kelsey was curious about Nicholas's boyhood home and his grandmother.

Nicholas shook his head. "Another time. We're on business."

The van arrived at what looked like a large barn house in the middle of an isolated wooded lot. All around the gravel driveway were pine trees, but Kelsey only saw the trunks. The canopy disappeared into the Carolina night.

An oversized garage door took up an entire half of the barn. The other half seemed to have been converted into living quarters.

The driver drove the van to the back of the barn where a smaller garage door opened. The fluorescent ceiling lights flickered on, and the driver drove the van in, parked, and turned off the ignition before he closed the sliding door.

Just then, Armin woke up.

Kelsey wondered if he had really napped or whether he was listening with his eyes closed. Then again, he'd been up most of the night working on his computer back in Savannah, and he'd had a long day.

All six people filed out of the van, with the three

men flanking Nicholas like he was some big shot mafia dude. Staring at him from the back, Kelsey began to wonder if there were things she hadn't known about her hairstylist friend of four years. She had trusted him all this time, but this afternoon's event gave her pause.

How had Nicholas suddenly appeared on Interstate 95 to rescue them from the fake traffic stop? His timing was impeccable. So had the two police officers who showed up in the same patrol vehicle.

Kelsey wondered what else would unfold.

"Welcome to Casa Bay." Nicholas spread out his arms. "Someone get over here and remove those handcuffs from my friends."

One of his men came running over to Kelsey and Armin. Using a cuff key, he made a quick job of releasing the duo from their handcuffs.

As Kelsey rotated her arms a bit to stretch the muscles, she wondered how Nicholas's people had a cuff key handy.

"Universal cuff key," the man lifted it up in the air.

"I see." Kelsey glanced at Armin. She suspected he was thinking the same thing. Why would Nicholas hang around with a group of people working for him and carrying cuff keys?

Nicholas ushered them into a second garage, a much larger one, that looked like a mini hangar of sorts.

Kelsey stared at the mammoth RV parked to one side of the garage. It was painted all black with some purple streaks here and there. Black and purple were Nicholas's favorite colors, although lately he'd been favoring various shades of gray as his clothing color of choice.

Someone came around the front of the RV. She was dressed in black from head to toe. With her hair a different cut and color, Kelsey almost couldn't recognize her.

"Zinnia?" Kelsey rushed to her. "I thought it was you."

Zinnia Zhang, who once worked for Roxanne as her bodyguard, only had to take a few steps forward before Kelsey gave her a bear hug.

"I'm so glad to see more familiar faces. It's been a rough two days."

Zinnia smiled and nodded. "Hope it's over soon."

Kelsey didn't ask what she meant by such a statement. Her eyes wandered to the RV door, where Nicholas was now standing.

"I'm sure you want a tour, but we have to make it quick. It's almost dinner time." Nicholas glanced at his Rolex, a gift from Roxanne.

They might no longer be friends and their summer fling had been over a long time ago, but Nicholas wouldn't throw away gifts. Just as Kelsey still wore the watch and bracelet that Roxanne's daughters had made for her, long after she no longer had anything to do with them.

"Why would we need to tour your RV?" Kelsey asked Nicholas as Armin came up to stand next to her.

Zinnia eyed Armin from head to toe, and instinctively, Kelsey stood a little bit in front of him, surprising even herself. She had no idea what she intended to say to Armin. He didn't move away from where he stood, so he must not have thought too much —not as much as Kelsey had been thinking anyway.

Then Armin stepped back.

Oh well. Kelsey had thought there was something blooming between them. Perhaps they'd be nothing more than friends, but she'd like to explore the possibilities before someone else more beautiful and still in her twenties, like Zinnia, had a chance with Armin.

If Zinnia set her eyes on Armin, Kelsey wouldn't fight the mixed martial arts champion for him. Kelsey would have to let Armin go.

"Why a tour? Maybe there's no need." Nicholas brushed something off Kelsey's jacket. "Looks like you picked up some cat hair from the van when you fell asleep."

Kelsey looked where he pointed. "You have a cat?"

"I do now. Grandma can't take care of all her cats anymore, so she gave me one." Before Kelsey could ask any more questions, Nicholas continued speaking. "Male. About five years old. A fawn Abyssinian. Answers to BitCat."

"So who named him?"

"I did. Grandma bought the cat five years ago when I was helping her to double her bitcoin profits. So she asked me to name him. Just as well because now he's my cat."

"I want to meet him." Kelsey knew Armin was looking at her, but she was genuinely interested in the cat—not the owner, Nicholas. However, this wasn't the time to explain to Armin. Maybe they'd have time later.

"He's in the house. He's not going with us in the RV. He'll stay with Grandma until I get back."

"Are we going somewhere in your RV? Where are we going?" Kelsey asked politely, but she was beginning to sense that Nicholas had more control over her situation that he let on. It seemed to her that he was trying to steer her toward something. At this point, it seemed fuzzy, but she knew the endpoint related to Braun-Dean.

As much as she hated the idea of it, dealing with the wake of Braun-Dean's money laundering schemes would stop Roxanne from coming after her once and for all. Unfortunately, Kelsey knew nothing about those illegal activities that the

Bonnie and Clyde duo had been up to in the last decade.

After all, Kelsey was only the third wheel or fifth wheel, depending on who was asked.

"I'll explain over dinner." Nicholas weaved his arm in Kelsey's and led her across the garage and up a couple of steps. He opened the door to the smell of pot roast permeating the landing that led to both the dining area and the open kitchen."

"Mmmm... Smells good. Who cooked today?" Kelsey asked.

Nicholas stepped into the kitchen and introduced his cook, who was standing at the sink loading the dishwasher and humming a tune.

Nicholas put his arm over the cook's shoulders. "This is Bernie. He has prepared a whole week's worth of meals for us that we're going to freeze or refrigerate for our trip. Plus tonight's pot roast. Good job."

Bernie nodded. "Thank you."

"So we are going somewhere," Armin mumbled.

Kelsey heard him. It was time to get down to business. "Where are we going, Nicholas?"

He preferred that his friends called him by his full first name, so Kelsey had never called him Nick, not even on the first day they'd met, when he was coloring Braun-Dean's toupee. Kelsey agreed with him that Nicholas Bay sounded better than Nick Bay.

Nicholas looked at his cook. "Is dinner ready?"

"Yes, in the dining room," Bernie said. "Once everyone is seated, I will serve the courses."

"Good." Nicholas led them to the dining area by the front entrance, the same one Kelsey had first seen when they'd entered through the garage door.

There were only four table settings—two on each side of the farmhouse table.

"Where are your men going to eat?" Kelsey asked.

"You worry about them. Why don't you worry about me?" Nicholas winked.

Armin cleared his throat.

Kelsey grabbed his arm and led him to the table. "Where do you want us to sit, Nicholas?"

Nicholas frowned. "Anywhere is fine."

Kelsey picked the side of the table facing the windows so that she could see what was coming even though it was dusk outside and soon everything would be dark in the woods.

Armin sat down beside her. Since the drive, he had been pretty quiet, and Kelsey couldn't wait to ask him what was on his mind. Needless to say, they had a lot to talk about the events of the day, but in front of Nicholas, Kelsey had to play the helpless damsel in distress.

She knew that Nicholas would come running if she needed his help. She just didn't realize that his men would shoot at those state troopers. Perhaps this was nothing new to them, but Kelsey felt uneasy now that she had discovered a darker side of Nicholas.

The barn house wasn't new, but it was warm and cozy. If Nicholas was an ordinary person, Kelsey would say that such a lifestyle suited him. City life did not.

However, Nicholas had never been a simple person. It would make more sense if he had quit his day job as a hairstylist. The more Kelsey thought about it, the more she believed that it was only a cover story for Nicholas.

*What do you really do, Nicholas?*

After Zinnia arrived to sit next to Nicholas across the table, dinner was served and worries were forgotten. Not!

As they enjoyed the roast beef that had simmered in beef bone stock with chunks of onions, carrots, and celery—but no white potatoes because Nicholas was on the keto diet—Kelsey thought about all the things that happened to her in the last three days, when both Tanaka and Armin had descended on Savannah.

Kelsey didn't think those two people knew each other, but their timing made her wonder.

"I can't believe you're a fugitive now," Nicholas said.

*A fugitive?*

"I can't believe that either. I'm actually a law abiding citizen," Kelsey said.

"For the most part."

"What do you mean?"

"Sometimes you have sticky fingers." Nicholas's voice was accusing, as though he knew her well and not afraid to say it in front of Armin and Zinnia.

"Are you calling me a thief?" Kelsey tried not to raise her voice.

"I'm not saying office supplies." Nicholas chuckled. "I'm talking about this mess you're in. Looks like maybe you have something that doesn't belong to you. They want it, so they're coming after you."

"What might that be?" Kelsey looked at Nicholas and then at Armin. "What do I have that they want so badly?"

Armin shrugged. He was eating a piece of carrot.

"Are you sure you didn't take something from Braun-Dean?"

"I took nothing he didn't give me," Kelsey protested. She lifted up both hands, jiggling the watch and bracelet on her wrists. "These are gifts from his two daughters."

"Gifts don't count." Nicholas dismissed what he might have considered to be trinkets.

Maybe Kelsey should put them in a box or storage somewhere instead of wearing them.

"Last night, wasn't the carjacker trying to take you somewhere to meet someone?" Nicholas asked.

"Meet someone?" Kelsey didn't remember telling Nicholas the details of the carjacking. She only recalled that Nicholas himself had been pushing a narrative that this was all Roxanne's doing."

"Today, someone clearly wants to frame you for murder of your ex-lover, and we all can guess that it's probably Roxanne herself."

One again, Nicholas pointed to a person they would consider to be bad enough to do all these things.

"Sitting in her jail cell?" Zinnia shredded a piece of beef on the plate with her fork. The beef separated easily. She ate a little bit of it.

Maybe that was why Zinnia remained in good shape. As for Kelsey, she almost wiped her plate clean and was hoping for seconds. Like in the next minute.

"She can still call the shots from the Fulton County Jail, as she probably already has." Nicholas buttered a bread roll. "For example, last night with the carjacker and this afternoon with the traffic stop."

Kelsey went through the notions that Nicholas seemed to try to plant in her mind. However, wading through the obvious, she noted his choice of phrases this evening.

*Looks like...*

*Maybe you have...*

*Clearly wants...*

*Probably already has...*

None of them were definitive proofs of anything. They seemed to be conjectures on Nicholas's part. Yet again.

And then if she backed up a bit to what Nicholas had said earlier.

*You're a fugitive now.*

It was as though Nicholas wanted her to think that she was. Nicholas was a good friend, but she didn't appreciate how he hadn't brought facts to the table.

"I'm in a nightmare," Kelsey said.

Armin turned to look at her. He had also finished eating. "With God's help, we'll get through this together."

"Since you have God, I guess you don't need me anymore." Nicholas made a face.

*Oh, the gall of him.*

Sometimes Kelsey didn't know what to do with Nicholas. He'd be kind to her and heartwarming one moment, and then another moment he'd say things like this. Would this be construed as a disrespect of Kelsey's belief? She wasn't sure. All she could tell was Nicholas had compared himself with God.

"Sometimes God brings people to the rescue." Kelsey sipped some water from her goblet.

"Are you saying God is in charge and not me?" Nicholas pushed.

Kelsey didn't think he'd been drinking since there was no wine or beer on the table. Sometimes when he did, he'd say whatever popped into his head and riled against Braun-Dean and high level campaign officials. Without alcohol lowering his guard, this might be what Nicholas truly felt about God. Nicholas wasn't controlling his anger this evening and was showing the slightly bitter side of himself.

Or perhaps he was diverting attention away from the things Kelsey should really think about. Like what? Exactly. Right now, all she could see was smoke and mirrors. The truth lay somewhere behind all this obfuscation.

There was only person on earth she could ask if she wanted clarity.

She glanced at Armin. He didn't look back at her. She wondered what he was thinking. Well, she'd have to find some alone time with him so that she could pick his brains.

It was time for Kelsey to change the subject. "In the garage, you mentioned that you were going somewhere in the RV."

"We are." Nicholas's fork in hand circled the table. "My RV only sleeps four because I have some computer equipment to take with us."

"Why should we go with you?" Armin finally asked.

"Do you have a choice?" Nicholas laughed. "There's a warrant for Kelsey's arrest for the murder of the former senator, whom most of us hated when he was still alive, and now two police officers are dead."

"I didn't shoot them, and..." Kelsey wasn't sure what she should do, but breaking more laws wasn't going to help. "And I think I should just turn myself in."

Armin nodded. "I know a few good defense attorneys in Atlanta."

"And then what? Let Kelsey sit in jail?" Nicholas sat back in his chair. "Just like Mean Dean? She's stuck there for the foreseeable future."

"That's because she committed a crime." Kelsey recalled the last year's events in Miami. Hu Knows had been heavily involved in it with two private investigators in danger. To be fair to Roxanne, her husband was also to be blamed for the hostage situation. They ruffled the wrong feathers and had to pay the price."

"Sorry I compared you with Mean Dean. You're not like her at all," Nicholas said. "You don't wish Braun-Dean dead, in spite of the domestic violence."

"I don't recall Roxanne ever wishing Braun-Dean dead." Kelsey's eyes widened. "Did you think that Roxanne killed her husband?"

"I wouldn't put it past her." Nicholas pointed a finger at Kelsey. "My point is that if she could kill her husband out on bail, she could certainly find someone to kill you inside your jail cell if you turn yourself in and get locked up."

"But I'm innocent of the charges."

"Does it matter?" Nicholas reminded her of the surveillance video. "It might be fake, but it would take a while to prove it. Someone who looks like you went to Braun-Dean's lake house and murdered him."

Kelsey drank more water. "But how long do I need to hide?"

"As long as it takes to clear your name."

"Who's going to clear my name?" Kelsey looked at Nicholas, then at Armin, and then back to Nicholas again.

"I know someone who can," Nicholas said.

"Who?" Kelsey leaned forward.

"The Steward."

Silence in the room.

That area of Braun-Dean's life had always been off limits to Kelsey. As long as he spent money on her, she didn't care where their money had come from. After she became a believer of Jesus Christ, it began to matter. She returned all the gifts that Braun-Dean had given her, including the beach house in Key West, the Porsche, every piece of jewelry, all the evening gowns, and three bitcoins he'd bought for her at their last Christmas together.

The only two things she had kept from their time together were the watch and bracelet from his daughters.

"Why would The Steward, whom I've never met and have nothing to do with, help me to clear my name?" Kelsey asked.

"Because you hold the key."

"I hold the what?" Kelsey laughed.

"My time with Braun-Dean was so long ago, Nicholas. Don't remind me of the bad memories. I've moved on."

"You might have, but nobody else has."

"What do you mean?" Zinnia laughed. "The former senator is dead. Whatever he had that wasn't distributed is gone now. No one can access his bitcoins since nobody knows the right passwords to his stash."

"He has ethereum and other cryptocurrency also," Nicholas said quietly.

Has?

It wasn't lost on Kelsey that Nicholas had spoken in the present tense.

"So what? He died before he cashed out his coins," Zinnia reminded him. "When he died, his multi-signature system stopped working. It matters not that his ex-wife and daughter still have their unique signatures needed to access the hardware wallet. They need Braun-Dean himself as the first signer."

"I told him he should've added two more people in the rotation, but he didn't listen," Nicholas said. "If he had five people, then he could ask three of five. If he died, which he has, then he still had four people to draw three signatures from. Now it's all moot."

Kelsey knew that Braun-Dean had used what looked like physical USB devices as his "hardware wallets" to keep the keys to his cryptocurrency investments. With the information on his wallets, he could buy and sell his bitcoins. In fact, when she had left him, she handed over one of those wallets back to him. She knew it was probably foolish to let go of the three bitcoins, but she also knew that he hadn't earned them above board.

"So how would they access the wallet then?" Kelsey asked. "Or are the bitcoins lost forever?"

"Not really," Zinnia started to say, and Nicholas picked up on it.

"Braun-Dean left behind a recovery passphrase that anyone can use to recreate the hardware wallet should something happen to him or the other people whose signatures were needed to access his crypto keys," Nicholas explained.

"A passphrase?" Kelsey had heard it before. Braun-Dean mentioned it a lot.

"You know how a password is: a secret word to let you pass." Nicholas's voice was kind. "A passphrase, therefore, is a bunch of words in a particular order that lets you pass."

"Oh." She already knew what it was, since Arun had helped her to invest in some cryptocurrency before she had lost them all, but now wasn't the time to show off.

"Sometimes called a seed phrase, the passphrase is the master key to Braun-Dean's crypto account."

"How long is this passphrase?" Kelsey buttered another piece of toast. All these carbs...

"It's usually twenty-four words. Sometimes it can be twelve."

*Sometimes it can be twelve.*

*Hmm...*

Kelsey wondered if those words had anything to do with the twelve-word memory games that Braun-Dean liked to play with her. For some odd reason, in the three years she'd been with him, he had made her memorize a list of ordinary words, and he'd always test her every month to make sure she hadn't forgotten. Those word games drove her nuts, but Braun-Dean was convinced that Kelsey had the best memory brain he had ever known.

That had also been the time when Braun-Dean encouraged her to go to law school. Her eyes for details and her ability to reason and think analytically—when she wanted to—had helped the former defense lawyer in quite a few fixes. Kelsey always brushed off the idea of going to college because she'd have to do that before she could go to law school for graduate studies.

However, she never forgot that she was supposed to have a great memory. Ironically, that had been the bane of her life now as she tried super hard to forget those three months of living as a mistress with Braun-Dean and then the next remaining three years living under his wrath and control. The only reason she had been able to escape from him was all due to Pilar Santiago, the private investigator whom Kelsey had met at the Miami hotel where Braun-Dean had been held hostage.

"Regardless of how many words there are, Braun-Dean stored the list in an encrypted file on a USB drive that he gave to his lawyer," Nicholas said. "Upon his death, the lawyer sent the file to The Steward for processing."

"Did he meet The Steward?" Kelsey asked.

"No one has ever seen or met The Steward," Zinnia replied for Nicholas.

"Then how was the file delivered?" Kelsey pressed.

"Through a proxy." Nicholas's warm response offset the edge in Zinnia's voice.

Kelsey appreciated Nicholas's patience. He rarely

mansplained things to her. He was a good friend, but she started to wonder about his ulterior motives now that he had told her to run from the police instead of toward them.

"Did you mean that Braun-Dean had to die before they—whoever they were—could see the file?" Kelsey wondered if the murderer knew that was the only way to trigger the release of the recovery passphrase.

"Looks like it, doesn't it?" Armin was probably thinking along the same lines as Kelsey. "A dead man's switch."

"A dead what?"

"Something activated upon the death of the person. For software, it's usually a pre-programmed switch. In this case, Braun-Dean's death triggered an action on the lawyer's part." Armin turned to Nicholas.

Nicholas nodded. "The Steward was supposed to make the bitcoins and other coins available to the beneficiaries of the will. The lawyer, who is also the executor of Braun-Dean's will, has instruction on the distribution once the crypto is cashed out—unless the beneficiaries want to keep theirs in crypto, in which case they would change ownership."

"Unfortunately, the lawyer's file did not contain the password to access the recovery passphrase. In fact, it contained an address to an old house in Chattanooga. Can you believe it?" Zinnia added. "The

Steward's been there for two days, trying to figure out what the password is. It's not even his money. He acts like it is."

"Chattanooga?" Kelsey was somewhat surprised. As far as she had known, Braun-Dean had not owned a house in Chattanooga. He had a vacation cabin near Pigeon Forge in the Great Smoky Mountains, but nothing in Chattanooga. Having said that, she had lost contact with him for a year since she left him, so he could have bought a house in the interim. On the other hand, Braun-Dean had not always told her everything, so this could be one of his many secrets from long ago.

In fact, the only reason Kelsey knew Arun Dhillon was due to Braun-Dean's doing. When he had given her three bitcoins for Christmas one year, he had also given her a burner phone with Arun's number on it, saying that she could talk to him about managing her bitcoins. Arun helped her sell it all before he passed away suddenly.

Kelsey had lived off the money until it was all gone. Now she barely had money for food. After this mess was over, she had to find a real job or go to college. She rather liked the idea of going back to school and getting a degree. It would be a lifelong dream of hers to graduate out of college. She'd be the first person in her family to do so.

"Are you saying The Steward is physically in Chattanooga right now?" Armin asked.

"He's on his way," Nicholas said.

Zinnia stared at Armin across the dining table. "Wouldn't you like to meet him?"

"So it's a he." Then Armin added, "Don't get me wrong. I'm for equal opportunity. What's his real name?"

Nobody replied.

"I'd like to know too," Kelsey said.

So far, the techno mumbo jumbo had gone a bit over Kelsey's head, but Kelsey was a fast learner. She tried to pick up the jargon so that she could participate in the conversation.

Bernie arrived just then with cheesecake slices. Kelsey didn't think much about his timing. The cook probably saw that they had all finished their dinner.

"Oh dear." Kelsey looked at the cheesecake longingly. "I'm on a diet."

"Decadent, right?" Bernie was all smiles. "Have a small slice if you can't have more."

"All right." Kelsey laughed. "Gimme a sliver. A tiny one, please."

Bernie did so and Kelsey devoured it. It wasn't overly sweet. Problem was, she wanted more.

"You're saying that instead of giving The Steward the password to the backup file, Braun-Dean is making him go to an old house of mystery in Chattanooga," Kelsey said.

"The password The Steward is trying to find hidden in the house will open the recovery file, which is supposed to contain the passphrase needed to recreate the wallet that contains the account information for his crypto stash." Nicholas ate his cheesecake.

"How much bitcoins are we talking about?" Kelsey asked.

"The equivalent of seventeen billion dollars," Nicholas said. "And counting."

"Wow." Kelsey nearly dropped her fork. She had no idea that Braun-Dean had amassed that amount of money. "All in just one wallet?"

"Hardware wallet."

"I know. You kept saying wallet as singular. Did you think that Braun-Dean would put all his bitcoins in one basket?" Kelsey knew that the former senator was paranoid enough to probably distribute all his coins in several places.

"The bitcoins are not in the wallets themselves," Nicholas said patiently. "The wallets contain private and public keys that enable the owner to access a blockchain out there somewhere where the bitcoins are stored."

Kelsey glanced at Armin. Armin didn't say a word. He was still eating.

"After Braun-Dean got out on bail, he started consolidating his crypto stash," Nicholas said. "This was his biggest bundle."

"Wouldn't his assets have been frozen after his arrest?" Armin asked.

"Good point," Nicholas said. "After all, the FBI is still investigating him for money laundering. However, his crypto investments are not under his own name and cannot be traced back to him. Only a few people know."

Zinnia made a face. "The man was a criminal all the way. Criminals do what criminals do."

"Well…" Nicholas chuckled.

"You disagree with me?" Zinnia's eyebrows rose. "What did I say about criminals that was incorrect?"

"The person who has all the keys to the hardware wallet owns the bitcoins."

"Oh, so you want them too?"

"I didn't say—"

Zinnia cut him off. "I thought you were better than that, Nicholas."

"No need to thank me for giving you a job after Mean Dean fired you."

His voice was pleasant and he even smiled, but those words could slice emotions a thousand times. Kelsey watched to see how Zinnia would react.

Knowing a little about her, Kelsey expected her to basically explode.

"She didn't fire me," Zinnia said. "I quit because she wanted me to do things that I didn't want to do, like spying on her own daughter. I'm a bodyguard, not an investigator."

That, Kelsey had also known. How could she defuse the situation? She had no idea if there was anything going on between Nicholas and Zinnia, but they were quarreling like they were more than friends.

"Is this a lover's quarrel we're witnessing?" Kelsey asked.

No one answered.

"Why don't we talk more later?" she suggested. "Let's just enjoy the cheesecake—which I have already finished."

Zinnia tossed her napkin on the table and stormed out of the dining room without another word.

"She's frustrated," Nicholas said. "So am I."

Wow. Nicholas sure knew how to make it sound like he was in the same boat as Zinnia. Earlier, the two of them had clearly disagreed on what constituted a crime. Zinnia's standards might be higher than Nicholas's.

*What about mine? What are my standards?*

Kelsey wondered if standing in the gray area now had already made her complicit to whatever Nicholas was up to. She had looked at him as harmless. Now she wondered if she had misjudged him. If he were willing to kill two police officers, there was no telling what else Nicholas could do.

Her heart sank as the conviction settled in.

*I made a big mistake, Lord.*

She shouldn't have come here with Nicholas at all. She should have taken Armin's advice and surrendered to the police in Savannah. Then they wouldn't have been stopped by the police on Interstate 95, and the officers would still be alive.

Maybe they'd get a good night's sleep tonight and figure out how to get out of here in the morning. Somehow they'd have to get past The Stylist of Spartanburg. No worries. Kelsey was sure she could handle Nicholas.

The person she might not be able to handle was probably The Steward. Braun-Dean had hated him, and often said that The Steward had stolen his money. Kelsey would rather have nothing to do with him, but it might be too late for that.

*Because you hold the key.*

Nicholas's words rang in Kelsey's mind. The Steward wanted something from her. Was this a physical key or just a proverbial key? Kelsey didn't know and didn't want to know.

Bernie returned with a jug of water to refill

Kelsey's and Armin's goblets. Nicholas didn't want any more water, and Zinnia hadn't returned to her seat.

Kelsey glanced at Armin as they sipped water. It tasted like tap water with mineral in it, and a hint of lemon. Kelsey was thirsty from the salt in the roast beef, so she drank the entire goblet of water.

"You do drink a lot of water, don't you?" Nicholas asked.

Kelsey nodded.

And nodded...

# CHAPTER NINE

Armin woke up on a couch that smelled musty. He opened his eyes to find cracks on the ceiling. The room didn't look like it was one in a barn. In fact, the architecture seemed to be somewhat Edwardian, maybe the nineteen-twenties era.

Slowly he sat up on the couch and oriented himself. The room was small and rectangular. There was a dresser pushed up against one wall, and a door next to it.

As soon as Armin stood up, he felt dizzy. He sat back down again and closed his eyes for a bit until the feeling passed.

*Was I drugged? How? When?*

The last thing he remembered was having dinner with Kelsey, Nicholas, and Zinnia. Armin remembered that Bernie the cook gave them cheesecake and refilled their water.

Armin didn't remember anything after that. Had Bernie slipped a Mickey Finn into his water goblet? That could have easily made him pass out and not remember a thing until he woke up in this place, wherever this was.

Had Kelsey been drugged too?

He prayed that no one had done anything immoral to her. Then again, her friend Nicholas would protect her, wouldn't he?

Armin worried about Kelsey because he cared, maybe more than he wanted to admit at this stage in their relationship.

Slowly, he rose again to his feet—he was still wearing shoes—and shuffled across the dusty floor to the door. He leaned against the doorframe.

"Is this room in the barn house? Am I still in Spartanburg?"

He turned the knob. It wasn't locked. Was that good or bad?

He opened it and looked outside. The hallway was long and the floors were painted. It was grimy and dirty white under a couple of pendant lights hanging from the ceiling.

"What is this place?" Armin asked no one. He was alone, and felt tempted to call out, "Anyone?"

Then he heard a woman cry. His first thought was Kelsey, but he couldn't be sure. He walked down the hallway toward the crying, all the time thinking it might be a trap. Still, his legs propelled him forward as the cries drew louder.

"Help!" was the first clear word Armin heard as he came to another door like his.

On the other side, someone pounded on the door and jiggled the doorknob.

There was a key in the knob. Armin turned it and slowly opened the door.

Someone opened the door away from him, and screamed.

"Kelsey, it's me!" Armin enveloped her in his arms. Her sobs eased off.

Kelsey stepped away from Armin and wiped tears from her cheeks. "What's going on? Where are we?"

"I have no idea. The last thing I remembered was drinking water at the dinner table."

"Bernie served us. He might have slipped some drugs into our drink. I need to tell Nicholas." She searched her jacket and pockets. "My phone is gone."

"Both of ours were left by the roadside in South Carolina, remember?"

"Yeah, but also remember that I have a second phone, the one that Tanaka gave me."

"Looks like they don't want us calling anyone."

"They who?"

"We'll find out, won't we?"

"Now I can't call Nicholas. I want to warn him to watch out for Bernie." Kelsey looked worried.

Nicholas? Armin was about to say that Nicholas was up to no good, not only Bernie.

"You and I were the only two people who got refills from Bernie," Kelsey said. "Nicholas watched us drink it, but Zinnia left the room."

"You still trust Nicholas?"

Kelsey nodded, to Armin's disappointment.

"Let me connect the dots for you," Armin said. "Nicholas told us that Braun-Dean had left seventeen billion dollars of cryptocurrency in a hardware wallet with The Steward that he can't access. After he died, his lawyer handed an envelope to his ex-wife in jail. That envelope contained recovery instructions that had somehow made their way to The Steward, who determined that you, Kelsey, of all people, have something to do with it. So Nicholas brought us to Spartanburg, and the next thing we knew, we both passed out. We woke up here. And you still trust Nicholas?"

"Well, he's saved me many times." Kelsey's voice cracked. "When Braun-Dean beat me up, Nicholas was the one who took me to a private doctor for treatment and stitches. When Roxanne chewed me out, he defended me, and brought me little treats to cheer me up. I can't forget what he's done for me."

"Braun-Dean abused you?" Armin wasn't sorry that he had died.

Across the hallway, a screen flickered alive. A video started to play. It was Felix Braun-Dean himself.

*Speak of the devil...*

"Welcome to my Password Escape Room." In a plaid jacket, Braun-Dean looked like a salesman.

"This must've been from a while back, when he had more hair." Kelsey pointed. "At least two or three years."

"If you see this video, it means you want to recover my hardware wallet without my multi-signature team. That means you need the password to the file where I tell you how to recreate my crypto wallet."

"Ah. So that's what Nicholas referred to at dinner," Armin said to Kelsey. "This is the password to the encrypted file that the lawyer gave to The Steward."

"He didn't want to make it easy for his beneficiaries, did he?"

"Contrary to what my crypto specialist said, I'm not stupid." On screen, Braun-Dean made a face. "With the help of my IT friend, Arun, I have created a failsafe system to ensure that only the right people gain access to my cryptocurrency account."

"He mentioned my brother in the video. Why would he do that?" Armin asked.

"Ironically, if you're watching this prerecorded session, it also means that not only am I dead, but my friend, Arun, is also dead." Braun-Dean frowned.

"Arun? He's been dead for three years," Kelsey muttered.

"This video is at least three years old then." Armin stepped closer to the screen.

Braun-Dean waved his chubby hands on screen. "If you have a heart, you might want to look into this. Why are both of us dead?"

At least Armin was looking into why someone would want to put a car bomb in Arun's family van. If it had been five minutes later, Arun's wife and daughter would also have perished on that driveway of their dream home.

"There are five doors through which you can form the password that will enable you to decrypt the file containing the recovery passphrase. Is that enough for you to recreate my hardware wallet? Hmm... We shall see." Braun-Dean gave a sly smile.

"That same old smile." Kelsey sighed.

"What does it mean?"

"Means he's cunning and he knows it. Smarter than everyone else and proud of it."

"To your right is the first of a series of doors," Braun-Dean continued. "There is a riddle you have to solve or a question you have to answer. If you can make it through the door, then the next door will open. If you cannot, you will have to stay there until you get through or you can backtrack all the way here, and this video will repeat."

"Was he like that when he was alive?" Armin asked.

"Oh yes. He was always solving puzzles—or attempting to." Kelsey walked toward the first door. "I ignored him as much as possible when he went into his zone or when he was in meetings with Arun."

Armin followed. "He mentioned that his crypto specialist thinks he was 'stupid.' Who was that person?"

"We don't know. He's simply known as The Steward and only Braun-Dean had met him. I was never invited to their tête-à-tête." Kelsey was looking for something all around the first door. There were nothing and no instructions. "Isn't there supposed to be something around here? Didn't he say we should expect a riddle or a question?"

"That's what I thought the video said." Armin

helped her look but there was nothing there. Not even a sign.

The only thing he could see was the doorknob. He turned it. It didn't help.

"What question are we supposed to answer?" Kelsey asked.

Suddenly a screen appeared on the door above the doorknob.

"Looks like a biometrics scanner." Armin wondered how much money Braun-Dean had invested onto this escape room.

Kelsey lowered her head to stare at it. Nothing happened.

"I don't think it's for your retina," Armin said. "If not, why would it be placed so low on the door, at waist level?"

"Ah." Kelsey put her right hand on the screen.

"Zuriel, why are you here?" Braun-Dean's voice came out of the speaker.

"Creepy." Kelsey shuddered as the door opened.

Kelsey and Armin stepped through the door.

"Does that mean the first word in the password is 'Zuriel?' If so, we better remember it." Armin looked around. "Nothing for us to write it down."

"We just have to memorize it." Kelsey didn't seem surprised. "When I was with Felix—I mean Braun-Dean—he would make me memorize long strings of random words. I told him it was crazy, but he said that if I played along with him, he would make sure that I never worked again for the rest of my life."

She chuckled. "Six months after we broke up, I found myself on food stamps. An irony of life, isn't it?"

Armin wanted to say that if Kelsey would stay with him, he would take good care of her the rest of his life. However, he wasn't sure if this was the time and place to talk about such things. After all, they were surrounded by her ex-boyfriend's voice.

"How do we enter our answer?" Kelsey asked.

Armin waved in front of the screen on the door, but nothing happened. Then he tapped it. A virtual keyboard appeared.

Kelsey typed in "Zuriel."

The door unlocked. Down a short hallway, a second door greeted them. It was also locked, as expected.

"He should've made each door a different color," Kelsey said. "It's so drab with every door brown."

"Maybe he was saving money on the cost of paint."

Kelsey didn't answer. A screen appeared on the door, much like the one they'd seen on the first door earlier. On it was another question.

```
What does Felix Braun-Dean want
for his seventieth birthday?
```

"Too bad he died before his sixty-seventh." Kelsey drew a deep breath.

"I see now why The Steward said you hold the key." Armin wasn't happy but he tried to hide it. "You were the closest person to the former senator."

"Roxanne was too. She could've done this."

"Not if she's still behind bars."

"Yeah."

"So what's the answer?" Armin asked. "What would he have wanted for his birthday had he been alive?"

"Wow. He wanted a lot of things. And we can't write any of them down."

Armin nodded. "We have to carry the data in our minds."

"I don't know if he wanted money anymore. He had so much of it," Kelsey said. "I want to say that he might want good health, but knowing him, he didn't care one way or another because he said he'd eventually die anyway."

"Was there something that he always said he wanted but never got?"

"Everything that Roxanne didn't want him to have." Kelsey laughed. "I'm trying to remember, but you know I spent the last year shutting him out of my head. I can't believe I have to dredge up the past right now."

"Would you feel better if we pray first?" Armin asked. "We need God's wisdom to proceed."

Kelsey nodded and then reached for his hands.

"What are you doing?" Armin asked.

"Don't we hold hands when we pray?"

"Some Christians do. We don't have to." He immediately regretted it.

Unfortunately the moment had passed.

Kelsey's face reddened. She clasped her hands, bowed her head, and waited for Armin to pray.

He cleared his throat. "Father God, we are in a crisis. We don't know how much danger we are in, but we need to get through four more doors. We're not even at the end of our quest yet, because this is only the first of a series of passwords and passphrases. At the end of our usefulness, we may not be alive."

Kelsey made a sound. "Sorry. Please continue."

"Lord Jesus, I pray now that You will deliver us through this valley of the shadow of death." He recited Psalm 23:4.

*Yea, though I walk through the valley of the shadow of*
*death,*
    *I will fear no evil;*
    *For You are with me;*
    *Your rod and Your staff, they comfort me.*

"Holy Spirit of God, show us who our friends are. Show us who our enemies are," Armin prayed. "Protect us from confusion. Show us the truth. In the name of Jesus, I pray. Amen."

"Amen."

When Armin opened his eyes, Kelsey was holding on to his sleeve. He wondered if Kelsey was scared. She didn't show that she was, but still.

Feeling bad that he had prevented her from holding his hand, Armin wove his fingers into hers. "Let's get to the second door."

"Okay." Kelsey looked serious, and her eyes were sad.

"Don't be sad. Let's do this together."

Kelsey nodded. "I just feel like my life is so unstable. I never know which way the wind blows and whether I'd be toppled over."

"Do you remember the story of the house built on a rock?" Armin asked.

"I might have heard it in Sunday school."

"Jesus is our rock. If we are anchored in Him, the wind will not hurt you. Matthew 7:24-25."

*Therefore whoever hears these sayings of Mine, and does them, I will liken him to a wise man who built his house on the rock: and the rain descended, the floods came, and the winds blew and beat on that*

*house; and it did not fall, for it was founded on the*
*rock.*

"Maybe I should memorize it," Kelsey said.

"While you're at it, you might also check out the Bible verses that talk about God being our rock," Armin said. He suggested Psalm 62:7.

*In God is my salvation and my glory;*
  *The rock of my strength,*
  *And my refuge is in God.*

"Thank you. I feel better now," Kelsey said. "I'm relieved that God is my salvation, my glory, my rock, my strength, and my refuge."

"For sure."

"Better than all the material wealth in the world. He is my true refuge—my shelter and sanctuary—unlike anything the world has to offer—"

She stopped suddenly.

"What?"

"I got it." Kelsey turned to the question on the door and reread it. "What he wants for his seventieth birthday is the world."

"The world?" Armin wouldn't have guessed. "That's a tall order."

"No doubt about it. Might be why he amassed all

these bitcoins by hook or by crook." Kelsey touched the screen and a virtual keyboard appeared. She typed in "world."

The lock clicked and the door opened.

"Two down, three more to do." Kelsey stepped inside the door, pulling Armin along.

The third door was identical to the other two. Without much ado, a similar screen also appeared.

```
Enter        one        non-alphanumeric
character.
```

"What is that?" Kelsey asked.

"Alphanumeric characters are the alphabet and numbers," Armin explained. "Non-alphanumeric characters are like ampersand, question mark, backslash, that sort of thing."

"Oh I see. Like hyphens and colons."

"Right."

"Which one should we pick?" Kelsey's eyes widened. "Or does it matter?"

"I think not. I think we'll let The Steward—if he's the one who locked us in here—figure out which one works for real. There's a limited number of characters on a keyboard, so they can easily run through the permutations. If they can't solve it, it's not our problem."

Kelsey agreed. "You're thinking any non-alphanumeric character will unlock this door."

"Let's find out."

"Your turn to do the honors." Kelsey stepped aside.

Armin randomly picked a dollar sign because he suspected that Braun-Dean loved money.

*Click.*

The door opened.

"Is this easy or what?" Kelsey leaned against Armin.

He didn't move, and neither did he smile. "I think that's the calm before the storm. We have two more words to decipher, and then we don't know what will happen to us once we exit this escape room."

Kelsey straightened up and said little as they entered the hallway. This time it rounded a corner. The door was the same drab brown, and a screen appeared on the fourth door.

```
Why did Felix Braun-Dean run for
Senate?
```

"I know that one. To help people." Quickly, Kelsey typed in "help people."

A deafening horn blared.

"What? I know I'm right," Kelsey protested. She typed in "people."

"Still wrong," Armin said. "Think about this some more. I didn't know Braun-Dean, so I have no idea. I hate that this is all on you."

"I need a thesaurus."

Armin liked Kelsey's optimism. Perhaps that had been why she'd survived three years of drug-induced torture in the hands of Braun-Dean and then fifteen months of misery trying to recover from the mess.

Of course, God had been her strength once she believed in Jesus, but Armin was also convinced that God had helped her through the dark times. God would send people to surround Kelsey and lift her up, people like Nicholas—whom Armin didn't even like.

"I'm sure of this, Armin," Kelsey said. "He told me many times that he hated being on the campaign trail because he'd rather be at home, but he did it because he wanted to help his constituents have a better life."

"So he had compassion on them."

"Right. His personal life was a mess, but that didn't take away from the fact that he'd fought for the state when he was in Congress. Even though he was there for only one term, he did a lot."

"Why did he think he wasn't reelected?"

"Because he was corrupt. I don't know whether Washington corrupted him or simply brought out the worst in him. He was taking bribes and kickbacks. He did a lot of insider trading."

Armin shook his head. "And he was never caught?"

"No, but the voters got wind of it and decided not to vote for him. He also had troubles with his ex-wife's overseas businesses that ran afoul in several countries."

"She wasn't arrested for any of those either."

"No. She's in jail for the Miami fiasco she master-minded. A small matter compared to international intrigue."

"I'll have to ask Cade and Pilar to tell me more about what happened in Miami," Armin said.

"After this is over, let's fly to Miami to see them. I missed their wedding because I was in rehab, but it's never too late to bring a gift."

"So we have plans for the future, but we're still stuck here at Door Number Three," Armin reminded her.

Kelsey closed her eyes. "Helping people. Compassion. What else?"

"If he was compassionate, then was he kind and sympathetic?"

Kelsey opened her eyes. "Kind to others, but extremely cruel to me—and to his own ex-wife and his own adult daughter, Paige, for that matter."

"I'm sorry." Armin didn't step closer to Kelsey because he didn't want her to project her perspective of men and her bad experiences with them on him. He wanted to be different. He wanted to wait for Kelsey to come to him when she was ready.

"I would never call him kind." Kelsey steeled her voice. "He was wicked."

"You can be wicked and still be benevolent."

"That so?"

"Yeah. In Matthew 7:9-11, Jesus talked about the evil man who gave good things to his own children."

*Or what man is there among you who, if his son asks for bread, will give him a stone? Or if he asks for a fish, will he give him a serpent? If you then, being evil, know how to give good gifts to your children, how much more will your Father who is in heaven give good things to those who ask Him!*

"He definitely gave a lot of good things to his adopted daughter. Whatever Carmelita asks, Carmelita gets." Kelsey looked like she was in deep thought. "He also gave a lot of money to no-kill animal shelters around the country. He didn't have pets of his own, but he spared no expenses to help those shelters."

"Interesting."

"Yeah. He was kinder to the animals that he was to me."

Armin could tell that Kelsey still had some past hurts. He was no counselor and had nothing to say to her. He decided to pray instead, that God would heal her from the emotional damages and psychological trauma she had experienced over the years.

*Set her free, Lord.*

"Even after he lost the Senate seat, Braun-Dean continued to do a lot of charitable works. He'd take up any speaking engagements they offered him if it could help someone in need, like the homeless or mentally ill."

"Charitable work. Hmm. How about charity? Let's try that word," Armin suggested.

"Okay." Kelsey typed in "charity" and heard nothing.

"I guess that wasn't it."

A message appeared.

`You have one more chance left.`

"Wait, wait. No!" Kelsey stepped back. Her hands were shaking again.

Armin held them until she calmed down.

"Kelsey, it will work out," he said gently. "We need a word that describes why Braun-Dean ran for Senate. It's not a hard word. He seems to be for the everyday people, right, so this is not going to be a big word."

"We've run through all the words. He liked to help

people. We said he was compassionate, kind, sympathetic, benevolent, charitable—in that order."

"In that order?" Armin was surprised. "Your memory is really good."

"Do you think I should go to law school, since I can memorize a lot of things, like old cases?"

First, she had to focus. "Let's talk about that after we get out. Right now we need to think about this question."

"Sorry. My mind wandered off."

"Rein it in for a second. All those attributes would make Braun-Dean altruistic." Slowly, Armin typed in the word 'altruistic' and waited.

You are close. Try a noun.

Armin typed in "altruism" and the door opened.

Kelsey let out a yell and started to jump up and down. She and Armin high-fived each other. And hugged briefly.

They stepped into the hallway before Kelsey spoke again. "The last thing I would call Braun-Dean is altruistic because that would imply that he was selfless. He was the most selfish person I know. All that charitable work was so that he could get a pat on the shoulder and be worshipped."

"He probably thought he was altruistic." Armin

led her to the fifth and last door. "So far we have formed quite a bit of the password with one word left to go. We don't know if some of the letters need to be in uppercase."

"Right. However, we will have the password that The Steward can process if we get the last word." Kelsey touched Armin's arm. "Thank you for being here with me and not letting me do this alone."

Armin wondered if Kelsey's love language might be Quality Time. In this strange place where there was no daylight, standing at the last door, Armin had learned a little more about Kelsey.

Kelsey tapped the door and a screen appeared.

`Tomorrow is...?`

"Casablanca!" Kelsey shouted.

"What?" Armin was puzzled.

"It's a thing between Braun-Dean and me." Kelsey quieted down.

Armin tried not to react emotionally. He tried to say something objectively. "Not the movie?"

"No, the city in Morocco." Kelsey started typing on the virtual keyboard. "Let's see if this works first, and then I'll tell you the story behind it."

It worked. The final door opened.

"Whenever work was hard, he would ask me to

complete a sentence," Kelsey recalled. "He would say 'Tomorrow is...' and I would name a place. If we felt like it, we would go to that place on our next vacation. It could be anywhere in the world. He was very generous to me like that."

"However, 'Tomorrow is Casablanca' doesn't sound grammatically correct." Armin felt like a wet blanket, spoiling her one good memory of her past life.

"Does it matter? It was our game."

"Why Casablanca?"

"That was our favorite place." Kelsey's voice cracked. "He's dead now, so it doesn't matter, and I don't think I'll ever go back to Casablanca on account of that."

"It's okay. We'll find a new place for new memories, okay?" Armin tried to temper his jealousy, but reminded himself that it didn't make sense to be jealous of a dead man.

Kelsey nodded. "Let's find a new place that's just for us."

"Us? Meaning..." He wanted a confirmation.

"You and me, silly. Who else?" She held his hand again.

Was something happening to them? Armin had no idea. It was as though they had simply slid into the first base of a relationship.

"To be honest, I don't want to remember him all, but this escape room made me do it," Kelsey confessed.

As they stood outside the escape room, a deluge of relief washed over Armin.

"That wasn't too bad, was it?" Kelsey squeezed his hand.

Armin nodded. "So we have the full password, with a caveat. Some of the letters might be in upper-case, not necessarily the first letter, and the non-alphanumeric character might not be the dollar sign. However, that's a space filler for now."

```
ZurielWorld$Altruism-
Casablanca
```

What had begun as a trial for Armin and Kelsey became a time they could spend together. The forced proximity they had to endure turned into something that drew them closer together.

Truly God had worked it out for their good. Romans 8:28 came to Armin's mind.

*And we know that all things work together for good to those who love God, to those who are the called according to His purpose.*

"Where's the exit?" Kelsey asked.

There was no sign anywhere. In fact, they were still in what looked like a similar hallway to the last four.

A screen appeared on one of the walls, and a video played. Braun-Dean was sitting in a director's chair, staring straight at the camera.

"If you have reached this far, congratulations. You must be either close to Zuriel, or maybe you're Zuriel herself." Braun-Dean's smile looked like he was nostalgic and missed the old times.

Armin glanced at Kelsey to see how she reacted. Her face was expressionless.

"If you are Zuriel, let me take this opportunity to apologize to you for causing you grief," Braun-Dean continued. "If you had been the one I'd married twenty years ago, we'd be happy together and you wouldn't have left me."

A grunt in the background startled Armin.

"Do you really want to leave a personal message?" The voice was familiar.

Arun. Clearly Arun.

Armin blinked away tears as he listened.

"Yes, I do. Why not?" Braun-Dean said. "Very few people will make it to the end because they don't know me as well as Zuriel has. Not even my ex-wife knows me that well."

Both men laughed. Arun didn't show his face in

the video. Neither did he speak again. Braun-Dean did though.

"I was in high school twenty years ago." Kelsey laughed. "I would never have married him. And no, we wouldn't be happy together if his character then is what it was at the end of his life."

Armin didn't hear what else Braun-Dean had said because Kelsey was talking over him and Armin listened to her instead.

"In conclusion, I hope that The Steward isn't giving you any trouble. I know he isn't the one standing there watching this video." He chuckled. "Goodbye and I hope you do some good with the crypto I leave you."

The video ended. All was quiet until an Exit sign appeared on the wall at the end of the hallway. Under it, the door opened.

Kelsey held Armin's hand as they walked through the door together.

Armin was surprised at the unexpected entourage that greeted them on the other side of the door. A tall twenty-something woman in stilettos stood in the middle of the party, flanked by a couple of men. They were muscular, so that was all they needed to flaunt in front of Armin. He wasn't going to rush toward them with a flying kick.

"Paige!" Kelsey looked surprised.

*Ah, so that's who she is.*

Paige Braun-Dean, the daughter of the dead man, and the former manager of his failed reelection campaign. Some news outlets had reported that Paige herself had sabotaged her father's first term in Congress, effectively destroying his chance of ever going back to Washington.

"What are you doing here?" Kelsey asked.

"To get Felix's passphrase. What else?" Paige's voice was cold. "Why do you think you're still alive, you homewrecker?"

# CHAPTER TEN

"I'm sorry. I was wrong." Kelsey's voice sounded like she had heard all sorts of accusations before.

Armin stood closer to Kelsey than to Paige Braun-Dean, who stared her down. He almost put his arm out to shield Kelsey, but he knew that wasn't helpful. Confession was good for the soul.

"Please forgive me," Kelsey added.

No excuses, no justification. Kelsey sounded genuinely repentant.

"As long as I live, I will never forgive you and all the other women in Felix's life who destroyed his marriage." Paige's left eyelid started to twitch.

"I'm glad you brought up the timeline," Kelsey said. "For the record, by the time I appeared on the scene, your parents had separated for several years, and for the most part, they weren't even on talking terms."

"You might have been Felix's last side chick, but he was still married, and you knew that."

"Yes, they were three months away from finalizing their divorce." Kelsey drew a deep breath. "How many times do I need to say I'm sorry?"

"Forever! You were a mistress. You will always be known as his mistress. You will never get that stain off!"

Fighting words.

And calling her own father by his first name instead of Dad was another blow to his fatherhood. Perhaps the discord between father and daughter had been deeper than anyone but God knew. It would be unsolvable now that Braun-Dean was dead.

Kelsey sighed. "Once they were divorced, I became your dad's only girlfriend. Remember how happy you were that he was no longer sleeping around but that he was faithful to one person for the next three years?"

"Even one day of you being with Felix before he divorced my mother is enough for me to hate you for life." Paige made a guttural sound of disgust. Now the edge of her mouth started to twitch.

"How many women had your dad slept with while he was still living with your mom, let alone when he was separated from her? Perhaps your investigators might be able to tell you because I can't count that high," Kelsey said. "Those are the women you might want to accuse of wrecking your parents' marriage first."

Armin was on standby, in case things got ugly. Mainly he only listened. He had already made up his mind to be on Kelsey's side, no matter what Paige said. But standing there in the lobby outside the escape room, he realized that this was a rare moment for Kelsey and Paige to clear the air. Perhaps they hadn't had the opportunity previously.

"You were Felix's last mistress." Paige's eyes were dark. "If you hadn't hung around, my parents might have gotten back together and not officially divorced."

"Do you think they would? They hadn't been living in the same house for years before your dad met me. Every time they got together to discuss their businesses, they argued and fought, and Roxanne would stomp off and they wouldn't talk to each other for months."

"They were still officially married."

"On paper, yes, but..."

"Who are you to judge my parents?"

Kelsey sighed. "I know you'll forever brand me as a mistress because of those three overlapping months. I wish I had never met your dad at the celebration party. I wasn't even on staff. I was only a volunteer who put up signs in people's yards during his reelection campaign. I don't know how many times I've apologized to your mom and to you, and yet you won't let me go."

"I will never forgive you for it. Neither will I forgive all the other women in Felix's life."

"Have you considered that the common denominator in all those affairs was your dad himself?" Kelsey asked. "Do you think life with him was wonderful? He was a violent man when intoxicated, and he fed me drugs to keep me in a stupor day and night. It was a nightmare living with him."

And yet she stayed for three years.

"In other words, I don't know how your mom stayed married to him for that many years, and how much she has suffered. I feel sorry for your mom," Kelsey said. "Braun-Dean was a filthy beast."

"That, I agree with you." Paige pointed at Kelsey.

"I submit to you that your father wrecked his own marriage. Go after him."

Paige's eyes darkened. "No worries. I already did."
*I already did.*

Those three words landed on the floor in front of Armin like an anvil from a cliff above them.

Did Paige have anything to do with her father's murder in Georgia the day before? Who was the woman in the surveillance video? Could it have been Paige in real life, with her face digitally replaced?

Armin waited to see what else Paige would say. Maybe there was something he could use against her.

"All that we have just discussed was in the past and we can't go back," Kelsey said. "As I mentioned, I moved on fifteen months ago."

"Are you expecting me to be eternally grateful you left Felix after two years? It's too late, woman." One of Paige's eyes twitched again.

This time a little light bulb went off in Armin's head, but he couldn't pinpoint why.

"Eternally grateful?" Kelsey's eyes were far away. "Speaking of eternity, at the same time fifteen months ago, I accepted Jesus Christ as my Lord and Savior. I'm born again now and my past no longer defines me. For that, I'm eternally grateful to God."

"What's that nonsense? You're already born. How can you be born again? Are you in a cult or something?" Paige laughed.

Armin figured she was trying to understand a spiritual concept with sublunary reasoning. He almost opened his mouth and compared Paige to Nicodemus in John 3, but he decided not to inject himself into the conversation.

"I'm saying I'm no longer who I was," Kelsey said.

"I have a new life in Christ now. I spend my time studying the Bible and going to church."

"Oh so pious. Like that can erase your past?" Paige mocked her.

"God has forgiven me the guilt of my sins so that my soul is at peace with God forever. However, here on earth, I'm still dealing with the consequences of my sins. Case in point: you and your mom are still after me."

"Whatever."

Armin gently squeezed Kelsey's hand to let her know that he was there. He did not agree with her previous decisions to live off Braun-Dean by being his lover, but that had been before Kelsey had become a Christian. There were other jobs Kelsey could have done to make a living, but who was he to judge her decisions back when she was an unsaved person? Romans 3:23 condemned everyone.

*For all have sinned and fall short of the glory of God.*

Jesus Christ had made all the difference in Kelsey's life. She was no longer old Zuriel the mistress, but now she was new Kelsey the Christian. Christ had changed the trajectory of her life, transferring her from the domain of darkness into the kingdom of light. Armin felt a verse popping into his head, but now might not be the time to "go preacher" on everyone with Colossians 1:13-14.

> *He has delivered us from the power of darkness and conveyed us into the kingdom of the Son of His love, in whom we have redemption through His blood, the forgiveness of sins.*

Paige's phone rang before she could say anything else. She picked it up. "You have what you need? Good. Do you want me to take them to you? No?" She paused, listening. "Okay. Will do."

She hung up. Motioned to her men. "The Steward is working on the password you figured out. I don't have to tell you that, but he wants me to."

*He wants me to.*

Armin realized that Paige worked for The Steward. That was a new piece of information he hadn't thought of. In his investigation, he hadn't put much weight on Braun-Dean's daughter because she seemed to have been out of the picture once his reelection campaign was over.

"Does The Steward already have the password?" Armin asked. How?

"Obviously he was listening in when you and that prostitute walked through the doors," Paige said.

Kelsey didn't respond to the name calling. It was

only a word, and Armin had more critical things to deal with right now—like maybe saving their own lives —than to defend Kelsey over a word. She was an adult and could handle criticism on her own.

He guessed that The Steward—or his people—had installed listening devices on one of them or both after they had passed out at the end of dinner. This meant he and Kelsey shouldn't be talking privately about anything. The Steward was still listening.

Earlier in the escape room, Armin had voiced his concern about not trusting Nicholas. He wondered now if The Steward had heard that conversation. To her credit, Kelsey sided with Nicholas.

Paige motioned to her men. "They will take you to the RV. You can eat what's in the refrigerator that Nicholas put there."

"Speaking of Nicholas, where is he?" Kelsey asked. "Is he okay? The Steward is not going to hurt him, is he?"

Paige didn't answer her. Instead, she said. "Don't try to leave the RV."

"Wait a minute," Kelsey said. "We got you the password. Aren't we free to go?"

Paige laughed. "Are you really naive or are you pretending?"

Armin knew better. Kelsey was smarter than she let on. She probably wanted Paige to say more. The more she talked, the more clues they would get about their present and future situation.

"Are you saying the passwords don't exactly work yet?" Kelsey pressed.

Paige didn't answer her, but Armin could guess what The Steward might be doing. He was probably running software to get all the combinations of the various upper and lower cases, plus non-alphanumeric characters. If he had a supercomputer, he could process it in days. Otherwise, he'd have a harder time.

Then again, from what Kelsey had told Armin in their many heart-to-heart conversations over the months, Braun-Dean hadn't been a complicated man. Moral flaws notwithstanding, he wanted to see people suffer a little, but not too much. Even though he and The Steward didn't seem to be the best of friends, the latter was still the manager of his crypto fund. Maybe he was trying to be nice to The Steward who held the key to his vault.

In this case, Braun-Dean had seemed to be only trying to make it slightly difficult for The Steward to get the recovery password, but not too difficult because he wanted his ex-wife and daughters to have the bitcoins he had saved up. Perhaps he had a heart after all.

That was to say, Armin bet two cents on the possibility that Braun-Dean only capitalized the first letter of each word in the password, and he probably had used the dollar sign in the middle. Then again, Armin hadn't met Braun-Dean.

So in the end, Armin didn't know. All he and Kelsey could do was to wait for the verdict. When it came, would The Steward let them go? The prospects of getting freed by their abductors were slim.

The two men who Paige assigned to take Armin and Kelsey to the RV suddenly grabbed their arms and handcuffed their wrists behind their backs. They did it so quickly that Armin didn't have enough time to wiggle free.

"Oh no. Not again," Kelsey exclaimed.

Being handcuffed again reminded Nicholas of the strange afternoon on Interstate 95, when he and Kelsey had been arrested by two police officers and then abducted by Nicholas.

He glanced at the two men taking them out of the door to the building. They were wearing thick jackets to stave off the winter cold. The masks prevented Armin from recognizing their faces.

Outside the building, it was already night. Stars twinkled in the sky.

"What time is it?" Armin asked.

"There's no reason for you to know," the bigger man said.

"Just tell me roughly. Is it midnight? After midnight?"

"You guessed it."

They stood on the terrace level of what appeared to be a multi-level stone house overlooking a large body of water. Armin couldn't see the other side of it, and it was dark out. There were some lights along the water, which was how Armin knew it wasn't a pool.

"Is that a pond?" Kelsey asked.

"Chickamauga Lake," one of the men replied. "In the daytime sometimes, you can see yachts sailing by."

So they were in Tennessee. Had to be. Armin had lived in South Carolina for a number of years, and did not recall a lake there by this name. He also recalled their dinner conversation in Spartanburg, when Nicholas had told them that The Steward was supposed to be on his way to Chattanooga to go to the address the lawyer had given him.

Spartanburg to Chattanooga was about four or five hours, depending on the drive. However, Armin had no idea when they had left Spartanburg after they had passed out. Had they been given more drugs to keep them sleeping until they reached Chattanooga? After they had arrived at the mystery mansion and had woken up, how long had it taken them to go through the escape room?

"So you've been here all day?" Armin asked.

"We waited for you to show up." The small man chuckled. "Zinnia is such a slow driver. I don't know why Nicholas made her drive the RV."

There were two dim outdoor lights illuminating what looked like steps going up the side of a hill from the terrace. Beyond that, it was too dark to see.

"I want to see Nicholas," Kelsey said.

"I'll tell him you asked for him," the smaller man said.

Speaking of Nicholas, Armin wanted to know how complicit the hairstylist was in this entire matter. Had Nicholas known about the drug in their water goblet? Was he behind it? Was he working for The Steward?

So many questions, and no answers.

He couldn't voice his concerns aloud because someone was listening. Not just the two men taking them to the RV, but also The Steward. As soon as they had time, Armin wanted to check their clothes for listening devices.

They climbed up the stairs to what looked like a circular driveway. There was a small stone house on the other side of the driveway, with a single sconce light next to the door. It looked like a guest house or a pool house.

Since they were handcuffed, it was impractical for them to bolt. Armin thought he could make a dash for it—even with his two hands tied behind his back—but then he wasn't sure how to convey that thought to Kelsey without the two men—and The Steward—hearing him. Besides, he didn't know if Kelsey could run as fast as he could.

Back in high school, Armin excelled in the hundred-meter sprint. He could probably get away. However, being handcuffed changed the entire dynamic of a potential escape. And where would he go? He wasn't familiar with this area of Tennessee.

Perhaps he should wait until the men removed the handcuffs.

They didn't enter the small house. Instead, they went away from it, walking on a cement sidewalk until Armin saw the RV parked on a driveway behind a clump of trees.

"Isn't this Nicholas's RV?" Armin asked.

"It looks like it from the outside," Kelsey said. "The same one we saw in Spartanburg."

"What I thought."

So Nicholas also worked for The Steward. Was this recent, or had he been working for The Steward all along, way before he'd introduced the crypto specialist to Braun-Dean?

# CHAPTER ELEVEN

Inside the RV, the two men removed their handcuffs and slammed the door on their way out. Armin rushed to the door but it was locked. He couldn't open it.

When he turned around, Kelsey was checking the windows. Armin hoped that she didn't think about escaping through a window again.

She tapped the window above the booth dinette. The scenery through the window changed from night to day. "Whoa."

Armin stepped closer to have a look. "It's a screen."

They checked the other windows. "All screens except the front windshield."

"When we see Nicholas again, I'm going to ask him how we got from Spartanburg to Chattanooga."

Kelsey checked out the refrigerator. "Is there water in here? Oh good. You want some? These bottles look cold."

"Yes, please." Even as he said it, he wondered if they should drink any water provided by Nicholas.

He stared at the bottled water as they sat across from each other at the booth dinette. He didn't say a word because he knew that everything they said would be recorded.

Kelsey seemed to know that too.

Perhaps they could talk about the past.

"What happened to us?" Armin asked.

"And for how long?" Kelsey added. "I should ask Nicholas. I wonder where he is."

"I didn't know he works for—or with—The Steward."

"Yeah. That surprised me. I know he has some crypto investments, but The Steward is expensive. He takes fifteen percent out of every transaction."

"Does he?" Armin was surprised. Ten percent seemed much to begin with, let alone fifteen percent.

"Fifteen percent of seventeen billion dollars is a lot." Kelsey drank half of the bottled water.

Armin waited to see what would happen to her.

"I think the water is fine," Kelsey said.

"I'll wait an hour and see."

Kelsey laughed at him.

The door opened, startling them both. Nicholas and Zinnia entered the RV.

Kelsey looked glad to see Nicholas. "What's going on?"

Armin wondered if Kelsey was really that unsuspecting of Nicholas and unguarded around him, or whether Armin himself was overthinking because he was jealous of the closeness between Kelsey and Nicholas.

Nicholas sat down next to Kelsey. He touched her arm. "Are you all right?"

Kelsey nodded. "How did we get here?"

"I don't know what happened, but both of you passed out at the dinner table," Nicholas said. "Turns out Bernie works for The Steward, and they needed you to walk through the escape room to extract the password. They didn't think you'd willingly agree to go to Chattanooga, so they decided to drug you. There was nothing Zinnia and I could do after that but go along with the plan."

It sounded logical to Armin, but he reminded himself to look beneath the surface. He didn't believe that Nicholas was simply a bystander. Since Kelsey had a good rapport with Nicholas—whoever he was—Armin let her do the questioning.

"I'm assuming they drove us here," Kelsey said.

"In my RV, no less." Nicholas sighed. "It took over

four hours of driving but you didn't wake up until we reached Braun-Dean's house."

"Who carried us into the house and put us in the escape room?" Armin asked.

"Those two people who escorted you to the RV just now," Nicholas said.

"Where's Bernie now?" Kelsey asked. "I'd like to have a talk with him. What a shame. He's such a good cook and I enjoyed his pot roast and the cheesecake, but the Mickey Finn..." Kelsey shook her head. "What a disappointment."

"We left him behind at the barn house," Zinnia finally spoke.

"That was it? No penalty?" Kelsey's eyes widened.

"He works for The Steward. I can't punish him."

"That so? I'd like to talk to The Steward too." Kelsey twisted the cap to Armin's bottled water. She took a sip. "Tastes okay."

She slid the bottle across the table to Armin. "I tested it for you."

Armin wondered what he should do at this point. He rarely drank from the same cup or bottle as another person. In fact, he wouldn't even drink from the same cup as his own mother, let alone a friend.

Kelsey waited.

Maybe she was trying to prove a point.

Nicholas watched him. He didn't seem to react to

what Kelsey was doing. Perhaps there was nothing between Kelsey and Nicholas, and Armin was only overthinking it.

Armin went for it. He picked up the bottled water and took a sip. "I hope this doesn't knock me out again."

Nicholas laughed. "No, it won't. Don't worry. The Steward rarely repeats the same tricks."

"Was that a trick?" Kelsey made a face. "A poor one."

Nicholas didn't respond to that. He turned to Zinnia. "Go check if they've refueled this RV."

"Why? Are we going somewhere?" Kelsey asked.

Armin waited to see if he felt dizzy or something. Nothing happened. The water was simply water—maybe with a bit of Kelsey's saliva in it.

Why had she done that?

"Yeah, The Steward is pleased that the password you found works," Nicholas said. "All he had to do was set everything to uppercase. Even the dollar sign worked."

"I knew that dollar signs were Braun-Dean's favorite," Kelsey said. "You've seen his signature. It has a big dollar sign in the middle somewhere."

"Yeah."

"What's in the encrypted file?" Kelsey asked nonchalantly, as though she was chatting with a friend.

This same friend who had helped The Steward to drug and drag Kelsey and Armin to Chattanooga. Even if Nicholas hadn't been the one who'd provided the drug that had made both of them unconscious for hours, he hadn't done anything to help them escape The Steward.

"It was supposed to contain twenty-four words, the passphrase that would enable The Steward to recreate the hardware wallet that could access Braun-Dean's crypto stash," Nicholas said.

"Supposed to?" Armin asked.

"There were only eight words in the file." Nicholas frowned. "The Steward is very disappointed."

"Why?" Kelsey asked.

"Because now he has to find the other sixteen words before he could recreate the wallet." Nicholas sounded patient with Kelsey, even though he had been involved in the scheme to use her knowledge of Braun-Dean for their own gain.

"Are you saying that Braun-Dean didn't put all the recovery words in one basket?" Armin knew that would have been the smart thing to do.

"He didn't." Nicholas leaned forward, hands clasped together on the table. "Let me tell you a story."

Everyone waited.

"Do you remember about two years ago, when you

were still going out with Braun-Dean?" Nicholas asked Kelsey.

"I try to forget many things. What am I supposed to recall?" Kelsey leaned back against the bucket seat of the dinette.

"The Steward had a brief falling out with Braun-Dean over the delivery of payment for the black market arms sales to Tehran?"

At first Kelsey didn't respond. Then she seemed to slowly recollect bits of information. "He didn't tell me anything."

"No?" Nicholas raised his eyebrows. "Roxanne wanted to make a scapegoat out of The Steward, and Braun-Dean agreed?"

"Wait," Armin said. "Two years ago? Weren't Roxanne and Braun-Dean already divorced?"

"They were, but they were still business partners." Nicholas turned to Kelsey. "You sure you don't remember anything? Do you remember the big bash in Atlanta at some mansion? Fundraising event that Braun-Dean attended though it wasn't for him? He went there to meet women, but I helped you stop him from embarrassing himself?

"Oh. That. I don't want to remember the bad things, Nicholas. Let's talk about something else."

"No, we can't. Sometimes we have to rehash the tough times so that we can prepare for better days. You know that, love." Nicholas pushed a strand of hair over Kelsey's ear.

*Oh, the "love" word is back.*

Armin tried to brace himself for more feelings he might not be able to contain. "Why are we talking about the past?"

"Because at that Atlanta fundraising bash, Braun-Dean met with another crypto specialist named Arun Dillon." Nicholas turned to Armin, his deep eyes on him. "Your brother."

"You knew this entire time that I'm Arun's brother," Armin said.

"Kelsey has told me about your late night conversations."

"Not everything." Kelsey shook her head.

"When Arun showed up at the bash and talked to Braun-Dean, he put himself on Roxanne's radar. Roxanne was always worried that Braun-Dean would stash his crypto somewhere else where she couldn't access. She could talk to The Steward and get an inside track on Braun-Dean's income streams, but she was no friend of Arun's. In fact, Arun wouldn't talk to her at all."

Armin wasn't sure what to make of Nicholas's story. "You're saying Roxanne killed my brother."

"That's what I'm telling you. Roxanne 'Mean Dean' Braun-Dean did it," Nicholas announced.

If Armin couldn't believe Nicholas most of the time, why would he believe him this one time?

*A liar lies.*

"Why are you telling me all this now?"

Nicholas raised a finger as though to tell Armin to be patient. He wasn't done with his story, apparently.

"The Steward grilled Braun-Dean's family attorney, and before he died, the man finally confessed that he had two envelopes. The second envelope was already delivered two years ago..." Nicholas stared at Armin. "To your brother."

Those eight words on a folded piece of paper in Arun's keepsake box!

It all made sense now.

"The Steward knows that your sister-in-law in Mumbai sent you a keepsake box," Nicholas said. "Do you recall sixteen words somewhere in the box?"

Yes and no. Yes, Armin recalled words on the folded piece of paper in Arun's box. No, there weren't sixteen words. Only eight. Should he tell Nicholas now?

Eight words from the lawyer's encrypted file plus eight words from Arun's keepsake box would only add up to sixteen words. In order to recreate the physical wallet, The Steward required twenty-four words. Or more. They wouldn't know unless they had all the words.

If the lawyer had only distributed two envelopes, containing their recovery passphrase, wouldn't they be twelve words each, not eight?

Therefore, even if Armin gave him Arun's eight words, The Steward would still be eight words short.

A third person, somewhere out there, held the remaining eight words. Who was this third person?

"Not for sure," Armin finally answered.

"Not for sure?" Nicholas asked. "What does that mean? The Steward likes precision."

"Are you on The Steward's side?" Kelsey asked. "Since when did you start working for him?"

Nicholas ignored her. He turned to Zinnia. "Show him the video."

On the video was a birthday party for Arun's baby girl. Armin recognized his parents and his sister-in-law. They were clapping as Armin's niece blew out the candles. His sister-in-law wrapped her arms around a caucasian man who Armin had never seen before. The man kissed her on the forehead.

"They're getting married later this year," Nicholas said. "Your sister-in-law's new boyfriend."

Firstly, Armin wondered about the deep fake video from the news report that caused Kelsey to be wanted for a murder she hadn't committed. Now Zinnia had shown them a home video all the way from Mumbai. Was that doctored too?

"What are you saying?" Armin asked.

Zinnia played another video. "This one is from yesterday morning."

This time Armin's sister-in-law and the man were driving somewhere.

"We've on a vacation, just the two of us." She was smiling from ear to ear. "We're going to a place where no one can find us. Isn't it mysterious and oh so romantic?"

"Anything to make you happy," the man added.

Then Zinnia made a video call. The same man appeared on the screen. He was wearing all black.

"You calling to check if I've done it?" the man asked.

"Sam, we have her brother-in-law here, so we want to confirm to him that we're not joking," Zinnia said.

"Tell him I never joke." The video panned across what looked like a hotel bedroom.

Someone was sleeping on the bed. A woman who looked like Armin's sister-in-law. She was tied up to the bed, and duct tape was over her mouth.

"Rita?" Armin's jaw dropped.

"Say hello to your brother-in-law." The man removed the duct tape from her mouth.

She had a birthmark on her neck, and it seemed to be in the same position as Armin's sister-in-law's birthmark. How precise could a deep fake video be?

"Armin?" His sister-in-law sounded shocked. "Call the police!"

That would be exactly what she'd say, from what Arun had told him. Armin couldn't believe a deep fake character could mimic a real person that well in the present day.

Before she could scream, the man taped her mouth shut again.

"Stand by, Sam." Zinnia ended the conversation.

"What is that all about?" Kelsey asked. "What is going on?"

Armin was baffled too. Which of the videos that Zinnia had just shown them was real? Were all three deep fake videos? If he assumed they were, but they were not, wouldn't he put his sister-in-law's life in danger?

What was the truth? Where was the truth in all of these things?

He felt like he was in Plato's cave, seeing shadows on the wall. It seemed that the truth was somewhere out there. Where, exactly?

Nicholas directed his attention to Armin. "Let me ask you again. Do you recall sixteen words somewhere in the keepsake box that your brother left you?"

This time Armin wanted to cave in. Even though he wondered if the video was yet another fake, The Steward had enough information about his family in

Mumbai. If they targeted Arun's widow, it would only be a matter of time before they go after the rest of his family, including Armin's retired parents.

Perhaps he could give The Steward some breadcrumbs. In any case the box was in Buckhead in uptown Atlanta. If he could get out of this present environment, wouldn't the chance of getting help increase?

Armin didn't want to leave Kelsey behind.

He glanced at Kelsey, who said nothing. To her credit, she didn't try to tell him what to do. If she as much as said a word, Armin would do whatever she told him to do.

He knew he would.

"Let me pray about this for a minute," Armin finally said.

"Pray?" Nicholas let out a laugh.

Kelsey put her hand on Nicholas's arm. "Please? Let him pray."

Nicholas softened. "Okay. One minute timeout."

Armin bowed his head, knowing that God would protect him even when his eyes were closed for prayer. Right now his problem was not knowing the truth. He did not believe the video from Mumbai about his sister-in-law, because this same Nicholas had given them a fake video about Kelsey murdering the former senator in the crux of this entire situation.

What was the truth? John 14:6 said that Jesus Himself was the truth.

*Jesus said to him, "I am the way, the truth, and the life. No one comes to the Father except through Me."*

Armin prayed that God would reveal to him the truth and show him what to do. Should he admit that Arun's box contained some words that could be a part of the passphrase? If he said no, what would The Steward do to him and Kelsey? If he said yes, then he had to go retrieve it.

He said his "amen" and then looked up. Drew a deep breath.

"My brother did give me a box, but it only contained memories of him, like the baseball he caught at a Braves game. Things like that." He turned to Nicholas. "Yes, there was a piece of paper, but I don't recall seeing twelve words. I think there were only eight."

"Eight?" Nicholas's eyes widened.

"My guess is that Braun-Dean split the recovery passphrase three ways," Armin suggested. "He gave eight words to you, eight words to Arun, and eight words to someone else."

"From what I know about Braun-Dean, that would make sense," Kelsey added. "He was paranoid like that.

226

You saw his video in the escape room. He wanted to stick it to The Steward."

Nicholas nodded. He seemed to buy what Armin and Kelsey said, even though they were simply speculation.

"The Steward had helped Braun-Dean so much that it's a shame there hadn't been more trust between them." Nicholas sighed. The rest of his attention was on Armin. "Where did you put the words you found in the box?"

"They're handwritten on a piece of paper," Armin said. "I left the paper in the box."

"Where's the box?" Nicholas asked him point blank.

"I missed my brother so much that I took it to work." It was true, but only half the story. He had taken it work because he had thought that the box itself was a puzzle box. Deshon had told him the story of Helen's associates chasing after puzzle boxes that were supposed to contain the map to Blackbeard's treasures.

Unfortunately, Arun's box was simply a box. However, taking it to work reminded him why he moved to Atlanta.

Nicholas chuckled. "So it's sitting on the desk for all the world to see."

"At first it was, but they didn't give me a big desk. So I put it in the drawer under my desk."

The box should've been at home, on top of the dresser in his master bedroom at his penthouse condominium five minutes away from the Hu Knows Atlanta office. It was fortunate that he had taken the box to work. There was no better place for it, except for a bank vault.

Hu Knows was protected by security around the clock. The front desk was trained to handle a crisis. There were four unknown entities taking up floors in the building, and at least two of them—according to Deshon—were fronts for undercover operations at the federal level.

Arun's box was safe in the building.

Armin knew he would get help if he took The Steward's goons to the Hu Knows office instead of to his house—which only had a Ring alarm, and with neighbors on both sides who were gone most of the year.

"Where's this office?" Kelsey asked.

"He works for Hu Knows now," Nicholas said. "Their white collar crime division in Atlanta."

"You didn't tell me." Kelsey stared at Armin.

"He started six months ago." Nicholas seemed proud of his intel.

Armin wondered where he had gotten it from. "Technically, I was only a consultant then."

"You're a CPA though." Kelsey still looked hurt.

"Which means I can work anywhere."

"But your office..." Nicholas's voice trailed off.

"There are only two of us working at the Atlanta branch at this time," Armin tried to allay Nicholas's concern. "The other person is on assignment, and I am here with you."

"On assignment?"

"I don't know where he is." It was the truth. Armin had no idea where Deshon was.

"In that case, you'll go back to your office and retrieve the box," Nicholas ordered. "If you lie even a little bit to me, The Steward will have no problem killing Kelsey, and there's nothing I can do."

"Let Kelsey go with me," Armin said.

"No." Nicholas's voice was harsh. "Kelsey is my insurance."

"Your insurance? Not The Steward's?" Kelsey made a face.

"Both," Nicholas corrected himself. Then he turned to Zinnia. "Get Sam and Bob here to take Armin to Atlanta."

"It's a four-hour round trip," Zinnia said. "Can The Steward wait that long?"

"He has no choice."

*Third person.*

The way Nicholas said it almost dispelled Armin's suspicion that Nicholas and The Steward were the same person. Perhaps Nicholas had spoken of his other persona in the third person for so long that he had gotten used to it.

On the other hand, they might be two different people. If Nicholas was only a lackey, he must have been promised a big reward from The Steward. Would The Steward murder anyone to achieve his goals? After all, someone had murdered the former senator to get to his crypto accounts. Was The Steward behind it?

"Wait. Remember what I said earlier?" Armin asked. "The paper I found did not contain sixteen words. I remember thinking about it."

Nicholas tapped his phone and texted something to someone. He didn't say what he was doing. Armin waited.

Kelsey leaned over and tried to read what Nicholas was tapping. He finished and put his phone away.

"Curious Kelsey, what am I going to do with you?" His thumb lightly rubbed Kelsey's jaw.

She let him.

Armin's blood started to boil.

How could she let him?

"Why did you have to text Paige?" Kelsey asked, puckering her lips.

Was Kelsey putting up a show? Armin waited.

"I want her to take a trip to the Fulton County Jail

to visit her mother," Nicholas explained. "Maybe she has the remaining passphrase."

"Maybe?" Kelsey gently lowered Nicholas's hand away from her face. "So you think that Braun-Dean split the passphrase into three, and Roxanne has the third piece, like Armin suggested earlier?"

Nicholas barely nodded. "He's not a genius. I can come up with that idea myself."

"Should I go with Paige to make sure she doesn't run away with the words?" Zinnia asked.

"No need. She can't do anything with the eight words that The Steward has. Nobody has seen those words but him." Nicholas looked at ease, like he was in charge. "Armin will retrieve his words and bring them here because he wants to come back to Kelsey."

"Why can't we all go? Let's just drive this RV to Atlanta." Kelsey smiled. "I want to know how it drives. It seems like a very expensive RV."

Nicholas seemed to study her. "If I didn't know any better, I'd say you're trying to lower my guard."

Kelsey blew him off. "You're my friend. Why would I try to do this or that to you?"

Nicholas looked touched by Kelsey's sentiment.

"The Steward may be trying to control you and order you around, but I think you're just trying to do your job because he's paying you," Kelsey said. "After this is over, we should choose to be free, okay?"

Nicholas blinked. Then he reached for Kelsey. His fingers ran through the ends of her hair. "You should wear it down more often. There's no need for highlights. Your brown hair is shiny and glossy."

"And no split ends, thanks to you," Kelsey said.

Nicholas smiled.

Armin had to trust that Kelsey knew what she was doing and she'd be fine waiting for him to return from Atlanta.

If he stayed with Kelsey in Chattanooga, neither of them would be rescued. If he sent Kelsey to Atlanta to retrieve the box—hoping that FBI Special Agent Tanaka would rescue her—it wouldn't work because Kelsey was not currently an employee of Hu Knows. She didn't know where Armin's desk was, and what Arun's keepsake box looked like.

Armin had to go.

He tried to make eye contact with Kelsey, but she was focused on Nicholas.

*Stay safe, Kelsey.*

# CHAPTER TWELVE

Driving Armin down Interstate 75 that ran from Chattanooga all the way through Atlanta were the same two men who had escorted Kelsey and Armin from the mystery mansion to the RV back in Chattanooga. The smaller man was at the wheel, and the bigger man was in the back of the sedan with Armin.

Armin had heard Zinnia calling their names earlier. Sam was the big man and Bob was the driver.

For the third time in two days, Armin was handcuffed again. This time, only one hand was cuffed, so that the other hand could eat breakfast, which was comprised of a chicken biscuit they'd picked up from a fast food place on the highway that opened at six o'clock in the morning before they crossed the Tennessee-Georgia border.

Armin was sitting on the right side, behind an empty passenger seat. Sam to his left was dozing off. Armin glanced at the dashboard clock between the two front seats. It was seven in the morning. The sun would rise in forty minutes at this time of the year.

Armin looked over his backseat companion, out the window facing east, but it was still dark. A new day would be dawning.

Sunrises over Georgia were often glorious, and Armin wished that Kelsey could have been with him to see it, especially from his top floor penthouse in the heart of Buckhead. They could drink coffee together and look to the east.

The hope of it was why Armin left Kelsey behind in Chattanooga and agreed to go on this fool's errand for The Steward, who might not even be a person in real life.

Armin felt bad for not staying in Chattanooga with Kelsey, but he made a calculated but risky decision to leave her with Nicholas on the belief that he wouldn't hurt her. He hadn't hurt her in the years they'd known each other, and Armin doubted he'd hurt her now—although with The Steward calling the shots, anything could turn sideways at any moment.

Armin prayed that Kelsey would stay safe until he returned.

Meanwhile, he had to produce the piece of paper that Arun had left him. It only had eight words, but Nicholas didn't know that.

Perhaps Arun had been mistaken. He would have to look at the box again to make sure. Maybe there was another piece of paper in there somewhere.

He couldn't believe that Arun would leave such an important piece of information on a piece of paper and tell no one. If his wife hadn't discovered it almost a year ago, it would have been lost forever.

Perhaps Arun had wanted to move it somewhere safe, but he had died before he got around to it. No one would ever know.

The vehicle passed Cartersville and headed south toward Kennesaw and Marietta. Armin looked out the window to his right. Somewhere over there was the Kennesaw Mountain National Battlefield Park, where the Union and Confederate armies had fought in 1864.

A few months ago, Deshon had brought Armin to see a reenactment of the Battle of Kennesaw Mountain somewhere near the national park. It was then that Armin had learned about General Tecumseh Sherman's march from Chattanooga to Atlanta to burn down the city during the American Civil War. The

Union army would go on to march through Macon and all the way to Savannah on the coast.

Here was Armin, traveling on the same route as Sherman, albeit on a faster steed: a horseless carriage.

He remembered that field trip because Deshon had gone out of his way to welcome Armin to Atlanta. He had also taken him to various area restaurants in Atlanta, from downtown to midtown and Buckhead, plus his favorite grocery stores and bookstores. Both were single and liked to hang out in bookstores when they were not working.

Now all his hopes were pinned on Deshon figuring out where Armin and Kelsey were without any GPS or tracking devices, without any phone calls or messages in bottles. Deshon had to grab clues out of thin air and look for Armin.

*Wait. Let me correct that.*

Armin reminded himself that he shouldn't put all his hopes on Deshon, a mere mortal. As a Christian in crisis, he should always remember to put his hope in God, as the Psalmist sang about in Psalm 42:11.

> *Why are you cast down, O my soul?*
>> *And why are you disquieted within me?*
>> *Hope in God;*
>> *For I shall yet praise Him,*
>> *The help of my countenance and my God.*

After all, Armin's life was in God's hands. He prayed that he had made the right decision. He was going to do something that could either kill him and Kelsey, or save them both.

Looking out of the window into the dawn, Armin second guessed himself. What a bad idea to leave Kelsey behind. However, if he had nothing to offer The Steward, both of them would die.

*Yeah, yeah. Justify it all you want. You left Kelsey behind. She will never forgive you for it. Forget ever asking her out.*

Armin recalled asking Nicholas to let Kelsey go with him to Atlanta. Nicholas said that The Steward wanted to use Kelsey as insurance. Kelsey didn't seem bothered by the separation. Maybe she didn't care about Armin all that much. Maybe she had a plan of her own. Maybe she didn't think she was in grave danger with Nicholas around.

Whatever it was, the whole mess jostled in Armin's head, and he felt sick to his stomach with an onset of fear that he might have made a grave mistake.

It was too late now.

The man beside him stirred as the traffic continued to pick up as they drove past Marietta. Rush hour had begun even before the sun rose. Such was life in Atlanta, something that Armin had to adjust to very quickly after moving here from South Carolina.

The driver cussed as he slammed on his brakes to avoid hitting the vehicle in front of him on Interstate 75. "I hate Atlanta traffic!"

"You want me to drive?" Sam chuckled.

"No, you can't see out of your left eye," came the reply.

"I can drive just fine, buddy."

"I know you can. Just pulling your leg to bring some levity into this situation."

"Levity? Where'd you learn such a big word?"

"I watch TV, dude." He laughed.

The sun rose as they were stuck in traffic. Right above the skyline, the sun's rays came straight into the sedan. Sam lifted up his left hand to cover his eyes from the direct sun.

And that was when Armin saw it.

It was the same scar that ran around his thumb all the way to his wrist.

He couldn't have seen it earlier because it was dark in Chattanooga when they had started driving. He could only see the scar now because it was daylight.

Armin almost couldn't breathe. Turned out that Sam was one of the cops—now established as impostors —who had stopped him and Kelsey in their Highlander on Interstate 95 the day before.

He wasn't dead.

Was this the time to confirm who he was? Or

should Armin not say anything, in case it made matters worse for him?

Armin closed his eyes and prayed for wisdom. He used the words in James 1:5 in his prayer, repeating them back to God. God had promised to give him wisdom if he asked Him for it, right?

> If any of you lacks wisdom, let him ask of God, who gives to all liberally and without reproach, and it will be given to him.

He opened his eyes to find Sam staring right at him.

"You sleeping?" he asked.

"Praying."

"One of those people."

Armin didn't ask for clarification and neither did he want to know who "those people" were. He was more worried about "these people" he was stuck in the car with.

Who were they working for? Armin would like to know, but again, it might be the wrong time to interview them and he might be the wrong person to ask such questions. He wasn't trained for any such thing. He was not a former police officer or an FBI agent. He wasn't a trainee private investigator. He didn't know how to use a weapon or fire a handgun. He didn't even know how to throw knives.

At Hu Knows, he primarily did his investigative work from the safety of his desk. He was simply a civilian CPA who was caught in this web he'd found himself in because he wanted to know why his brother had been murdered.

Located in uptown Atlanta, Buckhead had grown vibrant and crowded over the years, according to Deshon, who believed that the entire state of Georgia had gotten more crowded as people moved here from the north and west.

The driver knew where to go as he exited off of Interstate 75 onto West Paces Ferry Road, because Armin had given him the address earlier before they had left Chattanooga. It was then that Nicholas told them to take a photo of the words on the paper and text it to him.

That told Armin a lot. It meant that The Steward had considered two men disposable. Why? Because as soon as Nicholas handed the sixteen passphrase words to The Steward, they had no need for the two men anymore.

As for Armin, he had to fend for himself.

He was on his home turf now, and he prayed that someone armed would be waiting for him at the office when he walked in. If not, there would be cameras everywhere, much like the Savannah office. The probability of people working at the Buckhead office this morning was higher because Deshon didn't like talking to people on Zoom. He'd much rather have meetings in person and do things in a team, also in person.

Deshon was former military, so Armin felt safe with him.

Still, it was God in whom he must trust, not people, as wonderful as they might be. Armin prayed that no matter what, God would protect him and Kelsey from danger.

Before he moved away from Columbia, he had one last lunch with his Sunday school teacher at the church he'd attended for years. Knowing why Armin was leaving, the friend shared 2 Samuel 22:3, and told Armin that he'd pray that verse for him as the Lord led him. He wondered if Pastor Calman had been praying for him this week because he could use all the prayers he could get.

> *The God of my strength, in whom I will trust;*
> *My shield and the horn of my salvation,*
> *My stronghold and my refuge;*
> *My Savior, You save me from violence.*

The driver cussed again, jolting Armin from his

prayer. Armin looked out the window. Traffic was everywhere. Sidewalks were filled with pedestrians.

There were no slow days in this Buckhead haven filled with bookstores and health food stores, as well as old churches, concert halls, and business complexes, including the newly minted branch of Hu Knows.

They were inching forward slowly on the roads to Hu Knows, when Armin jiggled his handcuff. "Hey, you might consider removing this because it's daylight and people can look into the car and see me like this."

Sam didn't reply. He was tapping his phone.

Armin didn't know what he was doing and dared not lean over to pry. No sound was coming out of the phone.

"What's wrong with these people?" He swiped the phone and put it back into his jacket. "Keep asking me, 'Are you there yet? Are you there yet?' Of course we're not. We're in Atlanta, stupid. Can't you see the traffic?"

Armin almost laughed.

"You think it's funny now?" Sam said. "Wait until the show begins."

"What show?" Armin asked.

"Told you to wait and see." A snarl crept up his face.

"Dude, in this traffic, I don't know how we're going

to get out of here safely afterwards," the driver added. He seemed to be the thinker between the two.

"You don't worry about that. The Steward promised us safe passage."

"For all three of us?" Armin asked.

"As far as I know. Don't you want to go back to your Kelsey?" Sam eased, all innocent like.

*My Kelsey?*

They reached the building where Hu Knows took up the entire third floor. Armin tried to think about how he could alert the front desk to call for help.

Sam put on his mask and cap. There was no way the security cameras would be able to identify him.

"Here's a spot near the building." The driver coasted to an empty spot in the first row that wasn't for handicapped parking.

"This is a bad idea. Cameras are everywhere." Sam unbuckled. "How about you drop us off and then stay close? I will text you. Pick us up at the front entrance."

Sam turned to Armin. "I will be pointing my pistol at your hip as we go inside. If you don't want to lose your ability to produce kids, you will stay close to me and don't make a fuss. Anything strange, and I will text Zinnia, and your girlfriend dies. She has killed before and she will do it again."

*Killed before?*

"Who has she killed before?" Armin asked.

The man didn't answer. He reached over to remove Armin's handcuff. "If you bolt, Zinnia will kill her."

"I won't." Armin massaged his wrist. "When we go inside, we have to sign in at the front desk."

Truth was, they didn't have to, but Armin wanted the man in front of the security camera. If he could send a message to the receptionist to call 911, it would help. Whatever it was, their first stop had to be the front desk. He prayed that someone he knew was working today.

"I'm going to say that you're a friend," Armin added. "What name should I use when I check us in?"

"Sam is my stage name."

"Last name?"

"Whatever. I don't care."

"Okay. Let's make you Sam Smith."

Sam frowned as he exited the vehicle and came around the other side to open Armin's door.

They walked toward the entrance, with Sam standing slightly behind Armin with his hands in his jacket pocket.

The morning air was cool, and Armin could feel a whip of bitter chill. It was still mid-January. Would it snow? He looked up at the sky. It was blue and clear, with a couple of contrails crisscrossing it.

At the front desk, Armin waved hello to the receptionist, who was sitting down tapping her phone. "I need to sign in."

She smiled back and handed him a clipboard and a pen.

Armin wrote down his name. Then he filled in the rest of the columns with a message wherever and however he could fill them.

> *Help. Life in danger. Call 911.*
> *Call Deshon ASAP 404-73...*

He blanked out on the rest of Deshon's phone number. He moved on to the next line, writing down Sam Smith as his guest, adding a few helpful notes.

> *Man with gun. Dangerous.*
> *HKI on 3rd floor.*

Armin turned to Sam. "It's asking for your phone number."

Sam shook his head. Of course, he wouldn't give it.

Armin only wanted to show that he was still filling out the form. He handed it over to the receptionist. "Hope I filled out the columns correctly. Please check, and have a good day."

He turned to his abductor. "Let's go."

At the elevator, Armin didn't turn his face to look

at the front desk. He prayed that her training would serve her well. This building had several offices whose workers must be protected, so she'd know what she needed to do.

In the six months that Armin had been here, he hadn't met a single person from the other floors. He had walked past some of them when he and Deshon went out to lunch, but beyond the perfunctory southern hello, no one discussed the work they did. It was as though this building was yet another mystery box.

In the middle layer of this box was the Hu Knows Atlanta office, with nobody in it but Deshon and Armin. Deshon had said that they would add an office manager, but nobody showed up. Lawyers and paralegals came and went for meetings in white collar crime cases, but otherwise, business was slow.

Armin suspected that if nothing happened here in one year, Helen Hu would close the office. The rental in the heart of Buckhead was expensive.

As the elevator door closed and Armin pressed the third floor button, he wondered how he could disarm Sam alone. If Deshon was here, the two of them could do it together. Or maybe Deshon could do all the work, and Armin would run and hide behind a steel cabinet.

Deshon lived five minutes away in an old house with a small pool in the backyard. However, that was of no use, because Deshon was supposed to be in Savannah—no, his last known location was on Interstate 95 in South Carolina, chasing after Armin and Kelsey in the Toyota Highlander.

Was Deshon still in South Carolina?

Good thing Armin had asked the receptionist to call 911. That was the best thing he could do right now to save his life.

The elevator door opened to a wide hallway and a set of locked double doors. To one side of the door was an electronic keypad that kept the door locked. Armin pressed his six-digit numeric access code.

He knew that as soon as he did that, Deshon would be notified of his identity. That, plus the message to the receptionist downstairs, should be enough to save his life.

Hopefully.

Armin and Sam entered the sparse office space. As expected, nobody was there.

"Nicholas said that nobody works here most of the time," Sam said. "Looks like he was right."

"I told him that."

"He believed you. Nicholas doesn't believe anyone."

Must be due to Kelsey. Nicholas trusted Kelsey, and Kelsey trusted Armin. Therefore, Nicholas had no reason to think that Armin would put Kelsey in danger.

It also meant that Nicholas really expected Armin to return to Chattanooga.

"Where's your desk?" Sam held his handgun in front of him.

Whatever make it was, it looked lethal.

Armin had no experience with weapons, but now he wished he had. If he survived this episode, he'd asked Deshon to recommend an instructor he could take lessons from at a shooting range.

Or perhaps he should get some training on how to disarm a person holding a weapon.

Armin led Sam across the open office, past a seating area and a coffee nook, to a row of desks and workstations. There were no labels on the desks, but Armin had to go to his own desk because he was most familiar with it.

His desk was at a corner of a wall, with the right side of it up against the wall.

There were only six drawers, three on either side of the desk, and no matter how slowly Armin opened the drawers, he was going to come up against time and the business end of a handgun.

He sat down on his office chair, which was actually an oversized gaming chair for big and tall people. It was Deshon's chair but he'd upgraded, so he let Armin use the chair.

Armin began with the left drawers. Sam stood to his left, overseeing the operation. The drawers were filled with mostly snacks.

Sam laughed.

"Want some?" Armin asked.

Sam shook his handgun. "Keep going. No time to waste."

"Yes, sir." Armin scooted over to the right side of his desk. He leaned down to open the drawers, knowing that Sam's weapon was pointed at his back. The gunman couldn't squeeze into the small space. The right side of the table was too close against the wall.

He opened the first and second drawers. Note pads, backup hard drives, and more snacks filled the first two. The last drawer at the bottom, inches off the ground, was what he needed to get to.

Armin opened it, and there it was. Arun's box was next to two things he had forgotten about: pepper spray and bear spray. He leaned over the drawer, and pretended to rummage through the stuff.

"I need to get better organized," Armin muttered loud enough for Sam to hear.

"Hurry up!"

Armin picked up the bear spray, and recalled where he'd gotten it. Deshon was an outdoorsman, and he introduced Armin to his friends who'd gone camping in the Great Smoky Mountains, where they'd encountered black bears. One thing led to another and Armin decided he might go camping with them. So he bought bear spray.

He put down the bear spray. Deshon's friends had told him that it would be illegal for him to use bear spray on humans due to federal regulations on the product.

Well, what about in times of danger?

He rummaged through the drawer and found a can of pepper spray. He had just bought it because he had heard so much about crime in Atlanta that he'd thought he might need it when he walked in the city at night. So far he hadn't needed to walk around at night. Thank God he had removed the tough plastic sleeve that it had been delivered in, or else he couldn't have been able to use it now.

It was only a small canister of pepper spray that would hang off his keychain. He palmed it, and then picked up Arun's keepsake box. He held the box to his chest and slipped the pepper spray into his jacket pocket.

He turned around. "This is my brother's keepsake box."

"Open it and let's find the paper." Sam motioned for Armin to put the box on his desk.

"We need a bigger table. We may have to take the things out of the box to find the paper. There could be more than one piece of folded paper." Armin pointed to the other end of the office. "How about the conference room? It has a big table."

Sam nodded.

Armin led the way. Unlike the Savannah headquarters with its glass-enclosed conference rooms, the Atlanta office conference room was originally the chairman's office. Since it was a big room with a locking door, Deshon had turned it into a mini conference room.

Armin placed the box on the table that took up most of the space in the room. Sam watched Armin take things out of the box and line them up on the table. After a few minutes, he sat down in one of the chairs around the table. His handgun was still pointed at Armin.

Standing by the table, as Armin emptied out the keepsake box, he wondered how to spray Sam. Eventually, he found the folded piece of paper that was at the bottom of the box. He lifted it in the air. "I'm going to unfold this now and put it on the table."

Sam waited as Armin did as he said he would,

spreading the paper flat on the table. Unfortunately, the paper contained only eight words.

"That's all?" Sam looked disappointed. "That's what we came here for?"

"Uh-huh." Armin studied the words. "What did I tell Nicholas? I don't have sixteen words."

"What do the words mean?"

"They're computer generated keys to the vault, but not all of them. This is only a third of it. The Steward has another third."

"Who has the rest of it?"

"Nobody knows. Maybe Roxanne has it. Not my problem." Armin sighed. "You want to take a photo of this and send it to Nicholas? That would be faster than us hand delivering this."

"I still need to take you back to Chattanooga because Nicholas promised your girl that he'd bring you back—although we don't need you anymore once we have these words," Sam smiled.

"On the other hand, The Steward will not kill me until he has accessed the seventeen million dollars of crypto." Might as well tell him what was at stake. Maybe that would make the gunman consider his options.

"How much?" Sam's jaw dropped.

"What I thought when I first heard it," Armin said. "I suppose you're getting a cut of that. I know I'm not."

Sam frowned.

Armin hadn't been a psychology major in college, but he could tell that Sam was probably calculating what he wasn't getting out of the deal with The Steward.

"They made you do all the work and you only get minimum wage." Armin rubbed it in.

Sam got out of his chair. "I have to take a photo of this."

He fished his phone out of his jacket pocket. With his left hand, he logged into his phone and swiped until he found the camera app. The way he was barely able to tap the phone told Armin that Sam's left hand wasn't his dominant hand.

His dominant hand was holding the gun pointed at Armin, but Sam's eyes were on the camera app as he tried to get the paper into the frame. He was about three feet away from Armin.

"I'm told there should be sixteen numbers," Sam said. "Look for another piece of paper with eight more words."

"Okay." Armin stepped back from Sam, and leaned on the table so that Sam couldn't see what Armin was doing with his right hand as his left hand dug into the keepsake box to find more folded paper.

His right hand slid into his jacket pocket and he fumbled at the pepper spray until he felt that his thumb was on the trigger on top of the spray can and that he had a good grip on the canister.

"Oh man. That was blurry." Sam let out an expletive under his breath. "Let me try again."

His weapon hand wobbled.

*Now or never!*

Armin whipped out the pepper spray and pointed it at Sam's face, especially his eyes. The spray only hit the right side of Sam's face because the latter was looking down at his phone, trying to take photos of the eight words.

Startled, Sam yelped, and dropped his handgun and phone as he tried to wipe the pepper spray off his face. He turned toward Armin and growled.

Armin sprayed again. This time he aimed for both of Sam's eyes, partially blocked by his big hands. He sprayed side to side, aiming for that left eye that was still open. He was faster than Sam, and Sam howled as the chemical hit his retina.

Armin stepped back, turned, and sprinted toward the conference room door. He slammed the door shut, and randomly pressed the keypad to lock the door with Sam inside the conference room.

He ran through the office to the double doors they had come through earlier, opened it and ran out—

Straight into a group of police officers with their weapons up and pointed at him.

# CHAPTER THIRTEEN

Whether Nicholas was nice to her and cared for her, Kelsey knew that she was still a prisoner in this RV. Regardless of the custom features and burled wood and leather seats in the dinette, she was still unable to move about freely.

Disappointed that Nicholas worked for The Steward, Kelsey's friendship with him seemed to be unraveling as a certain sense of distrust crept in. Kelsey didn't want that because she genuinely liked Nicholas.

What now? Should she consider The Steward as harmless?

Since Nicholas had been the person who'd introduced Braun-Dean to The Steward, Nicholas must know something more about the crypto consultant than he'd let on these three years.

For now, she had to make the best of the situation and wait until Armin returned. He'd been gone for two hours now, and still no word from Sam or Bob about their excursion to Atlanta.

Inside her head, she was upset that Nicholas was against her. Yeah, holding her here against her will wasn't a good sign of their friendship. She most disliked people controlling someone else's freedom.

She could go in several different directions with her approach to handling Nicholas. Since he knew her, she was somehow limited in how she could disarm him. For now the best method was sincerity.

Nicholas was stretched out on the other seat that Armin had vacated earlier, and he looked relaxed. Of course he did. He could come and go from the RV anytime.

"Are you staying with me until Armin gets back?" Kelsey asked as casually as she could.

Nicholas made a face when Kelsey mentioned Armin.

"You don't like Armin, do you?" Kelsey was fishing.

She thought Nicholas was looking at her with certain longing, but she could be wrong.

"What's he to you?" Nicholas asked.

"To tell you the truth, if he wasn't Arun's brother, our paths would never have crossed. I spend more time with you than with him."

A small smile.

"I asked you if you're staying with me because I don't want to be locked up in the RV by myself. Who knows how long I'll have to wait."

"Be careful what you say, love." Nicholas sat up.

"I know you respect me, and I appreciate you for that." Kelsey drank more bottled water as she chose her words carefully. "When Braun-Dean was ugly to me, you always came to my rescue. You took me to the doctor and you nursed me back to health."

"I told you he's no good for you. You should have left long ago."

"It took me three years to walk out."

"I'm happy for you that you finally did."

"I grew some courage after God saved me."

"God again." Nicholas got up. "You want a beer? There are a few cans in the fridge."

"No, thanks. I don't drink anymore, remember? I'm sober twenty-four-seven. A teetotaler."

"No need to run through the thesaurus." Nicholas opened the refrigerator. "You hungry?"

"I haven't eaten anything since dinner at your barn house." Kelsey slid out of the dinette. "Was that last night or the night before?"

"Last night." Nicholas took out some eggs and bacon and placed them on the counter.

"Did you wash your hands?" Kelsey was at the sink, washing her hands. She dried them on a paper towel nearby. She stepped aside to let Nicholas get to the sink.

"I pity the man who marries you." Nicholas washed his hands.

"Hygiene is very important."

"To you." He reached around her for the paper towel. He still smelled of fresh laundry, like he had when he first came to the RV to sit next to her at the dinette. "Two eggs or three?"

"Two. Thank you. I want some bacon too." This wasn't the first time Kelsey had eaten breakfast with Nicholas. On the campaign trail with Braun-Dean, they had sometimes arrived at their hotel late at night with nothing to eat. Nicholas and Kelsey would go to the nearest diner that was open around the clock. If they couldn't find one, then Nicholas would whip out his portable stove, and they'd cook eggs in his hotel room—breaking all the rules. Breakfast was their comfort food.

Was Nicholas trying to put Kelsey at ease?

Nicholas had been the only other man that Braun-Dean trusted with Kelsey. Maybe Braun-Dean had known something she didn't, but one thing they had for Nicholas was trust.

That trust was now put to the test.

"Yes, ma'am." Nicholas looked for a frying pan.

"I don't understand why The Steward can't just let us go," Kelsey said. "Then we could go to Waffle House or someplace. Then you wouldn't have to cook."

"I won't have to if you cook instead." Nicholas offered her the frying ladle.

Kelsey didn't take it. "I like the way you cook breakfast better."

"The Steward can't let us go just yet, not until he gets the remaining sixteen words to the passphrase." Nicholas put slices of bacon on the pan. "So we wait until he gets to that point."

"And you have to cook for me."

"I don't have to. I want to."

"You're so nice to me. So why are you helping The Steward?" Kelsey genuinely wanted to know.

"I could use the money. I don't have many useful skills, but I've been helpful, and he's going to pay me. I'll take it, you know? Money always helps."

"Dirty money, though."

"Who's gonna know? Are you going to tell?" Nicholas heated butter on another frying pan.

"I have nothing to do with it."

"Good answer."

"Is The Steward paying you by the hour?"

Nicholas shook his head. "One percent."

"That little?"

"What's one percent of a billion dollars? Multiply that by seventeen, and you have a hundred and seventy million dollars."

Kelsey understood it now. They were splitting the seventeen billion dollars worth of crypto. How much of that would go to Roxanne, Paige, and the rest of Braun-Dean's beneficiaries?

Wait a second. Paige was working with The Steward. "How much is Paige getting?"

"You have to ask her that yourself."

"I gather that in the scheme of things, Roxanne is not included in the share?"

Nicholas flipped the bacon. "Don't know and don't care. I'll take the money they offered me. One percent is more than I expected. The Steward could have given me ten million dollars, and I'd take it."

"What's the catch?" Kelsey found two dinner plates. She placed them on the small island near the stove.

"I can always count on you to ask me that question." Nicholas plated the eggs and bacon.

"They look delicious."

"Catch, you say?" He carried the plates to the table.

Kelsey opened and closed drawers.

"The forks are in the drawer under the cabinet you took the plates from."

"Ah, okay." Kelsey picked out two forks and two butter knives. When she sat down at the dinette, she knew she would offend Nicholas again but without asking him for permission, she closed her eyes and thanked God for the food. She didn't offer to pray for Nicholas's breakfast because she had done that before and it had ticked him off.

She said a quick silent prayer for God to protect the food, though she had watched Nicholas cook it and didn't expect him to poison her. She also prayed for Armin's safety, and for Nicholas's salvation.

Nicholas was eating when Kelsey opened her eyes.

"There's no catch," he said.

"What?"

"You asked me earlier why The Steward agreed to pay me one percent. You thought that sounded suspicious."

Kelsey nodded.

"I negotiated the deal. As long as I don't have to kill anyone."

Kill? Kelsey clearly remembered that Nicholas had been with the people who shot at the police officers on the roadside in South Carolina. What about that?

"The Steward did all the work, hired all the people." It was as though Nicholas had read her mind.

"However, he doesn't show his face, so he needs boots on the ground," Kelsey said.

"Bingo. You got it. He needs supervisors, and I need money."

"A hundred and seventy million dollars."

"Not too much in today's economy, love." He finished his breakfast. "Even this RV costs me three million dollars."

Kelsey nodded. She wasn't surprised at the amount because she knew that Nicholas could afford it. He was one of the nouveau riche who had amassed his millions in the crypto market. Gone were the days of styling hair, though he'd still do it for Kelsey.

She had stopped asking him what his background was. She knew that being a hairstylist was only a cover for Nicholas. He had secrets that he didn't want to share with anyone. Touché.

"You like?" Nicholas asked.

"It's smaller than some houses but bigger than the camper van I had to live in for a week," Kelsey replied.

She didn't want to say that the multi-million-dollar RV looked like an ordinary touring bus. It might hurt Nicholas's feelings.

To her credit, Kelsey wasn't an ambitious person. As long as she had food, clothing, and shelter, she was content. She didn't care if she drove a used car or lived in a small house. It mattered not.

Therefore it had gone against her better judgment to get involved with Braun-Dean. A bad mistake for which she'd regret the rest of her life.

"With the money I earned from The Steward, I can pay for all of my grandmother's medical bills." Nicholas lowered his voice. "She won't be around forever, even though a number of people on her side of the family lived until past a hundred years old."

"That so? Amazing." Kelsey used to wonder how long she'd live on earth, but once she became a Christian, it didn't matter how much time God had given her on earth as long as she used it well. After all, her soul would live forever with God in heaven.

"How long do you want to live?" Nicholas asked.

"It's not up to me," Kelsey asked. "However, I can shorten it if I don't take care of my health. Otherwise, God determines the number of my days."

"God again." Nicholas sat back. "You really take your new religion seriously, don't you?"

"Well, it's not a religion in the common sense of the word as it is a relationship with Holy God through His Son, Jesus," Kelsey said carefully. "Men—people—made Christianity sound pious, like getting saved from our sins is some holy unattainable thing. While it is impossible for sinful me to be accepted by God on my own, He has made a provision in Christ for my atonement. His perfect Son sacrificed on the cross to save me from my sins. After He died and was buried, He rose again three days later to give me eternal life."

When Nicholas didn't respond, Kelsey recited Romans 6:23.

*For the wages of sin is death, but the gift of God is eternal life in Christ Jesus our Lord.*

"Let me ask you this." Nicholas uncrossed his legs. "If God has a Son, wouldn't that mean He has a wife too?"

"The Bible speaks in a language that we understand. However, God is not human, you know. He's Spirit. It says so in John 4:24." Kelsey recited the verse for Nicholas.

*God is Spirit, and those who worship Him must worship in spirit and truth.*

"Maybe it's a strange concept to you if I tell you that in heaven there is a triune Godhead, also known as the Holy Trinity. That is, God is in three Persons: God the Father, God the Son, God the Holy Spirit."

Nicholas held up a palm. "Stop right there. I'm not into the metaphysical. If I cannot see it, I won't believe it."

"Yes, it takes faith to believe." Kelsey didn't want to

argue with him. It was not easy to discuss life and death sub specie aeternitatis.

"Doesn't matter, love. I'm all for the here and now." Nicholas cleared the table and loaded the dishwasher. "You know who really determines if you live or die tonight?"

Kelsey waited for the answer.

"It's The Steward, that's who. He will decide if you live or die. God would have to go along with it."

Kelsey disagreed, but she didn't argue with him.

While The Steward was a mere mortal—if he was a real person and not a deep fake—he clearly had some power to kill. Even if it meant that he had to bear the consequences of his actions.

Kelsey had never met The Steward, but she had known for a long time what he was capable of. Braun-Dean had suspected that The Steward had stolen money from him. That was why he had gotten a second opinion from Arun Dhillon, a move that eventually led to Arun's death—although the jury was still out as to who killed Arun.

Nicholas had pointed his finger at Roxanne, but Kelsey believed that it was more likely that The Steward had ordered it. He had the means and resources. Perhaps he had also been the one who'd killed Braun-Dean.

Kelsey didn't feel fear. The Steward could get rid

of her and Armin, but she recalled a warning in Matthew 10:28 from a recently read-through-the-Bible study.

> And do not fear those who kill the body but cannot kill the soul. But rather fear Him who is able to destroy both soul and body in hell.

Fearing God instead of men made a difference in her attitude. Kelsey got up to find a dish rag to wipe the table clean. Then she followed Nicholas to the sitting area.

"These are leather seats. I had them reupholstered." Nicholas crossed his legs and stretched his arms across the back of the seat.

"I thought you bought the RV new."

"Yes, but I changed my mind after it was delivered. It set me back a little, but it's nicer now." Nicholas seemed too relaxed talking about spending money.

"How much time do you spend in this RV?" Kelsey asked.

Speaking of time, she glanced around to find a clock. No clock to tell her what time it was and whether Armin would be back soon.

"Sam and Bob are supposed to call as soon as they get the paper from Armin." Nicholas checked his phone. "Looks like they're half an hour late. I can call them, but Sam hates people who micromanage him."

"Aren't you the boss of them?"

"Sam's actually my uncle on my father's side," Nicholas said.

"Oh, I didn't know that. So you got him a job with The Steward?"

"Something like that. He gets paid well and stays out of jail."

*For now.* "Once The Steward gets what he wants, will he let us go?"

"You'll have to ask him. I'm just the lackey."

How can the lackey have three million dollars of spare change to buy this RV?

*A very rich lackey.*

"Seems to me that The Steward makes people around him do the crime so that he doesn't have to do the time." Kelsey watched to see how Nicholas reacted to the statement.

"Isn't that smart of him?" He laughed.

"Why wouldn't he let me go?" Kelsey asked. "I solved the password for him."

"One password. That's not enough."

"It opened the encrypted file and got him eight words, didn't it?"

"Only a third of the passphrase."

"Nonetheless, this is all I can do." Kelsey didn't

want to suggest or hint at anything that would make The Steward retain her further. She wanted Nicholas to think that she had outlived her usefulness, and convey that thought to The Steward.

"He might need you later for leverage." Nicholas stared at her.

"Me?" Kelsey felt uneasy at the stares, but this was Nicholas. He'd look at her and then leave her alone.

"Doesn't FBI Agent Tanaka need you?" Nicholas asked. "You can be a potential bargaining chip."

He knew about Tanaka because Kelsey had told him. She shouldn't have, but she was complaining about the camper van and Tanaka's name popped up in her rant.

However, all Nicholas knew was that Kelsey was supposed to help Tanaka with the case against Roxanne. Nicholas hated Roxanne, and even called her Mean Dean.

In any case, Kelsey had told him more than she should.

"I guess she's probably looking for me now." Kelsey hoped that Nicholas could relate it back to The Steward to scare him a little.

He didn't flinch.

"Can't The Steward do something with the eight words?" Kelsey asked. "Like maybe restore a third of the wallet?"

"It doesn't work that way, love. You need the whole passphrase."

"Isn't The Steward a genius?"

Nicholas's eyes brightened, as though the compliment was meant for him. "So The Steward is a genius in your eyes."

Was Nicholas himself The Steward?

Kelsey thought that was unlikely.

"I was merely saying that if he's a genius crypto specialist, couldn't he find another way to recreate the hardware wallet without having all twenty-four words?"

Nicholas shook his head. "Without the words, the seventeen billion dollars of crypto are essentially gone."

"You said they were words. Can't he find other words?"

"These are special words." Nicholas swiped his phone and logged in. "Come sit here and I'll show you."

Kelsey did so. She didn't sit too close to him, but close enough to look at the eight words on Nicholas's phone, which he'd written down in a text file. "Those look like ordinary words."

The first two words caught Kelsey's attention.

coffee

## whisper

They were the last two words in a list of words that Braun-Dean had forced Kelsey to memorize for him. On cue, she could hear "Twelve Days of Christmas" in her head, which she had used to memorize the twelve words from Braun-Dean. She had replaced each line with the words in order in the public domain lyrics.

*On the first day of Christmas...*

*On the balcony of abstract...*

Every time Braun-Dean had tested her and she got it right, he would give her a gold bar. She had accumulated enough gold to leave Braun-Dean, but then he'd stolen them all from her at the end. He'd called it a confiscation of property as a punishment for bad behavior, such as spending too much time with other men—not including Nicholas.

Braun-Dean was crazy.

Kelsey wished she could forget the twelve words, but they had been seared into her memory, like it or not.

She stared at the screen again. Since she already knew the first two words, all she had to do was commit the last six words to memory. Piece of cake.

She read those new words from Nicholas over and over again.

"Enough?" Nicholas asked, pulling the phone away.

"Let me look at them again one last time."

"Why?"

"I think they're curious."

"Curious? I've never heard of anyone describing passphrases as curious."

"These common words form the key to unlock seventeen billion dollars worth of crypto. Isn't that curious to you?" Kelsey tried to lead Nicholas to other thoughts.

"No." Nicholas put away his phone.

"Why did The Steward let you have a copy of the words?"

"He didn't. I did it myself. I was listening to you and Armin back in the escape room. I wrote down every word you two said at every door you opened. I used the password to unlock the encrypted file that the lawyer had sent to The Steward."

"All this time I thought The Steward had the passphrase file in his hand."

"You would be wrong."

"So you held the file hostage. Isn't that dangerous for you?"

Nicholas sighed, looking tired. "Since The Steward spends most of his time in the virtual world, he relies on boots on the ground to do his bidding. I'm his eyes and ears and arms and legs. I have leverage..."

"You want a bigger cut of the crypto," Kelsey said.

"Yes. You got it." Nicholas got up and made his way to the kitchen again, stopping at the coffee maker. "You want some coffee?"

Kelsey wanted to say, "Should I *whisper* yes?" But didn't. She didn't want Nicholas to know that she had memorized his list of eight words.

"No. Thanks," she finally said.

Nicholas poured filtered water into a kettle, then put it on the stove to boil. Then he poured coffee beans into a grinder. Before he could start the grinder, his phone chimed. He didn't say a word to Kelsey, but she remembered how his phone sounded when he received text messages.

He read it with an expressionless face.

He put his phone back into his pocket. "They got the words from Atlanta, but only eight words."

"Oh? Are they coming back? Is Armin okay?" Kelsey forgot that Armin's name bothered Nicholas.

Nicholas started the coffee grinder. It was too noisy for Kelsey to ask him another question. He poured the ground coffee into a French press. The water in the kettle hadn't boiled yet.

"Why did they text you and not The Steward?" Kelsey got up and walked toward Nicholas.

"Because I'm the assistant to the president, remember?" Nicholas chuckled. "Besides, The Steward doesn't have time to text."

Was The Steward even human?

The RV door unlocked, and Zinnia rushed in. "We have to go. The county sheriff is at the gate. We can't hold them off much longer."

*They've come to rescue me.*

Kelsey was excited—

"They're coming for you." Zinnia pointed to Kelsey. "Your arrest warrant, remember?"

Kelsey's heart sank. "I didn't kill Braun-Dean."

"They don't know that." Nicholas turned off the stove. To Zinnia, he said, "Let's go."

He grabbed Kelsey's hand and pulled her along as he followed Zinnia out of the RV.

It was late morning, but it was crispy cold outdoors. Maybe in the forties. There was a chill in the air. Kelsey was still wearing Armin's hooded jacket.

She let go of Nicholas's hand to pull the hood over her head. She zipped up the jacket all the way to her neck. Her knuckles started to feel cold so she dipped her hands into her pockets.

"Where are we going?" Kelsey asked.

"This way." A weapon appeared out of nowhere in Zinnia's hand. A small pistol that didn't seem like it had a lot of range, but up close, size didn't matter.

The path led down the hill. Nicholas gave up on trying to hold Kelsey's hand. He waited for her, and she knew she was slowing them down. Not on purpose, though. Kelsey wasn't very athletic, and going down a hundred steps or more with no guardrail hadn't been on her agenda.

"Don't fall," Nicholas whispered.

*Whisper.*

The word right after *coffee.*

Sometimes Kelsey was surprised at herself. In grade school, she was bad with numbers, but words didn't scare her. She could read a piece of literature and remember the nuances of each scene. She could read the news and remember it five years later.

Sometimes she wished she could forget. All the horrors of the past, these two days of running away from the law, and more running now downhill—literally and figuratively.

They passed the terrace and pool in the oversized mansion. Zinnia led them down steeper steps that looked like they could be treacherous in the rain or snow.

The ground leveled out, and Kelsey breathed a sigh of relief. She could not hear anything but their own footsteps. It was still winter, and there were no insects out. No buzzing ones, anyway.

Kelsey stepped on grass. When they skirted

around a grove of trees, Kelsey saw the dock. The trio ran toward it, with Nicholas still reaching out for Kelsey's hand. She kept them safe in her pockets.

If there was anyone whom she would allow to hold her hand, it'd be invited Armin, not uninvited Nicholas.

If Nicholas had any personal desire for her, then she'd have to disappoint him. Once upon a time, she had considered him to be a brotherly figure. Now that Nicholas seemed to be working for The Steward, Kelsey felt that their friendship would end soon.

They arrived at a speedboat, painted all black. It could seat five people, so there was plenty of room for the three of them. Kelsey had ridden in such a speedboat only one time, when Braun-Dean invited big-ticket donors for a spin on the Atlantic Ocean outside his vacation home on Fort Lauderdale Beach.

Was this his boat, since up there on the hill was his house?

"Is this..." Kelsey started to say.

"Yes, this is Braun-Dean's custom made speedboat." Nicholas pointed to the word *Braun-Dean* painted on the side. "Named the boat after himself, he did."

"I thought this boat was in Florida," Kelsey said.

"I thought so too, but Zinnia found it here yesterday. Paige said that Braun-Dean moved it a year ago."

Kelsey stepped back. "Uh...I don't think this is a good idea."

"What are you talking about?" Nicholas looked worried.

"How far does this lake go? Can we easily escape? Once we get onshore we have to run on foot, right? Do you have transport waiting?"

"You're asking way too many questions, love." Nicholas reached for Kelsey's hand.

"What are you planning to do? The police are at the gates already."

Zinnia pointed the gun at Kelsey's head. "Get in."

Kelsey had no choice. Nicholas helped Kelsey into the speedboat, and they sat at the back. Zinnia took the wheel.

Kelsey knew that the life jacket was under her seat. She pulled it out and put it on. She pointed to her life jacket and then to Nicholas's seat. He found his as well and put it on. He gave her two thumbs up.

The sleek carbon fiber hull slid easily into the water, and Zinnia took off in the fifty-foot speedboat. It went from zero to top speed in no time, and Kelsey clung to dear life as the speed rose over one hundred miles per hour.

*We're going to die!*

Kelsey gripped the seats underneath her. Since she had become a Christian, she no longer feared death.

However, there were so many things she hadn't done yet, like telling her grandparents about Jesus, falling in love, getting married, having children, and working in a dream job, for example.

*Oh and I haven't told Armin that I...*

Ah, none of that would matter if she died today. According to Paul in Philippians 1:21, going to heaven would be better than staying on earth.

*For to me, to live is Christ, and to die is gain.*

However, for the sake of the other Christians, Paul would rather live, reasoning it out in Philippines 1:24-26. If Paul thought he could be useful on earth, Kelsey also felt that God had something for her to do yet.

*Nevertheless to remain in the flesh is more needful for you. And being confident of this, I know that I shall remain and continue with you all for your progress and joy of faith, that your rejoicing for me may be more abundant in Jesus Christ by my coming to you again.*

Wow. Kelsey surprised herself by remembering these verses. She wondered if she was becoming more like Armin, who had a Bible verse for every situation.

The fact that she could remember such a long passage of Scripture...

She heard sirens.

They seemed to come from two sides behind the speedboat. She turned to look. Flashing lights and sirens on the water meant one thing: the police had blocked the mansion on all sides, including the waterway escape route. They had come prepared.

Nicholas seemed to be saying something to her, but all Kelsey could hear was the speedboat engine and the sirens behind them that were coming closer and closer.

Kelsey wondered if the police had the means to overtake a million-dollar speedboat whose top speed was nearly a hundred and fifty miles per hour.

There was nothing Kelsey could do to stop Zinnia. Whatever she did could endanger all three of them onboard, plus potentially the police officers chasing after them.

How dangerous would it be for her to jump out of a speeding boat?

Above them, a police helicopter arrived, hovering directly above the speedboat.

Kelsey saw more flashing lights and heard more sirens, but this time they came from the front, in the direction that Zinnia was taking the speedboat. Zinnia had no choice but to slow down the speedboat.

At that moment, Nicholas reached into his jacket, pulled out his phone, and tossed it overboard.

*Why did he do that?*

The engine noise and the sirens were so loud around Kelsey that she couldn't think.

*Lord, help us!*

It was all she could pray. Even so, she wondered if it was the wrong prayer. How could God help them if they ended up being branded as criminals? Kelsey hadn't killed anyone, but she had fled from the police when Nicholas picked her up from Interstate 95.

Behind them, the two police boats caught up. They sped up and flanked the *Braun-Dean* on both sides. Every officer standing facing them held their guns up.

"Stop the boat!"

Kelsey heard it loudly, coming through some loudspeakers all around them.

She also heard something about cutting the engine and dropping an anchor, but she might have been mistaken. Perhaps they were things she remembered Braun-Dean had said about his intoxicated boating friends when stopped by police patrol on the lake.

There was now a buzz of jumbled words in her ears.

Kelsey reached out to Nicholas and gently squeezed his arm. She shook her head slightly. "It's not worth it, Nicholas."

*I want you to live, Nicholas.*

Zinnia didn't get the memo. She sped up the boat instead.

Kelsey sank into her seat and covered her head, expecting the police to start shooting to make Zinnia stop the boat.

If Zinnia made the boat go at any higher speed than she had, they could be tossed out of the boat or the boat would capsize once it hit something along the way. They could all die. She suspected that Nicholas knew that.

He stared at Kelsey. She must've looked terrified to him. His shoulders sagged. He tapped Zinnia's shoulder.

Zinnia froze a bit, then nodded, and decelerated to a stop. She surprised Kelsey by her obedience to Nicholas.

*What is your real identity, Nicholas Bay?*

It took time for the speedboat to go from a hundred miles to zero. Surrounded by four or five police boats, plus the chopper above them, there was no way out for the runway trio, not with loaded weapons pointed at them in every direction.

Even Kelsey knew it was over.

# CHAPTER FOURTEEN

Kelsey slept for what felt like days in the hotel room in Atlanta. She climbed out of the king-sized bed and walked over to the window. She pulled the heavy curtains back to reveal a bright afternoon sun. Four floors down, the parking lot was half empty.

*What day is this?*

She checked her new phone on the table nearby. It was 4:19 p.m. on Wednesday.

"Can't be only twelve hours since I got here."

She recalled having had breakfast with Nicholas. Then he was making coffee. But before the water boiled, Zinnia came to evacuate the RV. They ran down a long flight of steps to the lakeside. Hopped into a speedboat at the dock. Chased by the county sheriff across the lake.

After the police arrested Nicholas and Zinnia, they took a statement from Kelsey before they handed her over to FBI Special Agent Tanaka, who was waiting onshore in an unmarked van. Inside the van were two agents, one of whom did the driving. They would be taking over the money laundering investigation from Tanaka, who would be taking two months off to recover from her broken arm.

"And you were never a fugitive," Tanaka told her in the van on their drive from Chattanooga to Atlanta. "There's no warrant for your arrest. The surveillance video at Braun-Dean's lake house has been doctored. Someone digitally altered the face of the woman in the video to yours. It was very good AI work, but our consultants are better. We sent them over to the Marietta PD since the local police handle murder investigations."

In this day and age, anything could happen.

Kelsey burst into tears. She was happy that the Marietta Police Department had found out the truth. She cared that she was exonerated. She didn't think she had it in her to stand trial for a false accusation that she had nothing to do with.

"Who are these consultants I need to thank?" Kelsey dried her eyes.

"Binary Systems did the work to unravel the fake videos, but the person who'd suggested a potential suspect was Armin," Tanaka said.

"Armin?"

"Yeah. He noticed that the woman in the surveillance video had a facial tic that matched Paige Braun-Dean's, whom both of you met after the escape room."

"That's a good observation. I didn't even notice." Kelsey sighed. "So she's arrested now?"

"Yes, for patricide. Tragic and very sad."

Kelsey wanted to call Armin to thank him, but his number was on her old phone somewhere in South Carolina. Maybe she could call the Hu Knows office in Atlanta and ask for Earl, then ask him for Armin's number.

Or maybe she was just afraid to talk to Armin again because now her feelings are going where they hadn't before. Once she had considered Armin to be a friend. Now she wanted to get to know him better. Did he feel the same way though? She feared that if she moved in that direction, she'd jeopardize their friendship.

That wasn't all the good news that Tanaka had brought her. There was that Interstate abduction in South Carolina.

"Local PDs in all three states only found out what

was going on when Sam and Bob were arrested at the Hu Knows office and parking lot respectively in Buckhead," Tanaka said.

"In the office?" Kelsey asked. "At what time?"

"As soon as they arrived. As far as I know it was around eight in the morning."

Kelsey recalled something. "Nicholas didn't get a text from Sam until past ten."

"That was the Atlanta PD, actually," Tanaka said. "To prevent him from being suspicious."

"So the second set of eight words that were supposed to have come from Arun's keepsake box?"

"Our consultants faked them."

Consultants again. Kelsey was more determined than ever to meet them and thank them in person.

"As far as I know, Nicholas had forwarded the words to The Steward." Kelsey wondered if The Steward might have noticed the words were fake. Then again, he couldn't have because he didn't have all twenty-four words yet.

"A moot point now that many people have been arrested."

"We don't know if Nicholas or The Steward masterminded the traffic stop on Interstate 95. Sam and Bob pleaded guilty to impersonating police officers —down to a movie prop patrol vehicle—and for making false arrests. However, they refused to say who they worked for."

"They were shot by Nicholas's people."

"That was a ruse."

Tanaka went on to say that the Georgia Bureau of Investigation, the Atlanta and Savannah police departments, as well as the South Carolina state troopers, were all looking into the possibility that the carjacking in Savannah was related to the fake traffic stop in South Carolina.

Since many local and federal agencies were working on it, the truth would be revealed soon.

"Nicholas may not be a suspect yet, but he's a person of interest," Tanaka said. "He's not the friend you think he is. He might be a snake in the grass."

"Let me rest and think about this, but I can say at this moment that since he didn't let Armin and me go, I no longer consider him a friend. A friend would not falsely imprison us."

It broke Kelsey's heart that Nicholas wasn't who he portrayed himself to be—the friend who cooked her breakfast, styled her hair, loaned her money when she was broke, and stood up for her when Braun-Dean and his ex-wife abused her.

This friend had now abducted her.

*Say it isn't so.*

Kelsey was exhausted, not having rested since she'd woken up in the mystery mansion after a drug-induced sleep. The strain of not knowing what was happening and not being free had exhausted her mentally.

The agents drove her back to Atlanta, where they put her in this hotel to rest while they recovered her purse and phone from the South Carolina state troopers, who had impounded Nicholas's rental Toyota Highlander that she'd left on the highway shoulder after being abducted by Nicholas.

Shortly after, one of the agents, Ulrich, returned to the hotel to ask Kelsey if she needed any food or snacks. Then he asked if Kelsey recalled the eight words that Nicholas showed her. She was tired from the ordeal of the day, so she could barely remember them. At Ulrich's insistence, she jotted down the eight words quickly without double-checking them.

Kelsey wanted to see Armin, but she was too exhausted to track down his phone number.

And here she was, waking up in the middle of the afternoon.

Leaving the window, she padded to the bathroom, brushed her teeth, and then decided to take a hot shower. The hot water felt good on her sore muscles. She only came out of the shower because the water had turned lukewarm.

She dried her hair with the hairdryer and then tied it up into a bun on the top of her head.

After changing into some clothes that Tanaka had left for her, Kelsey drank some water and wondered if she should eat an early dinner. After all, she had missed both breakfast and lunch.

She checked the binder on top of the table to see if she could order some dinner to be delivered to the room since she had no money to eat out. That way, the food could be billed with the hotel room cost. In fact, she didn't have her driver's license, credit card, or cash with her.

All she had was a new phone that Tanaka had given her, since her old one had been confiscated by Nicholas, supposedly in Spartanburg. She checked her phone to see if the agent had left her a message.

None.

She looked up media sites to see if there were any reports on the boat chase on the Chickamauga Lake. Nothing except some short video clips on social media sites from boaters nearby and people in their hillside vacation homes who had watched the whole drama unfold. The information was so erroneous that Kelsey was sure they had reported on some other incident, not the one she had been in.

*The intoxicated people onboard were arrested for speeding.*

Kelsey wasn't sure if Zinnia had been drinking, but she knew that Nicholas hadn't. And not all of them had been arrested. Only two people out of three.

Just as well that the information was scant. Otherwise, amateur journalists might meddle, and Kelsey's name would pop up, along with a host of details that might lead to Braun-Dean and his hidden seventeen billion dollars worth of crypto that the FBI wanted in conjunction with their money laundering investigations. That was evidence, after all. And dirty money.

She wondered what might have happened had Zinnia not stopped the boat. Would they have crashed into the police boats? Would they have been injured, maimed, paralyzed, or dead? Thank God they were all still alive.

Nicholas and Zinnia had surrendered without a fight. They were now sitting in jail in Chattanooga.

Kelsey googled Atlanta news to see if there were updates on the Braun-Dean murder. Several media outlets reported on deep fake videos.

"Marietta police have spoken again to the housekeeper at the Braun-Dean lake house, only to find out that she had lied about her whereabouts the night of the former senator's murder," the reporter spoke into the camera. "She had gone partying with her friends the night before and slept over at her sister's house. She was not at the lake house when the murder occurred at around four in the morning. Therefore, she personally did not see who walked into the house and murdered Braun-Dean. She simply believed the surveillance video and accepted it as fact."

Lying to the police.

"The detectives are continuing to make new discoveries, and we will bring them to you as soon as they happen—if we find out about them."

Kelsey thought the reporter was honest. Hmm, if she ever went to college, she might consider majoring in journalism.

She searched again and found more news online about the Braun-Dean family drama. In this video, the reporter was standing outside the Fulton County Jail.

"Roxanne Braun-Dean insists that she had nothing to do with the carjacker who abducted her deceased husband's former mistress," the reporter said. "She denies ever threatening Zuriel with anything except angry words that she now regrets."

Angry words?

Maybe Roxanne had a point, though it sounded like she had been coached on what to say by her defense attorney.

"The carjacker is still recovering from multiple gunshot wounds," the reporter added. "Strangely enough, he is not talking to the police—upon the advice of his defense attorney—although we are told that if he does talk, he could exonerate himself."

Off camera, the newscaster asked, "Do we know why he wouldn't talk?"

"Shelley, that's the mystery. Experts following this case say that they believe the carjacker, whose name is being withheld, works for someone powerful."

"He fears for his life, maybe."

"Maybe so."

Kelsey scoured more news from Georgia, but there was no word about Sam and Bob, the men who drove Armin to Buckhead, right into the arms of the Atlanta police—according to Tanaka. She said she'd let Armin tell her himself. It was enough for Kelsey that Armin was alive and well.

If only she could see him, she'd tell him what she thought of him while she had the opportunity. At worst, Armin could say they could never be more than just friends. But she had to know if he had feelings for her. If not, why else would he keep calling her for a year? It would be misleading, no?

In any case, the boat scare yesterday made Kelsey feel braver and bolder. She had to tell him.

Her phone rang. It was Tanaka.

"Sorry I can't pick you up. We have an emergency meeting that I cannot skip. How about you rest today?"

"Okay. No problem."

"I'll call you tomorrow."

"Anytime. How long can I stay here?" Kelsey looked around.

"Until this weekend when they deliver your purse back to you."

"Is there a police department I can drive to?"

"No. I'll send someone. You've gone through enough."

"Thank you."

"Oh by the way, Armin called me to ask for your new burner phone number. I didn't want to give it out without your permission."

Armin? "Text me his number and I'll call him back. I don't have his number on this new phone."

"As I thought," Tanaka said. "Look for a text in a minute."

"Thank you."

"Make sure you eat something and charge it to the room. Got to run now."

"Bye."

After Tanaka hung up, Kelsey checked the folder on the table. The only way she could charge meals to the room was to order from the hotel restaurant downstairs.

After this weekend, she would have to buy her own food and find new lodging. She wondered if it would be cheaper to rent a camper or a mobile home.

She would need to find a job to pay for rent and food. To find a job in a city such as Atlanta meant that she had to buy a car. More expenses.

All these years, she hadn't held down a proper job for more than six months. Before she had met Braun-Dean, she was only a volunteer handing out flyers and yard signs. They paid her an hourly minimum wage. No healthcare insurance.

After she had met Braun-Dean, she depended on him for everything because his schedule prevented her from getting a job of her own. They were always jet setting somewhere. If it wasn't to an exotic golf course somewhere, then it was to yet another fundraiser. All expenses paid, so Kelsey didn't need to shell out a dime.

Braun-Dean had pressed her down and oppressed her in their relationship, treating her as nothing but a punching bag—both literally and figuratively. After three years with him, Kelsey had lost all her confidence in her skillset and in her own self.

Her memory was still good, but she hadn't applied them to something satisfying.

She thought of the two reporters that she had watched on social media today, and was impressed. She reminded herself to pray for God's direction. Going to college would be a big move for her. Would she make the cut? Would she drop out? So many questions.

Ping.

A new text arrived. It was from Tanaka, but the message only contained a phone number. Kelsey tapped on it.

Someone picked up at the first ring. "Hello?"

She didn't recognize the voice. "May I speak with Armin, please?"

"This is he. Is this Kelsey?" he asked excitedly.

"Yes."

"Good. I was worried about you. Didn't know where Tanaka took you to after Chattanooga." His voice was the same as usual. Warm and calming on the phone.

Kelsey didn't feel nervous talking to him on the phone. He was kind but strong, and he made Kelsey feel that not only was she not in danger anymore, but that as long as he was around, she could walk around town freely without fear.

"I wanted to go to Chattanooga, but Tanaka told me that the local PD wouldn't let me into the mansion compound, which is basically fifty acres around that lake house."

"Fifty acres? Quite a big place. I had no idea."

"Me neither. So I stayed here in Atlanta and spent

a lot of time at the Atlanta PD," Armin said. "Then I went home and crashed."

"You don't have to explain."

"I want to. I don't want you to think I abandoned you."

It was a good thing they had time apart, albeit only for one day. "I thought Tanaka would send me to Savannah, but here I am in Atlanta."

"What are you doing for dinner tonight?"

"I was going to order room service," Kelsey said.

"How about we go out to a restaurant somewhere?"

"Is this a date?"

"It can be—unless you want me to invite Deshon. I'm sure he's single and free also."

Kelsey wondered what he was getting at. "Do you want to invite Deshon?"

"Frankly, no. He and I eat lunch out several times a week if we happen to be at the office at the same time. So I see him plenty."

"So it's just you and me this evening?" Kelsey asked.

"If that's alright with you, I'd rather just eat out with you alone."

"Fine. No big deal. We're friends, after all."

Silence.

Then Armin said, "What kind of food do you want and where would you like to eat?"

"I'm not new to Atlanta, but my memories of Atlanta are tainted by Braun-Dean. Wherever he took me, I went. So if I suggest any restaurants, it's someplace that he and I have both been to. You know what I mean?"

"I get it. So you want me to recommend a place."

"Yes." With Armin, Kelsey felt that she could be herself. She didn't have to keep up with anyone. She could just say what she pleased. "If you suggest a restaurant I don't want to go to because of the past, I will tell you."

"How about this idea? I'll text you five places. You pick one."

"No problem."

"Which hotel are you staying at?"

Kelsey gave him the hotel name and room number. "Text me when you're here, and I'll go outside. You don't have to park your car."

"Okay."

"So few words today?" Armin asked.

"Now that I've met you in person, it feels like our phone conversation has changed."

"Like how?"

"Like I used to be able to tell you anything that

popped up in my head," Kelsey reminded him. "Now I'm nervous. Don't want to say the wrong thing."

"I would say I'm the same here but I skipped lunch to work extra, and now I'm totally famished. So when it comes to food, I'm not shy about saying what I want, you know?"

"You mean otherwise you wouldn't?"

"Otherwise I'd keep it in my heart until I have the right opportunity."

"Got it. When do you think you'll get here?"

"Maybe fifteen minutes."

"I'll wait for you. Call or text when you arrive."

After she hung up, she wanted to read her Bible, but recalled that it was in her purse that was still in some police station somewhere in South Carolina.

Before she joined Tanaka in the undercover operation in Georgia, she had been reading her Bible faithfully. The events in the last forty-eight hours had thrown her off her routine.

She remembered that the last chapter she had read in Miami was Ephesians 4. Therefore today, she would read Ephesians 5. She looked up the chapter in the online Bible site she'd found. When she reached Ephesians 5:8-10, she realized that she must no longer go back to her old dark life, but she must walk anew in her new life in Christ that was full of light, hope, joy, peace, and the ever presence of God.

*For you were once darkness, but now you are light in the Lord. Walk as children of light (for the fruit of the Spirit is in all goodness, righteousness, and truth), finding out what is acceptable to the Lord.*

Kelsey checked her phone. No text message from Armin yet. Maybe he was caught in Atlanta traffic since it was the afternoon rush hour at the moment.

She kept reading her Bible, and stopped at Ephesians 5:11-12, which made her think about wanting to be a journalist. Maybe an investigative journalist. That way, she could expose "the unfruitful works of darkness."

*And have no fellowship with the unfruitful works of darkness, but rather expose them. For it is shameful even to speak of those things which are done by them in secret.*

Before she could read more Bible verses or even pray about her newfound calling, Armin had texted her. Out of his five suggested restaurants, there were ethnic restaurants she had never been to. Armin must've guessed that Braun-Dean was the meat-and-potato sort of guy and would have preferred steakhouse and seafood restaurants. He might even go for Mexican or Louisiana fare.

So Armin suggested one Chinese place, two Indian restaurants, and one Korean restaurant. The last line was left blank with a question for her.

> **ARMIN**
>
> Which cuisine would you like to try?

Kelsey picked an Indian restaurant. She figured that Armin would be able to tell her what was in the dishes, and they'd have some meaningful conversation. While she wondered if Indian restaurants in America could compare with restaurants in India, she also knew that Atlanta was a diverse cosmopolitan metropolis with almost every kind of major cuisine available to serve its international customers.

Armin liked her reply.

Fifteen nervous minutes later, Armin texted her to say that he had arrived and to apologize for being caught in traffic.

Kelsey quickly put on Armin's jacket—which needed to be dry-cleaned as soon as possible—and grabbed her phone and room keycard before she dashed out of the door. She looked back to make sure that the door closed properly.

Downstairs, she walked through the lobby to the front entrance, past several luggage carts, and then out the sliding glass door to the portico.

Armin was waiting for her by his Honda Odyssey minivan. He held another jacket. His first words to her were, "Got a clean jacket for you. Want to swap? I'll take that one to the cleaners tomorrow."

"Yes, please. This one has been through a lot." She took off the jacket and exchanged it with the clean one in his hand. "Ooh, nice and comfy."

He was all smiles as he opened the passenger door for her like a gentleman, and then ran over to the driver's side to climb in.

Buckled in, Kelsey felt self-conscious. "Were you smiling so broadly earlier because I'm wearing Tanaka's clothes?"

"Are you?" Armin pulled out of the hotel and onto a busy road. "My smile was for you. I'd still be happy if you wore pajamas to dinner. I mean, as long as you're with me, I'm happy."

"I see. Next time, I will try to win the ugly Christmas sweater contest for your sake."

"You do that." He laughed. "I dare you."

"I double dare you too."

"Maybe I'll suggest it to Deshon for the Christmas office party." Armin put his blinker on to turn onto a road. He seemed to know where he was going without a map.

"I'd never peg you as a minivan kind of guy," Kelsey said.

"But you know I'm a practical person."

"That, you are."

"I bought this van a while back when my parents lived with me in Columbia," Armin explained. "Relatives would often visit them from out of town, out of state, out of country. My rule of thumb was that we can only welcome as many visitors as would fit into this van. Otherwise there'd be chaos in the house."

"I remember that you said you have a big extended family, but I didn't realize they affected your vehicle purchase."

"Yep. Very much so. My parents have since moved home to India, and now that I live alone, this van feels too big."

"At least you have transportation that keeps you out of the rain going to and from work, right?"

"Right. You're a sensible person too." Armin said it as a compliment, it seemed.

They only made small talk this afternoon, but it was enough for Kelsey. Armin didn't demand anything from her, gave her personal space, and treated her as his equal.

They could be best of friends for a long time, if not for the fact that Kelsey had been longing to see him since the day before. She missed him.

Oh, could she allow herself to say it?

"I miss you," she said quietly.

"Say that again please." His voice was soft and gentle. He wasn't pleading but he sounded like he wanted a confirmation.

"You heard me though."

"Yes, but still... Just one more time."

Kelsey drew a deep breath. "Armin, I miss you."

Armin's right hand reached for Kelsey's left hand, but he didn't touch her. He waited for her assent. She interlocked his fingers in hers as her approval of him.

"I miss you too," Armin said.

Kelsey felt warmth in her heart, a feeling that she had found home.

# CHAPTER FIFTEEN

The Indian restaurant they decided to dine in didn't take reservations, but it would take over an hour to be seated. Kelsey and Armin decided to order a takeout dinner and eat elsewhere.

Armin was ready to invite Kelsey to his penthouse condominium, but he sensed that she wasn't ready to visit him alone, even though eating and talking were all they were going to do before the eyes of God.

He couldn't imagine doing anything with Kelsey that they couldn't do in public. The rest of it, he'd reserve for marriage.

Marriage?

Should he marry someday, he prayed that Kelsey would be his one and only wife, but for now, he had no idea what she thought of their present relationship, let alone future possibilities.

Armin found a parking spot under a street light. He cut the engine. It wasn't too cold outside, and they were wearing jackets, so he didn't need to keep the engine running.

He read the menu on his phone for Kelsey to consider which dishes she might like.

"I've eaten at an Indian restaurant a couple of times—with my friends, not Braun-Dean," Kelsey said.

Armin felt relieved because he'd hate for old memories to destroy their present happiness.

"However, it's been a while and I can't remember what I ate. I think I like both chicken and lamb, so I'm open to anything. Order for both of us, if you will."

"Okay. Do you prefer mild or medium spice? I gather we're not going to go too hot because it will be too spicy for even me."

"I prefer mild, but if you want to go for medium, I can try."

After placing the order for several meat and vegetable dishes plus naan and rice, Armin was told that they'd have to wait for half an hour. "Is that okay with you?"

Kelsey nodded. "We can chat. Lots to catch up. When I was on that speedboat, I thought I'd never see you again and never get to talk with you again, so this is nice. I don't care where we are. I'm just thankful to God that we can see each other again and talk like this."

"It must've been pretty scary on a speedboat. How fast did you go?" Armin asked, setting the timer on his phone for half an hour.

"Over a hundred miles per hour. I don't know what that is in knots. All I knew was that I thought we were going to die."

"So you prayed?"

"I don't remember if I prayed much, but several verses in Philippians 1 popped into my head." Kelsey waved her hands about. "I mean, it felt surreal. The engine was loud. Zinnia had a gun. Police were chasing us in their speedboats. And all I could think of was that passage of scripture in which Paul said he'd rather go to heaven, but for the sake of the Christians around him, he'd stay on earth."

"The Bible is also an anchor."

"Anchor. That's a good word. I'm just thankful the police came in time before Zinnia crashed the boat. If it's really the speedboat that Braun-Dean bought and customized it a while ago, then it's an old one, and I don't know who maintained it in that big empty house in Chattanooga."

Armin liked to hear Kelsey talk, but Kelsey was quiet all of a sudden. He didn't want to pry, but... Was she thinking about Braun-Dean's speedboat or Nicholas in the boat?

"Do you think he's okay in jail?" Kelsey asked.

Armin's heart sank. She was thinking of Nicholas.

Actually, he shouldn't feel jealous. Nicholas was a suspect. He wasn't going to get out on bail. If The Steward did not appear, Nicholas might be the one to shoulder the blame. Since he appeared almost everywhere The Steward had stirred up trouble, Nicholas wasn't as innocent as he had portrayed himself to be.

No doubt Tanaka had spoken to Kelsey about Nicholas. Armin didn't want to add to it.

"He has such a fragile heart," Kelsey added.

Nicholas? Fragile? Was she kidding?

Suddenly, his entire evening was ruined. Armin wanted to rein in his emotions, but he couldn't help considering bad boy Nicholas to be a love rival.

Firstly, he had to fend off past Braun-Dean's memories that were harassing Kelsey.

Secondly, he had to put up with present-day Nicholas who seemed to have rented space in Kelsey's mind.

Was there a place in Kelsey's heart for Armin?

The alarm on his phone went off.

"I'll go get the takeout." Armin unbuckled his safety belt.

"Do you want me to go with you?" Kelsey asked.

He had guessed once before that her love language was Quality Time. But this would be only a short walk to the takeout counter at the restaurant. She could sit in the car and wait, no?

"S-sure." His mouth had said it before he could bridle it. Sigh.

They both exited the car. Kelsey held Armin's hand like it was the most natural thing in the world for her.

"You know, Braun-Dean and I never held hands," Kelsey said.

"Oh?" And then his mouth said a foolish thing. "Nicholas?"

"Just once. Yesterday when we had to leave the RV, he held my hand, but only briefly."

Armin frowned. Well, how could he be jealous? He and Kelsey had been separated for only one day. Before that, they were friends with something developing between them. Today, he was feeling envious that she had spent more time yesterday with Nicholas than with him.

Envy.

Weren't there a number of Bible verses about envy? He let go of Kelsey's hand and searched the Bible app on his phone. There it was. Proverbs 14:30.

*A sound heart is life to the body,*

*But envy is rottenness to the bones.*

"What is it?" Kelsey asked.

"Looking up a verse." He stepped onto the sidewalk and opened the door of the restaurant for Kelsey. He handed his phone to Kelsey before he went to pay for the food.

Kelsey was still holding his phone when Armin picked up the paper bag of food.

She was smiling from ear to ear as they returned to the minivan.

"What?" Armin asked.

"Found you another verse."

"Oh?"

Armin put the takeout bag in one of the backseats, then opened the passenger side door for Kelsey. She climbed in.

Before he closed the door, she handed the phone back to him. He didn't read it until he sat down in his driver's seat and buckled in. The verse was from Proverbs 23:17.

*Do not let your heart envy sinners,*
    *But be zealous for the fear of the Lord all the day.*

"Didn't I say he only held my hand briefly?" Kelsey asked. "Why does it bother you so much?"

"Uh..." Armin wondered if his own love language might be Physical Touch.

Kelsey lifted her right hand toward Armin. "This is the hand he held. If kissing it will override his unrequited love, then please do."

*Unrequited?*

Armin felt childish and foolish. He had filled this precious evening with envy, when he could have spent the time focusing on Kelsey and their budding relationship.

He cleared his throat. "May I suggest two places we can go eat our dinner privately and talk about anything we want without fearing that strangers are listening in. One is my condo. It's on the top floor and we can see the city lights from the windows. The other is the Hu Knows office, where we have a large conference room that we also use for dining."

Before Kelsey could pick one, Armin's phone rang. It was Iseul Kim from Binary Systems. He put his phone on a stand that he'd mounted on the minivan dashboard. He turned on the video mode.

"Whassup?" Armin asked.

Iseul's face appeared on the screen. "Cayson tasked me to call you if we find anything with your brother's USB drive."

"Yes?" Armin tried to sound all businesslike. He

wanted to show Kelsey how he handled female associates.

The co-founder and CEO of Binary Systems, Cayson Yang led a number of projects himself. In each project, he'd assign an assistant to fill in for him when he rotated through the various projects. This time, the assistant position went to Iseul Kim, one of his network specialists.

"We decrypted the drive, but it's empty," Iseul said.

"Empty?"

"What I said. Are there any other devices hidden in the keepsake box that we need to look at? Our super-computer array can try to break the password if needed."

"As far as I know, there's nothing else. You can x-ray the baseball and other memorabilia, but I doubt you'd find anything in them."

Iseul sighed. "All right. So we're back to only those eight words Arun wrote on a piece of paper."

"Wait. What?" Kelsey asked. "What about the other eight words from Nicholas?"

Iseul didn't answer.

"Oh sorry. This is Kelsey Murphy. I'm with Armin right now. When Tanaka picked me up yesterday from Chattanooga, she had two other agents with her who were supposed to take over for her since she has a broken arm. They drove me to my hotel in Atlanta. After they dropped me off, Agent Ulrich returned alone to ask me for the eight words from Nicholas. I gave them to him. Wouldn't that have made sixteen words?"

"Agent Ulrich has taken an emergency leave to care for his grandfather who fell down the stairs." FBI Special Agent Tanaka appeared on the screen. "We're trying to contact him. My guess is that he was so worried about his grandfather that he forgot to hand in evidence."

"Miss Tanaka! Aren't you supposed to be on sick leave?" Kelsey asked.

"Well, I was, but now I'm glad I haven't." Tanaka shook her head. "I can't believe Ulrich hadn't said a thing before he left."

"More importantly, to whom has he given the eight words?" Armin asked.

He couldn't imagine why an FBI agent would work with The Steward, but the monetary rewards were greater from The Steward than anywhere else. He paid in percentages.

The fact that even an FBI agent could be bought off showed the power and reach of The Steward. No wonder the former senator Braun-Dean had been fearful of him, so fearful that he had enlisted a second crypto specialist to balance out The Steward.

Unfortunately for the second specialist—poor Arun—The Steward didn't like competition.

"How did Ulrich know to go to you?" Tanaka asked.

Kelsey shrugged. "I didn't say much on the drive between Chattanooga and Atlanta, did I?"

"Not that I recall." Tanaka smacked her lips. "What in the world? Who does Ulrich work for? Tell me again what he asked you."

"I don't remember his precise words, but he said that Nicholas showed me the eight words and he wanted to know if I remembered them." Kelsey thought she was repeating herself.

Armin's jaw dropped. "Did you tell anyone that Nicholas showed you the words?"

"Come to think of it, no." Kelsey seemed sure. "The only people in the conversation were Nicholas and I. No more than an hour later was the very last time I saw Nicholas. Maybe he'd told Zinnia about showing me what they had decrypted. I don't know. All I know is that I saw him throw the phone over the speedboat into the lake."

"The RV might have listening devices," Armin said. "Remember the escape room? They heard every-thing we said to each other."

"They sure did." Kelsey nodded. "I wouldn't put it past them to bug the RV."

"Maybe when Nicholas threw his phone into the lake, he made The Steward upset," Armin said.

"If Nicholas finds himself in danger, he will do something," Kelsey said. "It seems to me that The Steward was making Nicholas a scapegoat. He had to retaliate, so he threw out the thing that would make The Steward mad."

"Are you defending him?" Armin asked.

"Not at all. Just speculating."

"Nicholas told me that was the only copy of the words. He hadn't turned them over to The Steward because he wanted to negotiate a larger compensation. Apparently one percent wasn't enough." Kelsey looked out the window. "But why would The Steward come after me?"

"You saw the eight words," Armin suggested.

Kelsey nodded. "That, I did."

"Do you still remember them?" Tanaka asked.

"If I'm not stressed out, I can. If I'm stressed, I won't remember anything."

"But if you're not stressed you can remember the words." Armin thought for a second. "In the right order?"

Kelsey nodded. "Could you send me Arun's list?"

"Sure." He handed Kelsey his phone. "Find it in the photo album. I took a photo of Arun's handwritten note."

"The Steward is after you, Kelsey," Tanaka suggested. "I need both of you to go somewhere safe. For example, you come over here to the Binary Systems HQ right now. You look like you're talking to me from your car—I can see your backrest. Where in town are you?"

"We're in West Paces Ferry, and it will take us an hour to get to Alpharetta, thanks to the rush hour traffic on I-75, I-285, and I-85." Armin depressed the gas again as he had done a lot.

"Yeah, this is a bad time, but I'd feel better if Kelsey is with me here—where I can see her and make sure she's safe."

Tanaka didn't have to explain, but Armin could read between the lines. She had just found out that an FBI agent had tried to steal a part of the crypto recovery passphrase. Her thought might then go to the worst possible scenario. She might lose her asset, Kelsey, if the rogue agent returned for her—for whatever reason.

"We just picked up our takeout and the food might get cold by the time we get to Alpharetta," Armin said.

"The two of you are having dinner together?" Tanaka asked.

Even the great agent didn't know what happened under her watch. Armin simply smiled. "This is our first date."

"Ah okay. Takeout, you said? Where were you planning to go?"

"Either the Hu Knows office or Armin's condo," Kelsey replied.

"Hmmm... The office is safer," Armin said. "It has security twenty-four-seven, and even the receptionists are armed and trained—plus pepper and bear sprays."

"I heard." Kelsey's eyes were on her phone. She was tapping in a notepad.

"Sam looked like a bear, but it was too risky." Armin made a U-turn and eased into a not-so-busy street leading to Hu Knows.

"Then go to the Hu Knows office," Tanaka said. "I have to run. Keep your phones with you at all times."

"Thank you." Armin tapped the hands-free phone stand. "Call Deshon."

Deshon answered immediately. He looked like he'd just come out of the shower, wearing only a towel.

"Hey, get away from the camera," Armin warned him. "Kelsey is with me in the van."

Deshon turned off the video. Audio worked too. "Got a problem?"

Armin explained to him as quickly as he could, and then asked him for backup. "We don't know what Ulrich will do, and we think he's rogue at this point. Considering all the things that have happened so far..."

"Gotcha. I'll bring my Humvee. It has a push bar," Deshon said.

Deshon was proud of his refurbished High Mobility Multipurpose Wheeled Vehicle, which he had purchased at a military surplus auction. He'd spent a lot of money making the Humvee road ready to pass DMV requirements. Then he had it painted bright cherry red, so that no one would miss seeing his gas-guzzling Humvee on the road.

"Then come now. We're maybe three or four minutes away from the office. Can you track us?"

"I see you on my GPS. All right. I'll be right there to escort you to safety."

He was gone.

Traffic was light and there were just a couple of cars in front and behind Armin's minivan. Armin thought he should make small talk with Kelsey. He wasn't sure if she was listening since she was busy on her phone.

Suddenly she stopped tapping—

And screamed as she pointed to Armin's window. A pickup truck had crossed the intersection, was barreling straight at the driver's side.

Armin could see the driver's face, with his bulging eyes and wrinkled skin. He was wearing a baseball cap turned backwards that covered half his forehead. His cheekbones were stuck in a perpetual grin. He was missing a couple of teeth, and the rest of them were jagged, as if rotting away.

Armin's minivan was stuck between two vehicles, so he was unable to move out of the way. It was too late for him to climb out of the minivan to outrun a three-hundred horsepower pickup truck.

"Get out now!" Armin ordered Kelsey.

"Let's go!" She pulled at him, knowing it was futile. He was stuck in the driver's side with only seconds to spare.

Armin felt that this was the end. "I love you, Kelsey! I've loved you for months. Sorry it's not working out. I'll see you in heaven—"

A deafening crash drowned out Armin's confession.

Armin turned to look as an oversized red Humvee pushed the pickup truck sideways all the way down the left lane, nearly crushing it, pushing it to the raised divider in the middle. The pickup truck was stuck.

As soon as the screeching stopped, Armin jumped out of the driver's side and ran around the minivan to get Kelsey, but she was already out of the vehicle and running toward Armin. They met on the sidewalk near the front of the minivan, hugging each other.

Deshon came running toward them as sirens blared all around them. "You two okay?"

"Thank God you made it on time, Deshon!"

Armin's knees wobbled, and he leaned on Kelsey for support. His arm was around Kelsey's shoulders, and her arms were around his waist.

Deshon pointed a finger in the air. "Soli Deo gloria!"

Police vehicles and firetrucks arrived on the other side of the road and parked in front of the Humvee. Deshon went to tell them what happened.

Two officers came running toward Armin and Kelsey, just as shots rang out.

Armin and Kelsey dropped to the sidewalk. Armin spread his entire body on top of Kelsey.

"Shots fired!" the police officer yelled into his radio

Armin prayed for safety as Kelsey clung to him. He heard more shots, and then officers yelling and boots running across the sidewalk. The officers were all talking to one another but Armin's concern was Kelsey.

"You two okay?" The police officer nearest them put his weapon down.

"Yes. Thank you." Armin helped Kelsey to her feet.

About fifteen feet away from them on the grassy knoll, a man was on the ground. He was not moving. Officers surrounded him.

He looked dead.

"I need to sit down." Kelsey's knees buckled.

Armin sat with her as Kelsey's phone rang. He heard Tanaka's voice on the phone because he was sitting shoulder to shoulder with Kelsey on the sidewalk.

"I'm on my way." Tanaka said something about metro Atlanta traffic.

"Take your time. Armin and I are not hurt."

Just then Deshon approached them, together with a police officer. He took statements from Armin and Kelsey and then let them go.

"Do you have water?" Kelsey asked. "I'm thirsty."

Armin took her to his minivan, still parked on the right lane of the road. All around them, vehicles started to drive away, directed by the traffic police.

Armin retrieved a bottled water from the cupholder between the two front seats. "This is all I have. Unfortunately, I've already drunk half of it."

Kelsey took the bottle from him and finished the rest of the water. "I heard what you said in the van. Did you mean it?"

"Did you want me to mean it?" Armin knew that this was the only woman he wanted to spend the rest of his life with, but he had yet to hear her say the same of him.

When Kelsey said nothing, Armin added, "Yes, I still mean it."

Kelsey's lips quivered, and she hugged him tightly.

"I also fell in love with you during our phone talks. I don't know when the feelings began."

"I would venture to say in the last ten months or so?"

Kelsey nodded. "Less than a year, anyway."

Her stomach rumbled.

"I'm sorry our dinner is ruined. Wish I'd brought a cooler and put our takeout in it." Armin frowned. "This is the longest drive from the Indian restaurant to Hu Knows."

"Thank God we're alive though."

"Yes." This time, Armin's stomach also rumbled.

"You know what the Bible says. Man does not live by bread alone. We'll be fine."

"Matthew 4:4." Armin knew his Bible, but not every verse. He was glad that he knew that one when Kelsey referred to it.

*But He answered and said, "It is written, 'Man shall not live by bread alone, but by every word that proceeds from the mouth of God.'"*

Armin held her hands. "After we finish up here, would you like to have a late dinner with me?"

"Let's just eat inside the restaurant this time," Kelsey said. "This is Atlanta, so a lot of places open late into the evening."

"I don't know if it's safe for us to be in public." Armin knew they were not out of danger yet. The Steward was still at work. Since Nicholas was in jail in Chattanooga, Armin started to doubt that he was The Steward.

For now, his primary concern was Kelsey's safety.

Tanaka couldn't protect Kelsey any longer since she had been taken off the case and put on sick leave.

Armin should put in a request with Deshon—and therefore, with their boss, Helen Hu—to offer Kelsey a job as their office manager in the Atlanta branch so that she could come under the protection of Hu Knows. The international private investigative firm provided twenty-four-seven security if their staff was in mortal danger.

Meanwhile, as long as Armin was around, he'd protect Kelsey.

No. They would both protect each other.

With God's help.

But of course.

# CHAPTER SIXTEEN

J ealousy notwithstanding, Armin had a bigger problem of life-and-death to resolve. The bizarre incident on the road outside Hu Knows —with the near wreck and an active shooter—had sobered him up and slapped some reality into him.

As he sat on an armchair in the sitting area of the Hu Knows Atlanta office in Buckhead, Armin felt smaller and smaller in front of Deshon and Tanaka, who had arrived after Deshon picked up chicken biscuits from a nearby Chick-fil-A, their dinner for the night.

Deshon and Tanaka were at a whiteboard on wheels, arguing about something on the diagram that Deshon had drawn on the whiteboard.

But Armin couldn't hear them. All he could hear

was a little voice that kept telling him he was inadequate to protect the woman he wanted to be with more than any other woman in the world.

He glanced over at the couch. Kelsey was lying down, watching Deshon and Tanaka. She had kicked off her shoes and her toes were wiggling in her socks. She had also taken off Armin's jacket and used it as a blanket over her chest and shoulders. The room felt fairly warm, but Armin was happy to see his jacket being put to good use.

And yet this wasn't the time to romance Kelsey.

First, he had to make sure they both not only stayed alive but also thrived freely without interference from...

From who exactly?

The close shave earlier had thrown Armin off his game, and he had forgotten the counsel of the Word of God. It had been easier to pull out verses here and there when he was an observer of other people's problems. But when the problem was his, he shook a little.

There was Deshon, former military. There was Tanaka, a federal agent.

And here was Armin, an accountant who had never handled a weapon or taken any self-defense class.

Inadequate didn't even begin to describe his

dilemma of wanting to be Kelsey's protector and defender.

He closed his eyes, rubbed his temple. Where was his bearing? Where did the verses go when he needed some encouragement?

Then he answered his own question. The Bible was still there. God was still there. Whether he had been shocked by how close he'd come to being hit by a pickup truck or being shot by an active shooter, God was still there.

His grace hadn't left the room.

Slowly, Armin recalled the 2 Corinthians 12:9 verse that Pastor Kim had preached at Midtown Chapel late last year.

> And He said to me, "My grace is sufficient for you, for My strength is made perfect in weakness." Therefore most gladly I will rather boast in my infirmities, that the power of Christ may rest upon me.

Slowly, another Bible verse emerged in his memory bank. Philippians 4:13 reminded him that God would strengthen him.

> I can do all things through Christ who strengthens me.

"Makes no sense!" Deshon tapped the whiteboard with the red marker, its cap on tightly.

*Tap! Tap! Tap!*

Armin sat up straight, and almost raised his hand. He had lost track of what they had been talking about.

"Stop that. I can't think with all that noise." Tanaka walked away from the whiteboard and sat down on the armchair next to Armin.

"Aren't you supposed to be on sick leave?" Deshon reminded Tanaka.

He remained standing by the whiteboard. No one seemed to be paying attention to the scribbles and arrows on the board anymore.

"Me?" Tanaka put a free hand over her forehead. Her other arm was still in a cast. "I resigned on the way here."

"Because your firing arm is out of commission and you're basically useless?" Deshon ribbed Tanaka.

"No, Mr. Kernaghan. Because I raised the issue about Ulrich going behind my back to get the passphrase from Kelsey alone." She sighed. "Apparently some very powerful people think I was in the wrong for not getting the list of eight words from Kelsey myself on the way from Chattanooga to Atlanta. They didn't realize that if I'd pressed, Kelsey wouldn't remember a word."

"That's right," Kelsey finally spoke. "I had just memorized the words on the same day."

"How did you produce the words for Ulrich then?" Deshon asked.

Kelsey shrugged. "I thought I remembered them when he came to the door. He had a disarming smile or something and the words came to my mind, but like I said before, I might have misremembered the order."

"Which is very important," Armin said.

"All that is fine, but not enough to make you quit," Deshon said.

"Well, I didn't fully understand the technical mumbo jumbo and didn't appreciate the importance of the passphrase. That's what they told me." Tanaka grinned. "They suspended me—even though I was leaving for my sick leave today—and put Ulrich in charge."

"Let me guess." Deshon placed the dry-erase marker in a magnetic cup that held two other colored markers. "Ulrich suddenly appeared again and went back to work."

"What about his grandfather?" Kelsey asked.

"He's stable now in the hospital," Tanaka said. "In a few days, Ulrich will move him to an assisted living facility, where he will receive care twenty-four-seven as he recovers from the broken bones."

"So he's not a suspect," Armin said.

"Not now."

Deshon stepped away from the whiteboard. Armin noticed that the only spot he could sit was on the same couch as Kelsey. Feeling possessive, Armin pointed to his own armchair, as he got up and moved to the couch that Kelsey was on.

Kelsey pulled up her legs to make room for Armin at the other end of the couch.

He almost said, "Thank you, love," but stopped. The last thing he wanted to do was to remind Kelsey of Nicholas, how he'd called her love all the time.

*Hmm...*

Come to think of it, Armin had never called his ex-girlfriends "love"—or "honey" or "sweetheart" for that matter.

Did Kelsey like those sort of words?

"You could come work for Hu Knows." Deshon sat down facing Tanaka.

"Don't you need to ask Helen?" Tanaka asked.

"She put me in charge of the Atlanta brand, and I make all the hiring decisions." He pointed to Armin and then to himself. "We're the only two people working in this office right now. We could use a third investigator, if you want a change of scenery to deal with white collar crimes with us. All the other types of cases are still handled from the Savannah office. Earl is in charge of it."

"I'll think about it later. Thanks for the offer." Tanaka turned toward Kelsey. "Right now I'm stuck in this case and yet I can't work on it, you know?"

"We're away from everyone now, so you can talk freely." Deshon waved his hand.

"Roxanne and Paige are both in jail in Georgia," Tanaka said. "Roxanne for money laundering and arms sales to rogue generals overseas. Paige for suspected patricide. She's not confessing but the evidence is stacking up. I think her trial will go to a jury. If convicted, she's going to be in prison for a long time."

"It's too bad because she's only twenty six," Kelsey said.

"Nicholas and Zinnia are also in jail in Chattanooga, accused of false imprisonment," Deshon added.

"Even though they insisted they themselves were also prisoners."

"Does that mean they will be out on bail soon?" Kelsey asked.

Armin frowned. "What's wrong with the criminal justice system? Why do criminals get out on bail?"

"Due process." Deshon put his feet on the table. "Nicholas hasn't killed anyone. He's basically The Steward's slave."

"Zinnia will not make bail," Tanaka said. "She

confessed to everything via her lawyer to the Chattanooga police. She took the blame for everything."

Kelsey sat up. "She's taking the fall for The Steward."

"And Nicholas slips away," Armin said.

Kelsey nodded. "Exactly."

"I thought you and Nicholas were friends," Deshon said.

"We were, until I realized that he was complicit in The Steward's matters."

"When did that happen?" Armin could guess, but he didn't. He waited for Kelsey to explain.

Kelsey's eyes teared up. "For three years, he was practically my best friend, almost a close brother. He defended me when Braun-Dean yelled at me. He protected me from him. I lost count how many times he'd given me first aid. I will never forget Nicholas's kindness to me."

"If he was truly kind, he would've reported the abuse to the police." The words came out just like that, but Armin did not regret it.

"I know. Stockholm Syndrome, I guess." Kelsey drew a deep breath. "I can look back now and see how stupid I've been. Having said that, I wanted a friend, and Nicholas was there for me. He asked me to run away with him, but I refused."

"Oh?" Armin was somewhat pleased to hear that Kelsey had rejected Nicholas a while back.

"I think he wanted me to be more than just a friend to him. As far as I was concerned, he was the big brother I never had. In my eyes, he was the Good Samaritan, but not boyfriend material. That hurt him a little. But since I stayed with Braun-Dean, he also stayed. We both needed money, and Braun-Dean was the money machine."

Armin told himself that Kelsey was sharing her past, and that in vocalizing her feelings she might be able to let them go. He couldn't be angry about it, and there was no need for him to be jealous of a shadow from the past.

"However, we can't be friends anymore. Nicholas has changed." Kelsey wiped tears from her eyes. "The Steward offered him one percent of the seventeen billion dollars of crypto, and suddenly Nicholas was a different person."

"You only found out about that when he held you captive in the RV," Tanaka said.

"Captive? It didn't feel like that, but I guess it was because he wouldn't let me leave. He also threatened Armin, and I knew then that I was a pawn."

"Maybe his feelings for you were genuine," Tanaka suggested. "They might explain why he never tried to hurt you."

Kelsey nodded. "However, when Sam and Bob, the two fake cops, took orders from Nicholas, I half-wondered if Nicholas might be The Steward."

"Remember how he kept us in handcuffs for two hours until we reached his barn house in Spartanburg?" Armin asked.

"I remember."

"Thing is, his men had the cuff keys in his barn house," Arun said. "Why would he?"

"He himself didn't have the keys." Kelsey paused. "Only his men."

"I see what you mean." Not touching any incriminating evidence was a good way for Nicholas to absolve himself from blame. Armin gave Kelsey a fist bump.

"You two, speak up," Deshon said. "Stop this brain talk. Speak it out so that mere mortals like Tanaka and I can participate in the discussion."

"Speak for yourself." Tanaka rolled her eyes.

"Oh, I see we're going to have a smooth sailing working relationship from here on out." Deshon grinned at Tanaka.

Armin stretched and went to the whiteboard. He flipped the whiteboard over. There were some stray marks on it. "Can I erase all these?"

"Sure." Deshon stepped around the armchair to get

something out of the refrigerator nearby. "I'm still listening. Go ahead."

In the middle of the board, Armin wrote Nicholas's name and drew a box around it. "Nicholas is an erstwhile hairstylist by trade, and his last job as one was with Braun-Dean's reelection campaign three years ago."

"Right." Tanaka took a bottled water that Deshon offered to her. "When Braun-Dean lost his senate seat, a lot of people lost their jobs, including Nicholas."

"What has he been doing since then?" Deshon put down the other bottled waters on the coffee table between the couch and the armchair.

"He has money from his crypto investments," Kelsey said. "He has been living off of that."

"He's rich enough to buy a million-dollar souped-up RV." Deshon turned to Tanaka. "There, I said what you can't say."

"I'm no longer with the bureau as of rush hour this evening. Besides, you already looked into Nicholas's finances. It's not information only private to the FBI."

Armin continued. "So we've established that a jobless Nicholas has amassed a good fortune from his crypto investments. Suffice to say that he might not need to find another job if he could simply live off his crypto."

"We also know that a part of that money has gone

to buy the RV," Kelsey said. "I mean, people buy RVs, so it's not suspicious. After all, Nicholas uses it as his main home. That way he can travel to see his grand-mother in Spartanburg and then back to Atlanta without having to pack and unpack a suitcase."

"Is there really a grandmother in Spartanburg?" Deshon asked.

"I've never met her, but he has always talked about her," Kelsey said. "She practically raised him. Why would he lie about family?"

"Because he's lied about other things, it stands to reason that he can't be believed." Armin wondered why Kelsey had defended Nicholas again. He told himself to remain objective and to try to understand how Kelsey weighed things.

"I'm not disagreeing with you, but I'm saying he has a good cover story." Kelsey looked around the room. "If his character is in question, his defense team might call me to the stand to testify in court. I'll have to tell them about all the good things he's done for me—his company and care and compassion."

Tanaka nodded. "Nicholas has rescued Kelsey many times, and even paid for food and shelter when she was penniless after she left Braun-Dean."

"I could've..." Armin started to say.

Kelsey shook her head. "We didn't know each other then. Besides, it was only for a month or so. I needed an address when I renewed my driver's license. I was in-between jobs, so to speak."

"Regardless of what he's done, he didn't do it to Kelsey. Is that what you wanted to convey?" Deshon asked.

Kelsey nodded. "Nicholas never showed anger in front of me—except a flash of it when I worried about Armin on the day he ordered Sam and Bob to take him to Atlanta."

"Worried?" Armin asked. "You worried about me?"

"I knew you'd ask that as soon as the word 'worried' left my mouth."

Kelsey didn't directly answer his question, but Armin felt good that she cared for him even before they decided to go out on their first date night—which didn't turn out the way he'd envisioned.

He returned to the board. He noted a few things about Nicholas. "He's a crypto millionaire. Check. Nothing against that. I'm just writing down all that we know about him."

"He's close to The Steward," Kelsey said.

"How so?"

"He gives orders to Sam, Bob, Zinnia, the people in the barn house." Kelsey paused. "Wait. There might be overlaps with the people in the barn house. We don't know who they really work for. But Zinnia clearly works for The Steward, and she takes orders from Nicholas."

"If I remember clearly, Zinnia also talks to Nicholas like The Steward is a third person altogether." Armin wrote down some of the names mentioned.

"When I was with him in the RV, I was at ease with him because he's friendly," Kelsey recalled. "I felt no danger with him, and he made me think we could just wait for Armin to return with the next eight words."

"I had expected to go back there, but not with Sam and Bob. I thought Tanaka would take me back to Chattanooga, but I was told that it would be a police rescue mission, and that I'd better stay in Atlanta and wait for Tanaka to bring you home." Armin tried to read Kelsey's face.

"In general, we want to keep civilians out of trouble." Tanaka lifted her arm. "I can't protect you with this. Besides, it's a local police operation. I only waited at the side until they released Kelsey to me."

"I'm glad we're fine," Kelsey said.

"For now. The Steward is still out there somewhere." Deshon finished his bottled water. "I could eat a second round of dinner. Ramen noodles, anyone? I can cook a big pot."

Everyone raised their hands.

"Hey Kelsey, how did you get Nicholas to show

you the eight words he extracted from Braun-Dean's encrypted file?" Armin's hand was ready to write down more notes on the board.

"I wasn't a threat to him." Kelsey's eyes looked far away.

Actually, Armin thought so until he realized she was looking in the direction of the kitchenette near the conference room. Deshon disappeared behind a wall.

"I chatted with him and listened to him," Kelsey added. "I don't know what else I did, to be frank. But somehow he let his guard down and showed me the words on his phone."

"The phone that he threw into the lake." Tanaka shook her head. "Which they can't yet dredge up."

"They won't find it!" Deshon yelled from the kitchen area.

Kelsey got up, went to the board, and selected an orange marker. Was that her favorite color? Armin wondered. Or maybe he was overthinking it.

She wrote the numbers one through twenty-four vertically along the left side of the board, near the edge. She hummed something Armin couldn't decipher as she wrote down single words at the bottom of the list, from line seventeen through twenty-four.

The room was silent as Kelsey began to sing "Twelve Days of Christmas" with nonsensical words, and writing down selected words as she went along. She continued singing until the last line.

*On the twelfth day of walnut, my ketchup sent to me twelve jaguars leaping...*

When she finished, she had filled out line seven through fourteen, since she had filled out lines seventeen and eighteen earlier.

"Armin, you fill out the first six words from Arun's paper." Kelsey handed the orange market to him.

"You have the middle eight words." Armin was beyond surprised, and yet he shouldn't be. These were words generated to protect Braun-Dean's crypto account.

Kelsey nodded. "The middle eight words plus two before and two after."

Armin was puzzled.

"I didn't piece it together until I was stuck in the RV with Nicholas," Kelsey explained. "When I saw that the first two words on his list were the last two words on the list of twelve words that Braun-Dean made me memorize over three years, I knew what I had, but then the boating incident threw me off. Today is the first chance I have to put this list together."

"Your memory is amazing," Armin said.

"I can only remember things when I'm not stressed."

"You're not stressed now."

"Not when I'm with you." Kelsey held Armin's hand.

Deshon cleared his throat. He was approaching them with a giant pot, presumably with ramen noodles in it. Steam was coming out the side of the lid.

Tanaka called Cayson and put him on the speakerphone. "We found the last eight words in Kelsey's song."

"How?" Cayson asked.

"Braun-Dean split up the recovery passphrase and left it with three different people."

"This third person..."

Armin opened his mouth, but Tanaka shook her head.

"Anonymous source," she said.

Armin understood. The FBI agent still didn't trust Ulrich, her colleague who had taken over her role. In other words, she trusted Binary Systems, but not the people outside of it.

"We still don't have the account password," Cayson said.

"Is that my problem?" Tanaka laughed. "I just quit today."

"For real?"

"Yes. I don't even know if my arm will recover properly."

"What did the doctor say?"

"Two months."

"You need the rest. Ulrich seems to be doing fine."

"Glad he is. I'll send you the twenty-four words."

"Ruby?" Cayson said.

Armin was surprised that Cayson knew Tanaka by her first name. They might have worked together in the past. Armin didn't know and couldn't guess.

"Yeah?" Tanaka looked at Deshon, whose eyebrows rose.

"Remember that The Steward also wants these twenty-four words," Cayson said. "However, he can't clone the hardware wallet unless he has the account password. Looks like Braun-Dean has taken that last piece of the puzzle with him to the grave."

"Thanks for the warning." Tanaka hung up. "Funny. That's what Roxanne told Ulrich yesterday."

"What did she say?" Armin asked.

"Roxanne said that her daughters were convinced that Braun-Dean had taken the account password to his grave."

"Did they guess or do they know something we don't?" Kelsey touched the stone bracelet on her wrist.

Armin didn't know why she did that. Maybe she remembered something else that she wasn't saying at the moment.

Meanwhile, Armin himself tried to process what Tanaka just said.

*To the grave.*

Armin turned to look at Kelsey, his jaw dropping and his eyes sparkling.

Her eyes widened, and she nodded.

And they high-fived each other.

"What is going on here?" Deshon had somehow produced four bowls while Armin wasn't looking. "You two doing that brain-wave thing again?"

Armin smiled. It wasn't that uncanny to him. It was pure logic. They had looked at the same set of data and had reached the same conclusion. He could easily guess what Kelsey and Tanaka had in mind.

"Oh, I see." Deshon seemed to have caught on too. "However, let me remind you that the Cobb Medical Examiner is still doing an autopsy on Braun-Dean's body."

"When will they release him for burial?" Tanaka asked.

"Next week, I think."

"Braun-Dean had always said that he wanted his body buried within three days of his death," Kelsey added.

"I think a murder investigation overrides that." Deshon didn't smile. "But the Cobb ME team are doing their best to fast-track this due to media scrutiny. Investigative reporters have unearthed the bribes that Braun-Dean took during his time in the Senate."

Armin wasn't surprised. Still, the man was now dead, and justice was either served or not served, depending on who you asked. "When is Braun-Dean's funeral?"

Even as he asked the question, Armin scrolled on his phone to find the answer. "Okay. Got it. Roxanne's lawyer has announced that they would hold a small family-only funeral in a Marietta funeral home, but no address is given."

Everyone nodded.

Kelsey turned to Tanaka. "How does one break into a cemetery?"

"What?" Deshon stopped in his tracks, a fork in his hand.

Slowly, Tanaka nodded. "If I'm thinking of where you're thinking Braun-Dean's going to be buried, we can just walk in. There are no gates."

# CHAPTER SEVENTEEN

Felix Braun-Dean's funeral was held on a rainy Monday the following week. That afternoon, a hearse carried his coffin from Marietta to his final resting place.

To Kelsey's surprise, Braun-Dean wasn't buried at his family crypt at Oakland Cemetery in Atlanta. It turned out that his will had stated a special burial place for him in the compound of his Chattahoochee vacation home.

"That could bring down the price of that entire estate." Deshon placed a hand on the steering wheel of his Humvee.

Ahead of them was darkness, with hardly any vehicles on either side of the road.

"Why do you say that?" Tanaka countered him

from the front passenger seat. "I've seen nineteenth century homes with burial plots in their backyard."

"Common then, but not in the twenty-first century, wouldn't you say?"

"Are you trying to make me agree with you?"

There they went again, Kelsey thought. Arguing with each other like squabbling siblings.

Kelsey tuned them out, and looked through the Humvee window to the darkness outside. She knew that they had arrived in Tennessee on Interstate 75 from Atlanta, and had skirted the Chattanooga Metropolitan Airport, as they headed north toward Lake Chickamauga.

The drive hadn't been nearly two hours so far, and Kelsey was wide awake even though it was in the middle of the night. She glanced over at Armin, who was fast asleep like a baby in an insulated black leather jacket that made his torso look bigger than he looked in the other jacket.

She, too, was dressed in all black to blend in with the night. They had all been issued earpieces so that they could securely communicate with one another should they become lost in Braun-Dean's vast estate. Armin and Kelsey wore over-the-ear earpieces, while Deshon and Tanaka opted for earbuds.

Armin's eyes were still closed, but his hand reached out to hers and held it for a while.

*Are we moving too fast?*

Kelsey wondered if the speed of their relationship —from friendly chats to date nights—was borne out of a sound judgment. She knew they'd better pray about it because God would know what was best for them.

It had been one year since Kelsey had known Armin. Most of that period was on the phone, and via texts and emails. Kelsey sincerely believed that God had brought them together, thanks to Arun, their initial connection.

Now that they had met, Kelsey realized that she and Armin both genuinely liked each other in real life. That first date a week ago—albeit a botched one—hadn't been a fluke or an emotional episode. They had eased into dating seamlessly.

Holding hands with Armin felt like the most natural thing in the world to Kelsey.

In her heart was a lightness. God had freed her from the shackles of her past. She had a new beginning in Christ. She was starting over.

And she was falling in love again.

This time, it was a different kind of love. It wasn't the erotic love of her past life before she was saved in Jesus Christ, but now it was a Christian love that must be handled carefully before the eyes of a holy God.

This love that Kelsey had for Armin was clean and

wholesome, and began with God Himself, as Kelsey recalled from 1 John 4:9-11.

*In this the love of God was manifested toward us, that God has sent His only begotten Son into the world, that we might live through Him. In this is love, not that we loved God, but that He loved us and sent His Son to be the propitiation for our sins. Beloved, if God so loved us, we also ought to love one another.*

So were Kelsey and Armin dating or not? She wasn't entirely sure at this point except to say they had just started holding hands. She knew that Armin would agree with her if she said that they would proceed carefully, continue to pray, and get to know each other as they journeyed on.

If God had put them together, then God would also make it clear to them whether they would remain together. Kelsey made a note to herself to contact Midtown Chapel—Armin's new church and soon to be hers also—to get some counseling on Christian relationships from a biblical worldview. For now, she knew that she and Armin would not sleep together for as long as they were dating. Until marriage.

Marriage?

*Oh, it's too soon to think of that. Although...*

She turned to look at Armin. He had stirred from

his power nap, and was looking straight at her in the dim light of the dashboard that shone between the two front seats.

"What were you thinking of?" Armin asked.

Kelsey blushed and cleared her throat.

Deshon turned into a somewhat empty lot surrounded by trees, and parked his vehicle. He looked through the side rearview mirror. "He's here."

"Who's here?" Kelsey asked.

"Our backup." Deshon waited for a pickup truck to park next to them. "Armin, scoot to the middle, will you? We have a new team member joining us."

Armin unbuckled and moved to the middle of the bucket seat. He was sitting thigh to thigh next to Kelsey.

A man exited the pickup truck, and Deshon waved to him and pointed to the backseat. When the man opened the passenger side door on the driver's side, Kelsey felt the biting wind rush into the vehicle. She shivered. Armin put his warm hand over hers.

The man closed the door and sat in the seat that Armin had vacated.

Deshon unbuckled and turned as far as he could. So did Tanaka. Their faces were about a foot away from each other between the two front seats.

They said nothing to each other.

Was something going on between Deshon and

Tanaka? Kelsey couldn't tell, and this was not the time to speculate.

"Everyone, this is my good friend from my Army days, Jonathan Aberdeen." Deshon handed Jonathan his communication earpiece. "I texted him before we left Buckhead, and I'm glad he's free this evening."

Jonathan smiled. "I'm losing sleep tonight, but Hu Knows is paying me, so here I am."

"Didn't know you were driving behind us," Tanaka said. "Did you follow us all the way here or what?"

"No. I drove in from Knoxville and waited for y'all."

"Whatcha doing in Knoxville? I thought you were in São Paulo."

"I go wherever there's work." Jonathan didn't say more.

Kelsey wondered how Tanaka and Jonathan knew each other, but Tanaka knew a lot of people.

"Meet Armin and Kelsey," Deshon said. "Unarmed civilians—although I hear that Kelsey can somewhat shoot."

Kelsey bowed her head in embarrassment. She wasn't sure if Deshon was referring back to the carjacker episode, but she wasn't going to pick a fight now.

Yeah, she could shoot, but maybe not to kill. It was

best if she took up a job that required zero handling of weapons. She would feel safer that way.

Armin gently squeezed her hand and whispered in her ear. "It's okay. Don't worry about it."

"Hello, fellow gravediggers." Jonathan waved.

Kelsey waved back.

"We need someone to stay in the Humvee and drive us away once we get what we want." Deshon paused. "I don't think we should let Ruby drive with one hand."

*Oh, it's Ruby now.*

But he was right. Tanaka wasn't a hundred percent with her arm in a plaster cast and supported by a sling. However...

"I just need to keep the Humvee idle and monitor you," Tanaka said. "I can drive with one hand, seriously. I can't do car chases though."

"Any other volunteers?" Deshon's lips tilted up in a sly smile.

No one volunteered.

"Don't you think it's a bit late in the game to be asking for volunteers?" Tanaka frowned. "Are you always this disorganized?"

And there they went again.

Armin cleared his throat. "Didn't we already discuss this back at the office in Atlanta? Kelsey and I are going in. Deshon and Tanaka are going with us. Jonathan stays in the car."

"I changed my mind." Deshon pointed at Jonathan. "I think he needs to go with us. There are two of you, and I'm not sure if I can protect both of you if something should happen."

"What could happen?" Kelsey asked.

No one replied. Maybe they didn't want to scare her.

"You don't have to protect me," Kelsey added. "I'm not that fragile. Ask Tanaka."

"We want you safe because if you're stressed out, you can't read the signs," Deshon reminded her.

Kelsey didn't know what to say about that. She wasn't sure if she could pull this off. She and Tanaka believed that Braun-Dean had taken the last password to his grave. Based on his love for puzzles and the endless months he'd made Kelsey memorize random words—that turned out to be two thirds of the recovery passphrase—it was likely that Braun-Dean had been trying to get the last laugh.

"If we find nothing here, we need to get out alive to plan our next steps." Tanaka touched her earpiece. "Good idea to give all of us earpieces, Deshon. I'll monitor the security."

Deshon nodded. "Whatever you do, don't call Cayson. Don't want to get him into trouble."

"I can't promise you that," Tanaka replied. "I'll do my best to keep y'all safe."

"Y'all?" Deshon chuckled. "Welcome to the south, Ruby Tanaka."

"I think my pickup can outrace your Humvee," Jonathan said to Deshon.

"But my Humvee is bulletproof and has a second gas tank in the trunk."

"No way."

"Yes way. Plus, it has camo skin."

A camouflage skin. That was new to Kelsey.

"Like an invisible digital cloak?" Jonathan's eyes widened.

Deshon nodded.

"Say it isn't so." Jonathan seemed impressed.

"That's why we can chat in here without fear, although we should get going now."

Everyone agreed.

Kelsey wondered if she was seeing the beginnings of the Atlanta branch of Hu Knows, Inc. Armin and Deshon were already working there. Kelsey and Tanaka had both been offered jobs. Jonathan seemed to be a freelancer.

Deshon turned back toward his steering wheel. "Buckle in everyone. I'll get us as close to the Braun-Dean estate as I can, and some of us can hop out."

It took another five minutes through winding roads

before they reached the locked gates. Deshon made one pass and then returned. He parked the Humvee by the side of the road.

"I gather you've already dealt with the security cameras," Jonathan said.

"You gather right. We have an hour of power blackout, at most." Deshon didn't say more.

Kelsey was certain that Binary Systems hadn't been involved because they were above board. Deshon must've hired external hackers to take down the security system at the Braun-Dean estate.

Deshon got out of the vehicle. Tanaka followed him, and Kelsey followed Tanaka. They rounded to the driver's side, where Armin and Jonathan stood next to each other. While Armin was tall and somewhat skinny, Jonathan was more built and muscular.

"Don't scratch my Humvee." Deshon wagged an index finger at his Army buddy, who was climbing into the idling Humvee. "Or I'll deduct it from your super expensive hourly fee."

"It's my emergency rate, buddy. Next time, give me a month's notice and it won't be a rush." Jonathan smiled. "You're fortunate that I happen to be in Knoxville this evening. I was driving out of town when you called."

Kelsey thanked God for the timing. With Tanaka's arm in a cast, they could use an extra pair of hands.

In the dark night without any street lamps above them and with the Humvee headlights turned off, Kelsey felt uneasy. She stepped closer to Armin in the faint light of Deshon's flashlight.

Armin put a warm hand on her shoulder. "Stay close. I brought bear spray."

Kelsey nearly burst out laughing and had to cover her mouth because she was making too much noise. Then she realized she herself was unarmed.

"Shhh." Jonathan turned to Deshon. "Need more training with these people. They might get us all killed."

Killed?

Kelsey shivered a bit in the January night as she and Armin waited for Deshon to climb over the fence and unlock a side gate for them. If Kelsey could scale the fence like Deshon, they would've saved time.

The night temperature dropped to the forties when they walked through the woods toward the circular driveway that Kelsey and Armin had been to before.

"It should be...here." Deshon stopped.

"What's here?" All Kelsey could see in the waning moonlight was the small stone guest house across from Braun-Dean's mansion, the one they had walked past the other night.

This was Deshon's first time here, but he had the GPS. "It says we have arrived."

"Arrived where?" Armin and Jonathan asked at the same time.

"That's what I want to know." Deshon drew a deep breath. "We have fifty minutes—or less—before the power returns."

Kelsey took out her phone and turned on the flashlight app. She scanned the circular driveway, but didn't have to do much of it because she spotted something outside the guest house. There were fresh flowers on the front porch, in both vases and on wreaths. Lilies and white roses everywhere.

"I think I know." Kelsey led the way to the stone guest house. If Braun-Dean was buried on the estate, wouldn't it be in...

A private mausoleum?

The front door was locked. Padlocked.

"Let's check the back." Deshon had a handgun to his side, pointing down at the ground.

Kelsey and Armin were sandwiched between Deshon and Jonathan as they walked around the small house. The other night, they had walked away from the house on the sidewalk that led down the winding lane to the RV parked somewhere beyond the grove of trees over there.

This time, they walked around to the back of the

house. Two funeral wreaths decorated a low gate connected to an equally low brick wall that closed the backyard. Beyond the gate, a pair of closed wrought iron doors greeted them.

"This isn't a guest house, is it?" Armin asked.

"I'll stay out here." Jonathan crouched down behind the brick wall.

Deshon opened the gate. Thankfully, it didn't creak. He picked the lock on the iron doors, and then they were inside the stone building.

On the vestibule, there was an altar of some sort beneath a hanging chandelier, but there was nothing religious. No cross, no star of David, no stained glass. On both sides of them were marble walls with names engraved on each rectangular plate.

She was right. This was indeed a mausoleum.

Kelsey stepped toward one of the names. "Ceridwen Burditt. She died in 1972."

"This one is a Smith, and here is another Burditt." Armin pointed to a wall of smaller rectangles. A columbarium. "No Braun-Dean."

There was not a single Braun-Dean anywhere.

"Did Braun-Dean buy this property with the mausoleum on it?" Kelsey asked.

"And built the mansion near it?"

"I know we missed something in our homework."

Deshon shone his flashlight around the vestibule. He stopped. "Stairs over there."

As soon as they reached the bottom step, Kelsey regretted coming. There she stood beneath the mausoleum, surrounded by dead people in sealed chambers or crypts.

All around them were more crypts with most of the end panels etched with names, together with their dates of birth and death. Some of the panels were blank, which could mean there might not be caskets behind them.

"Look here." Armin read off a plate. "Sarah Burditt passed away on July 15, 1899."

"Is this mausoleum that old or did they move the bodies here after they built it?" Deshon asked.

"I didn't expect this." Kelsey walked around slowly, reading names, looking for Braun-Dean's name.

There it was.

Just like the other marble panel, Braun-Dean, the only name unlike all the other etched names.

This was her viewing. A way to say a final goodbye to her abusive ex-boyfriend of three long years. Whatever it had been, it was all over now. Scars remained, though, not buried with the past.

Armin gently squeezed Kelsey's hand, reminding her that by accepting him as her new boyfriend, she had moved on. The old had passed away.

"God has made all things new," Armin whispered in her ear.

Armin's words triggered Kelsey's strong memory to flip through her mental filing cabinet. She reached Revelation 21:5.

*Then He who sat on the throne said, "Behold, I make all things new."*

"What are we looking for?" Deshon mumbled. "Why are we here? What is life?"

"The account password," Armin whispered.

"I know. I'm just trying to lighten up the mood—"

*Click.*

Kelsey heard it first. She shut off her phone flashlight. Deshon followed with his flashlight.

The crypt turned pitch black. Whether Kelsey opened or closed her eyes, it mattered not. The windowless room was dark as dark could be.

Kelsey looked around in the darkness, adjusting her eyes—

And there they were.

Letters and numbers from the engraved coffin plates appeared all around them, glowing in the dark in three rows.

Kelsey tapped Armin's hand.

"I see them too," Armin whispered. "But where's the beginning of it? Where's the end?"

From what Kelsey remembered of Felix Braun-Dean, he liked his things to be in a particular order. He read from left to right, top to bottom. It was as simple as that.

Kelsey picked a random starting point and tried to remember letters and numbers as she read them from left to right until she reached the letter she had started with. Then she repeated it until she saw a pattern emerging.

```
noGoodbYe
,92
CataLina
```

That would've been the simplest formation. She could've also started reading at "Catalina" or "92" or the comma. One way or another, she had discovered the account password. Let Binary Systems sort out the order and whatever else needed.

"No goodbye comma ninety two Catalina," Kelsey whispered to Armin and Deshon.

"Oh, I see it now," Deshon said.

Kelsey was surprised that The Steward hadn't discovered this mausoleum already.

She took another turn around the room to double-check her finding. Two more numbers flickered, then faded away. She wanted to cry. Poor Braun-Dean must've been so ultra paranoid that he'd have to do this. Either that, or whoever he had hired to make the letters and words light up didn't account for the power outage in the estate.

Or... This mausoleum, with its surprise crypt, had a lighting system of its own.

In any case, Kelsey picked up the last two digits. She was about to tell Armin and Deshon what it was when Armin spoke.

"Who's Catalina?" he asked.

"My mother," a voice in the dark said.

A familiar female voice. That couldn't be...

The lights came on.

Several people marched down the stairs. They were armed. In the middle of the procession was none other than Carmelita Braun-Dean in the flesh. Gen Z millionaire and the apple of her adopted father's eye.

"Thank you, Zuriel." Carmelita walked toward Kelsey.

"Carmelita?" Kelsey was stunned. "I thought you were out of the country."

"Surprised?" Carmelita stood five feet away from Kelsey as her men disarmed Deshon.

They patted down Armin, and found something in his pocket.

"What's this?" The man lifted the canister in the air. "Pepper spray?"

"Actually it's bear spray," Armin explained. "I used up the pepper spray and had no time to reorder it."

The man threw the whole canister at Armin, hitting him in the forehead. He staggered back.

"Armin!" Kelsey reached for him before someone yanked her back.

Carmelita's men zip-tied Kelsey's hands behind her back. They did the same for Armin and Deshon. They also removed all of their earpieces.

Kelsey turned to Carmelita. "What's going on?"

"Don't even try that on me." Carmelita grunted in disgust.

Kelsey had no idea what she meant.

"All these pretenses. I'm done with them." Carmelita stepped closer to Kelsey. "You know what's going on, Zuriel."

Carmelita knew her real name, but had refused to call her by that tonight.

"I genuinely don't understand why you're involved." Kelsey thought of the stone bracelet she still wore on her wrist. She reached for it with her other hand.

Carmelita smiled. "That bracelet is how we found you here."

Kelsey gasped. "You put a tracker on me? When?"

Why hadn't Hu Knows checked?

"When Felix borrowed your bracelet for two days." She laughed.

Another daughter who refused to call her father Dad. Kelsey felt sorry for Braun-Dean. He seemed to have lost both of his daughters.

"That was a long time ago," Kelsey said.

"So? It still works, doesn't it?"

"What did you do?"

"Might as well tell you. I convinced him that you could be cheating on her. After all, you're half his age, and there're many prospects on the campaign trail."

"So Braun-Dean spied on my whereabouts?" Kelsey didn't know what to say.

"He was until the day he died. Can you imagine that?" Carmelita's voice was sharp. "He couldn't leave you alone. If he'd paid that much attention to my mother, she would still be alive today."

Carmelita trotted over to a sealed chamber next to Braun-Dean's. Slowly, she ran her finger over the engraving. "Catalina Burditt was my mother's name."

Burditt?

"So this land belongs to your mother's family," Armin said.

Carmelita nodded. "The mansion next door was built by my grandfather on top of an old log cabin he shouldn't have torn down. It was a house filled with family history. But what's done is done."

"Are you Braun-Dean's adopted daughter for real?" Kelsey asked.

Carmelita sighed. "I'm the daughter that Felix wished he had. When Roxanne murdered my mother twenty years ago, Felix adopted me because I reminded him of the woman he couldn't have."

"Roxanne did what?" It was news to Kelsey and she could barely process it.

"I know, right? She got away because Felix protected her." Carmelita turned around to face her captives. "You can be sure that Roxanne will pay for her crime. Felix already had."

"So let the law work," Deshon said. "Why all these?"

"The law is taking away the seventeen billion dollars that Felix accumulated." Carmelita returned to Kelsey. "Felix should've just told me the account password. Then none of these would be necessary."

"Did you ask him?" Kelsey tried to keep the conversation going.

By now, Jonathan outside and Tanaka in the Humvee had both heard their conversation. Kelsey prayed that there was enough time for them to call 911, and for the police to get here before anything happened to them.

"I asked him." Carmelita's face was cold. "He refused to give me the account password until the very end."

"The very end of what?" Kelsey asked.

Carmelita's face changed ever so slightly under the light. Then she returned to a poker face. "He said he couldn't remember the password. He was the greatest liar I've ever met."

That part might be true. Kelsey couldn't refuse Carmelita. Braun-Dean could lie at the drop of a hat. He'd developed that skill. Roxanne wasn't very far behind. Both of them had made a notorious pair.

"You saw your dad to the very end?" Kelsey tried again.

"He's not my dad."

"He gave you so much."

"Not enough."

"He loved you more than he loved his other daughter, Paige," Kelsey reminded her. "Isn't that enough?"

Carmelita frowned. "He cut off my allowances."

*You were twenty-five years old.*

How much longer should Braun-Dean continue to subsidize her jobless lifestyle? Kelsey dared not make her point because Carmelita could hurt her.

"Seventeen billion dollars should have gone to my mother. He told me that he loved her and would give her the world," Carmelita continued.

"How did you know what your dad told your mom?"

"She wrote me a letter to be read on my twenty-first birthday. I'm her only survivor. So why wouldn't he give me the world?"

Kelsey had no answer for Carmelita's logic.

"He treated you as his own daughter." Kelsey kept her voice down.

"He wanted all of us to think so. Inside, it was eating him up. He had lost the opportunity to have a child with my mother. That's why he dated you—to have a child of his own." Carmelita chuckled. "Only, he was infertile."

Infertile? Kelsey didn't know that. In fact, Braun-Dean had made it sound like she had been the problem in those three years they had been together.

Well, that meant...

Paige wasn't his daughter either.

Kelsey didn't want to recall the past, but now the past might be handy as a survivor tool to prevent them from being killed—or at least delay the torture of dying.

"Braun-Dean told me he'd leave half of his estate to you," Kelsey said.

"So it's Braun-Dean now? Why so formal?"

"We broke up a long time ago. Frankly, I don't want to be dragged into your family affairs." Perhaps *affairs* might have been the wrong word, but she'd said it, and there it remained in the cold air between them.

"Felix said many things." Carmelita touched Kelsey's arm. "He promised me all of the seventeen billion dollars of crypto. Then he made a deal with Roxanne to split it with her if she didn't testify against him. She went to jail. He made bail. It's never been fair to all the women Felix slept with, including you."

"Me? I've moved on. I don't owe anyone anything."

"He didn't want to let you move on, Zuriel." Her voice steeled. "I told him it was unfair to you if he left you the account password when you're no longer in his life. All he had to do was spit out the password and we'd be done."

"Couldn't The Steward have found a way to recreate the hardware wallet without this last password?" Armin asked.

Kelsey would rather that he hadn't said a thing. She felt that she had a conversation going with Carmelita, stalling her long enough for the police to come. They were probably outside already, but this underground crypt seemed to be soundproof. Kelsey couldn't hear anything from above. Not even footfalls.

"The Steward?" Carmelita laughed.

Kelsey wasn't sure why she'd laugh. "Do you know him?"

"Him? Wrong pronoun, Zuriel." There was a mischievous look in Carmelita's eyes.

"You mean The Steward is a she?"

Carmelita ignored her question. Her eyes were misty. "Felix wouldn't listen. So we had to..."

"Had to what?" As far as Kelsey had known, Paige had been arrested for Braun-Dean's murder. What exactly did Carmelita do? Had she been involved in the Marietta crime? "We? Who was with you—"

"Why should I explain to you?" Carmelita snapped. "You're not my therapist."

She turned to her men. "You have the recording?"

One of them nodded. "All of it, ma'am. We have the password."

Carmelita faced Kelsey. "We don't need you anymore."

"On the contrary, you do," Kelsey said quickly.

"Oh?"

"Better not kill me off before you recover the crypto stash," Kelsey warned. "After all, I'm the keeper of your father's secrets."

"You're stalling."

"I'm telling you the truth. For example, you could've gotten the password from this crypt yourself. Maybe you've been here this afternoon after Braun-Dean was buried.

Carmelita didn't reply.

"However, you didn't get the password. Why?" Kelsey asked.

"It's another dead man's switch," Armin said.

Kelsey nodded. "Because Braun-Dean had set it up such that someone else—not you—had to be here in person before all these letters and numbers showed up like Christmas lights. Am I right?"

"You knew Felix well." Carmelita clapped in a mocking way. "I don't know why he had chosen you, but this crypt has been wired to only respond to you, Zuriel."

"I don't think it's over yet." Kelsey was only speculating, but she had to buy time. For some reason or other, the Chattanooga police weren't here yet, and singleton Jonathan was no match for Carmelita's armed team.

Armin nodded. "You might find that when you try to recreate the wallet, it might be empty."

Deshon concurred. "Did you think that Braun-Dean was going to let you get to his money that easily? Otherwise, why hadn't The Steward gotten it already? He's the crypto king, isn't he?"

Carmelita smacked her lips. "I guess we'll have to take you with us, Zuriel. But only you."

"We go together." Kelsey made a circle with her hand in the air. "I go, they go. They stay, I stay."

"You're difficult." Carmelita signaled to her men.

Ushered up the stone stairs, Kelsey walked slowly, trying to listen to what was going on outside.

The chandelier cast an eerie glow on the vestibule, but the door to the outside was closed. One of Carmelita's men unlocked the door. The night air greeted them—

"Chattanooga Police!"

In the floodlights, Kelsey saw police officers in vests and a SWAT team behind shields surrounding the mausoleum. Between the SWAT team and the gate, dead bodies were strewn on the sidewalk and grass.

Kelsey heard a noise, and dropped down to the ground instinctively, as shots fired all around her. She closed her eyes and prayed for God to keep her and Armin safe. And Deshon and Jonathan and Tanaka out there somewhere.

Eyes still closed, she felt strong arms dragging her away. She could smell grass and dirt.

The gunfire ceased.

Kelsey opened her eyes to find Armin holding her in his arms on the grass. "You again."

"Me again." His wrists were bleeding where the zip tie had been.

Kelsey didn't know what type of zip ties Carmelita's men had used on them and what their tensile strengths were, but Armin had managed to break his.

And he had protected her again.

"Let's get the ties off you." Armin helped her to sit up as the paramedics arrived.

Across the grass, Jonathan was cutting off the ties around Deshon's wrists.

Beyond them, Chattanooga Police were handcuffing Carmelita and her entourage.

"Kelsey!" Tanaka ran over to her.

"Thank you for calling 911," Kelsey said to Tanaka.

"Jonathan and I both did," the former FBI special agent said. "However, he was chased into the woods. Thankfully, he survived and found me."

Deshon regrouped with them after a paramedic had treated the cut and burns on Armin's wrists. His wrists were bandaged, but he still smiled. He lifted up Kelsey's hands. "Are you all right?"

"I'm fine. Do you need stitches?"

"No need."

The police officer was taking a statement from Tanaka and Jonathan, eyewitnesses of the events outside the mausoleum. They would get Kelsey, Armin, and Deshon soon.

"How can it be that easy?" Armin asked.

"My thoughts exactly." Kelsey massaged her wrists. "Why had the Chattanooga Police taken so long to get here?"

"They were here." Tanaka didn't say more.

"Let me guess." Deshon stared at Tanaka. "The FBI held them back because they were listening in."

She didn't answer.

"It's now a sting operation, is it not?" Deshon asked. "Have you really quit or are you still working for the FBI?"

"I'm done. Truly." Tanaka sighed.

"We could've died underground—before I could even marry and have kids."

"I know they were all armed and dangerous." Tanaka leaned toward Deshon. "I'm sorry you have to whine like this."

"Hey—"

Deshon stopped talking.

Just then, Kelsey spotted FBI Special Agent Ulrich coming down the sidewalk, wearing a vest and surrounded by his team.

"What did I say?" Deshon made a face.

# CHAPTER EIGHTEEN

E scorted by FBI Special Agent Ulrich, the Hu Knows team arrived in Alpharetta, Georgia, shortly before five in the morning. Cayson Yang, the chief executive officer of Binary Systems, greeted Armin, Kelsey, Tanaka, and a very grumpy Deshon himself at his high-security headquarters. Jonathan had begged off going with them, and left Chattanooga in his pickup truck to go to his next free-lance job.

At the Binary Systems, Armin was happy to see Cayson again. This was one of the few times he'd actually met Cayson in person. His colleagues at Hu Knows had worked with Cayson and his cousin, Leland Yang-Joule, many times in the past.

Deshon had said that Armin might be shuttling

back and forth between Binary Systems and Hu Knows in Atlanta, just because of their white collar crime investigations, which were becoming digital crimes.

Cayson seemed to work in a relaxed atmosphere. He wore a sweatshirt and somewhat matching sweatpants, and he walked around in a pair of Oofos sandals. He was not harried, nor did he look tired from having stayed up all night, waiting for this account password.

After eating a free croissant from the Binary Systems' dining room, Armin joined the rest of them in a workroom. The small crowd gathered around Cayson at the work table as he accessed a small silver USB drive, which he connected to a laptop.

"There are other ways to clone this hardware wallet," Cayson said.

"Now you tell us." Deshon looked like he should go home and go to bed.

"This is how Braun-Dean would have wanted it done." Ulrich stood further back, standing next to Tanaka.

Tanaka nodded. "The money doesn't belong to the Braun-Dean family, and he knows it."

"Right." Ulrich concurred with Tanaka. "The money came from illegal arms sales to terrorists. Roxanne and Braun-Dean were building up their nest egg overseas. They weren't planning on going to jail."

"Braun-Dean feared for his life because The Steward was coming after him, so he came up with these schemes to protect his crypto stash," Tanaka added. "I only wished he hadn't involved Kelsey or other innocent people."

"So many players, so few answers," Armin said. "Nicholas. Zinnia. Paige. Carmelita. The Steward. How do they fit together?"

"Don't forget Roxanne and the deceased Braun-Dean himself, the source of our present woes." Deshon nudged Tanaka.

She ignored him. "I think we leave it to Ulrich and his team to sort that out. I'm no longer in the FBI, but this is an ongoing investigation. We'll talk about it around the campfire when all of this is over."

"For now are we free to go?" Armin asked.

He thought about Arun, who'd been murdered because he was helping Braun-Dean. It seemed clear from the mausoleum encounter that Carmelita knew a lot about The Steward.

Armin had come to Georgia to find justice for his brother, and it was still elusive.

Cayson reached for the piece of paper on which Kelsey had written down the account password for Ulrich. Armin knew that Kelsey had only cooperated with Ulrich because Tanaka had asked her to. Kelsey trusted Tanaka's judgment, and Armin decided that he would also.

Cayson typed it all in.

```
noGoodbYe,9297CataLina
```

They all held their breath.

The wallet unlocked.

"It works!" Cayson announced.

Armin gently squeezed Kelsey's hand. She nodded. She looked at peace. Armin wouldn't know what he would have thought of her if she had held back those two digits in the password from the FBI. He had missed the flicker in the crypt, but Kelsey had seen that the mnemonic password had a four-digit number in the middle, not two.

In the end, Kelsey had told the truth, and that had made the difference.

To Armin, it was more than that. Kelsey had passed the truth test. Would she tell the truth even if she wasn't sure of the situation? She had explained on the drive here in the FBI van that she only trusted Tanaka when it came to law enforcement.

Earlier, Ulrich had apologized for approaching Kelsey alone in her hotel room, but his explanation was that he wasn't sure whom he could trust in the bureau either, including Tanaka. They still hadn't found the supposed FBI agent at the Savannah Memorial Hospital ER who'd told Kelsey to wait at a campground—where she was eventually carjacked.

"It's over." Tanaka hugged Kelsey with her one working arm.

"Is it really?" Deshon's eyebrows rose.

"For us, yes," Tanaka replied. "I've been trying to keep Kelsey safe for a year, and at the end of it, I was hurt and Kelsey got into trouble. Thanks to Armin and Deshon, we're able to come out of this fine, and now we can all go home and get some sleep."

"Not so fast." Ulrich put his hand up.

"I'm no longer in the bureau," Tanaka said.

"I know, even though I wish you'd reconsider."

"I won't. Hu Knows is offering me a job that's easier." Tanaka turned to Deshon. "Cushier, right?"

Deshon shrugged. "You still have to work, but we'll let you recover from your broken arm first."

"See?" Tanaka smiled to Ulrich. "I'm not going back."

Ulrich nodded. "A change of scenery is good. But what I was trying to say was to Miss Kelsey here."

Kelsey straightened up. "Me?"

"Yes, ma'am. There's reward money for this."

"Oh?"

"How much?" Deshon asked for her.

"It's one point two million dollars." Ulrich

extended his hand. "Maybe it can help you move on. I know you've gone through a lot in the last four years."

"Wow." Kelsey started to cry. She was speechless.

Armin put his arm over her shoulders. "It's taxable income, but you still come out ahead."

"Armin!" Deshon said. "Can't you be nicer to her?"

"Can't you be nicer to Tanaka?" Armin had no idea why he blurted that to his direct supervisor at work.

Ulrich laughed. "I think you all need to go home and get some rest, don't you think?"

"Yeah, just leave this to Agent Ulrich and me." Cayson was busy typing.

On his laptop, Cayson reported the amount of cryptocurrency that Braun-Dean had stashed away. "At today's rate, we're looking at over eighteen billion dollars in total."

"How did it go up by a billion dollars?" The number was staggering, even for an accountant such as Armin.

"Better cash it before it bottoms out." Cayson laughed.

"It won't bring my brother back," Armin said.

Everyone was silent.

"I'm sorry." Kelsey put her hand on Armin's arm.

"Who killed my brother?" Armin asked. "All for eighteen billion dollars? What's the price of life?"

"So sorry." Tanaka and Deshon both chimed in.

Armin couldn't help but remember 1 Timothy 6:10, a warning verse to white collar criminals.

*For the love of money is a root of all kinds of evil, for which some have strayed from the faith in their greediness, and pierced themselves through with many sorrows.*

"What's this?" Cayson said as he accessed the online portal where Braun-Dean usually went to buy or sell his cryptocurrency. "How many dead man's switches did the former senator set up?"

"Two so far," Armin said.

"This might be the third." Cayson clicked on the video, and turned up the sound.

A wheezing Felix Braun-Dean appeared on the screen. He looked gaunt and had lost a lot of hair compared to the last video in the mystery house in Chattanooga.

"If you see this video, I'm probably dead," Braun-Dean said. "This is the last time I'm updating this video. I don't think I will be able to do another one."

Silence in the room.

"I'm going to try to record this in case the video disappears afterwards." Cayson went to work.

"Good idea." Ulrich came around the table to where Cayson was sitting.

Armin and Kelsey followed, and so did Tanaka and Deshon, even though the latter two did not stand next to each other.

Braun-Dean went on and on about his love for Catalina Burditt, including how he wished he'd had more spine and stood up to Roxanne instead of letting his wife end up killing the love of his life.

"The Chattanooga PD would want to see this confession." Ulrich swiped his phone and started texting. "Catalina Burditt was murdered in Chattanooga twenty years ago."

Armin couldn't see what he was texting, but he could guess.

"Don't blame Carmelita." Braun-Dean wiped away his tears.

"What did he mean?" Kelsey asked.

"Don't blame her," Braun-Dean repeated. "She's had a hard life. Mother was killed. Father died in prison. All she had left was me. I did my best. I really did. If you see her, please tell her that I did the best I could."

Braun-Dean paused. "I love both of my daughters, even though I know they're not mine. I don't know why they both think that I love the other more. Maybe

I do, maybe I don't. I just feel sorrier for Carmelita than for Paige. Paige still has her mother, you know?"

He leaned forward toward the camera. "Whatever you're doing, girls, please stop. You've already dealt with Arun. You took away my confidant. You've already put Roxanne behind bars. You--"

"Stop!" Armin shouted. "What did he just say?"

Cayson rewound the video and they watched that part again.

Armin held back tears. "Braun-Dean knew who killed my brother."

"Got it." Ulrich was on his phone again. "I'll text Atlanta PD."

Cayson resumed playing the video.

"I want to plead with my daughters to please don't cause trouble for Zuriel," Braun-Dean said. "Let her go. She has been very nice to you, putting up with me, and tolerating Roxanne's emotional abuse."

"He's not a saint himself," Tanaka said.

Kelsey said nothing. Armin held her hand.

"I want to say more, but there's an electrical storm coming this way, so I'm going to save this file and then upload it to the portal," Braun-Dean concluded. "If I feel like it, I might edit this video tomorrow or add to it. Oh wait. Tomorrow won't work out. My daughters are coming over for dinner. Alright, everybody. Time to sign off. This is me, Felix Braun-Dean, old and weary and exhausted with life."

He ended the video.

"Did you hear that?" Armin said. "Paige and Carmelita both were going over to his house for dinner. When was this video recorded?"

"I can find out." Cayson made quick work of it. "Nine days ago."

"The night before Braun-Dean drowned in the bathtub," Tanaka said.

"Maybe they drank too much, and left him afterwards," Deshon suggested. "He could've accidentally drowned."

"That wouldn't have explained the surveillance video," Armin said. "Remember the false arrest warrant for Kelsey?"

Cayson nodded. "We found out the video was AI, but it was generated using a real person. Potentially Paige."

"But who sent out the video to the news media?" Armin wondered. "Carmelita, perhaps?"

Kelsey agreed. "After all, back at the mausoleum, she didn't sound like she loved her non-biological sister very much. She seemed competitive and felt that Braun-Dean had treated Paige better."

"Make a copy of the video for me," Ulrich ordered Cayson. "I'm sending a copy of it to the Marietta PD."

"This mess has tentacles." Deshon shook his head.

"Out of our hands." Tanaka turned to Ulrich. "Your problem now."

Armin blinked. Of all the people in the investigation, it had to be Braun-Dean who ended up spotlighting his daughters as the prime suspects. As long as Armin had an answer regarding his brother's murder, he would be satisfied, and his parents could finally have a good night's sleep after three years of not knowing.

"If you all hadn't found the recovery passphrase and the account password, we would never have triggered this final video from Braun-Dean," Cayson said.

Kelsey cleared her throat. "Which is why the reward money needs to be shared among us."

"Don't include me," Tanaka said. "I did most of the work while I had a badge."

"The one who needs it most is Kelsey," Deshon said. "At this moment, she has no job, no house, no car."

"I don't need the money," Armin said.

"We'll sort it out later." Ulrich got off his phone. "I've notified three PDs about three crime scenes in their jurisdiction—including that cold case in Chattanooga. This is going to be an interesting year, and January isn't even over yet."

Tanaka stretched her working arm. "I've booked a

room at the same hotel as Kelsey, so if someone can give us a ride, it would be appreciated."

"You mean me, right?" Deshon asked. "After all, I'm the one with a vehicle. We left your rental and Armin's van at the Hu Knows parking lot last night."

"I can give you two ladies a ride back to the hotel," Ulrich said.

Kelsey was still holding Armin's hand, so he figured she didn't want to let go just yet.

"Actually, Kelsey and I have something to talk about, so we'll go back to the office with Deshon." Armin was happy to see Kelsey nod slightly to him. "I'll give her a ride back to the hotel after breakfast."

"Breakfast? Didn't you just eat?" Deshon wasn't getting the message.

"Ulrich, I'm ready to go." Tanaka patted Kelsey's shoulder. "Talk with you later. Good job the last couple of days."

"Thank God for teamwork." Kelsey hugged Tanaka.

Armin and Kelsey followed Deshon to the Humvee outside.

"Sorry for making you stay up longer." Armin opened the door for Kelsey to get into the backseat. "I wanted to see you."

"I know. We haven't had any time alone."

Armin buckled in on the front passenger seat, as

Deshon drove them away from the Binary Systems office. They hardly spoke on the thirty-minute drive to the Hu Knows office.

To stay awake, Deshon turned on some classical music, but Armin dozed off anyway. He woke up a couple of times to hearing Deshon laugh aloud at something Kelsey said. Those two were wide awake.

"I look forward to working with you." Deshon wiped tears from his eyes. "We just need to make sure you never have to exit out of a camper van again."

"I know, right. If not for Armin and Earl, I don't know what might have happened to me. They arrived just in time and called 9 1 1."

"Do you know who the carjacker worked for?"

Kelsey shrugged. "Tanaka said he hasn't confessed yet, but the possibilities are not endless. Considering that the two fake cops worked for The Steward, and so did Nicholas and Zinnia, there's a possibility that the carjacker also worked for The Steward. After all, they had the same modus operandi. They tried to scare me, but not kill me."

"Someone is protecting you."

"God."

Kelsey replied so quickly that it warmed Armin's heart knowing that she was growing in grace as a Christian. The thought was still on his mind when they arrived at the Hu Knows office.

"Are y'all going upstairs?" Deshon pulled up next to Armin's van.

"No," Kelsey said. "I think Armin wants to go to breakfast. You want to come with us?"

"Oh no no no." Deshon put the Humvee in park. "I'm going home to sleep for two days."

"All right. Thank you." Armin got out of the Humvee.

"To be on the safe side, I'll wait here until you two get inside the van and lock the doors."

"There's twenty-four-hour security here, remember?" Armin waved to a security vehicle parked nearby. The security guard driving it waved back.

"Yes, I see George over there." Deshon put his vehicle in gear. "Then I'll let you two go. Let's take the day off, and I'll see you tomorrow."

"Sounds good. Thanks and drive safely." Armin appreciated Deshon's care, but was it necessary now that the bad players had been arrested? Still, he understood the concern.

Kelsey walked around the van to the passenger side, and Armin caught up with her. He unlocked the van, but instead of opening the door for her, he held her hands in his.

"I'm going to miss you when you go back to your hotel and I go home."

"We have time to talk over breakfast, don't we?"

"I suppose. I just want to see you every day for the rest of my life." Armin inched toward her.

"Is that even possible?" Kelsey asked. "Hu Knows might require you to travel, and then we'd be separated, even if it's just for a day or two. So we won't always..."

"Come to work at Hu Knows, and we'll travel together."

"What can I do?"

"We need an office manager, someone who can write reports."

"I can do that."

"Good."

"But I also want to go to college and study investigative journalism," Kelsey said. "With God's help, I will go forth."

"I'll support you."

"Thank you, but I need to learn to be independent. The reward money will help, but I can also get a day job."

Armin's heart warmed. He felt proud of how far Kelsey had come from just a year ago when they had first made contact with each other. At that time, she had been unsure of herself, unable to find her footing in life, and unclear about her future path.

Now she sounded confident, and showed that she was truly a different person from the Zuriel she had been for three long years. Whether Armin's parents agreed or not, he knew that this is the woman he wanted to be with for the rest of his life.

"You look like you want a hug but won't initiate it." Kelsey pulled him closer.

"You read my mind."

Without another word, Kelsey hugged him tightly. Then she lifted her head and pecked him on the cheek.

"Do that again," Armin whispered.

Kelsey didn't comply with his request. Instead, she cupped his face in her palms. Her hands were cold, but Armin didn't care.

Her lips found his, and they kissed away the morning cold at the dawn of a brand new day.

# EPILOGUE

Fifteen months later, The Steward was still at large, but the Braun-Dean money laundering case had been largely resolved. The FBI white-collar crime division had confiscated the now eighteen billion dollars worth of bitcoins that Felix Braun-Dean had squirreled away. Roxanne Braun-Dean confessed to money laundering in exchange for lighter sentences for her two daughters.

Armin was relieved that Kelsey's life was out of danger, but he felt sorry for the Braun-Dean family's dysfunction. Patricide was no small matter, and the two daughters—one a stepdaughter to Braun-Dean and the other adopted—had done an unspeakable crime.

Paige and Carmelita revealed that they had gone to visit Braun-Dean at his Marietta retreat expressly to access his hardware wallet. Instead of giving them what they wanted, Braun-Dean mocked them and told them he had removed them from his will. The two sisters tortured him and then drowned him in the bathtub.

Paige was the actress in the surveillance video. Carmelita hired AI creators to deep fake her face, morphing it into Kelsey's.

"How could they even think the money was rightfully theirs?" Armin thought aloud at his desk at the Hu Knows Atlanta office.

Carmelita confessed that she had summoned The Steward, but she had no idea who the person was. Back at the mausoleum in Braun-Dean's lakeside home in Chattanooga, Carmelita had let it slip that The Steward might be a woman. However, Armin wondered if it might be more than one person. Regardless, it wasn't his problem anymore.

He was happy that he and Kelsey had gotten out of the mess alive and well. With a white-collar investigative job at Hu Knows, Armin felt that he had a new career he could enjoy. Not that he hadn't liked his CPA job in South Carolina. However, after his brother had died, Armin needed a change of scenery.

In Atlanta, he enjoyed working for Deshon and with Kelsey. Perhaps later, their office might expand, but he liked it quite the way it was now.

Armin was happy that Kelsey decided to work at Hu Knows, even though she didn't have to. The FBI had sent her the reward money for her work in the Braun-Dean case. She had enough funds to pay for four years of college. However, she wanted to save up to buy a house.

As for transportation, Armin had bought her a car she could drive from her rental apartment to school and work.

Kelsey didn't want to just go to school and see Armin after work hours. She wanted to be with Armin during the day too, and Deshon needed an office manager. Kelsey didn't want another person—especially a single woman—taking the job.

Armin chuckled as he recalled her momentary jealousy. He felt that he belonged to her and only her.

In the Hu Knows office, Armin had moved from the corner to a bigger space where he could finally walk around the desk. Instead of a wall, he had a good view of not only the front door, but also the front desk, where Kelsey worked part time during the school year while she attended Georgia State University to study journalism.

The last day of April was also the last day of Kelsey's spring semester final examinations, and thus the end of her freshman year in college. Armin had been on pins and needles all morning, waiting for Kelsey to finish her exams and show up at work.

He was ready. He had been ready since their first kiss back in January of the year before, and had prayed about this many times since then.

Glancing at the door and seeing no one, Armin placed a palm on his own chest and willed himself to calm down. He would know if this was God's will for him and Kelsey if she said yes.

*Your will be done, Lord.*

If Kelsey said no, then Armin would live with that. He could still see her every day at work, especially all summer when she would be working full time.

He eyed the small red velvet box on his table. He had purposefully not bought a big diamond ring because he wanted Kelsey to wear it to class, but he was afraid she'd lose it in downtown Atlanta. Sure, the ring was insured, but he didn't want her to be upset about it.

At the end of his long and wrangling decision-making, Armin decided that he'd give Kelsey just one engagement ring to rule them all.

If she wanted to find an everyday engagement ring to wear to work and school, he would take her to shop for a set of couple's rings that she could lose and it wouldn't put him out by seven figures.

Today's ring was a brilliant three-million-dollar

round diamond that he'd bought at the Tiffany store at Phillips Plaza across the street from Lenox Square Mall in Buckhead. This one, he wanted Kelsey to wear on their wedding day.

*Maybe I'm overthinking this.*

Kelsey might say no.

His stomach churned.

*Please don't say no.*

What if Kelsey wanted to pick her own engagement ring? Well, then it wouldn't be a surprise proposal, would it?

Armin got up from his chair and made his way to Kelsey's desk, where a monitor off to one side of the workstation showed the hallway outside, the only entrance into the Hu Knows office. Kelsey wasn't in charge of security, but Deshon wanted to keep the video live so that they could see who entered and left the office.

Speaking of Deshon, Armin reminded himself that he had to pick him up from the Atlanta airport the next day. Deshon had gone to Greece to have a meeting with the big boss, Helen Hu. Once a year, the top directors of the private investigative firm met for a few days to discuss the company. Hu Knows was still privately owned by Helen and her mother, but the latter was hoping to sell her shares back to Helen's sister, Sabine, who wasn't in the business.

Armin's cell phone rang before he could sit down in Kelsey's chair to look at the security monitor.

"Hey man." Armin walked back to his desk. "Are you at the airport yet?"

"Packing now." Deshon was on audio only. "I have a meeting with Hugo in Brussels, and then I'll be home in Atlanta. You still picking me up?"

"Yeah, taking your Humvee and letting you pay for gas."

Deshon laughed. "You look cooler when you drive my Humvee than when you drive your family van."

"Kelsey doesn't care either way."

"I know she doesn't." Deshon paused. "Speaking of Kelsey, I'm sending her to Tokyo to meet up with Ruby."

"When?" Armin knew right away he wanted to go with Kelsey, even if he had to pay his own way. After all, he had enough money earned from his cryptocurrency investment to take Kelsey traveling—although he'd made a big dent in his savings by splurging on the diamond ring.

"Tonight. Didn't she finish her finals this morning?" Clearly, Deshon remembered Kelsey's school schedule. "This afternoon, I need one of you to go to Binary Systems to pick up a USB drive from Cayson."

Half an hour drive. Armin wanted to volunteer.

"Then Kelsey is going to fly out tonight and hand it over to Ruby," Deshon said.

Ruby Tanaka hadn't returned to the FBI. She now freelanced like Jonathan. Her first contract assignment was with Hu Knows, but she would've done it on her own. She wanted to go after The Steward, who was rumored to be attending an auction in Japan.

"You sure you can't just send it on a VPN or tunnel or something?" Armin asked.

There were pros and cons to digital data transfers, but it would save time and money.

"Not this one." Deshon switched from audio to video. He was wearing a white T-shirt and a pair of jeans.

"But you're talking to me on the phone, telling me about the USB drive," Armin reminded him.

"Oh, the irony of it." Deshon laughed. "Trust me. I have my reasons."

Armin didn't want to think too much about this either, but his guess was that Deshon had taken into consideration that a third party might be listening on both ends of the conversation.

Which meant that Kelsey could be in danger if she traveled alone.

"I can go with her," Armin volunteered.

"Hu Knows won't pay for two people to deliver one USB drive, you know?"

"I'll take a week of vacation—or however many days you need her to be in Japan."

"You're kinda clingy, aren't you?" Deshon's eyebrows rose. "Something I don't know?"

"We've been dating."

"I know that, but seems like you're escalating it."

*Escalating it?*

"Escalating what?" The female voice joining the conversation made Armin spin around in his chair.

Kelsey closed the office door behind her. Standing there, in a pretty floral dress and platform sandals, she looked like she was ready to be proposed to. Her hair was tied up in a ponytail, and she had very little or no makeup on.

She put down her purse on her desk, and walked toward Armin, smiling.

Armin cleared his throat. "Good morning, Kelsey."

"It's after twelve o'clock." She pointed to the clock on the wall above her desk. She'd hung that one up so that everyone could be mindful of their time at work.

"Congratulations on finishing your freshman year!" Armin high-fived Kelsey.

"Yeah, congrats!" Deshon said over Armin's phone.

Kelsey leaned over to see who was on the screen. She waved. "Hey Deshon!"

Deshon waved back.

"What time is it over there?" Kelsey asked.

"Seven p.m. I'm seven hours ahead of you. Should've taken a nap this afternoon, but I guess I'll sleep on the short flight to Brussels." Deshon sat down on his hotel bed. "Armin, let me talk to Kelsey for a minute."

Armin handed his phone over to Kelsey.

Deshon told Kesley what he'd already said to Armin. "All expenses paid."

Kelsey looked excited. "I'll go."

"You don't have a choice since this is work. Remember the 'some travel' part of your work contract?"

Kelsey nodded.

"I'm not going to outsource this. Jonathan is unavailable. I have a problem to solve next week. Helen is pregnant and on bed rest—even though she's still working. Everyone else is too busy to go. But you —" Deshon pointed at the camera. "You're on summer break from school and your full-time work starts right now, so your first assignment is to go to Tokyo for four days. I'll email you the details. You fly out tonight. Book the tickets as soon as we get off the phone."

Kelsey nodded. "I can do that."

"I want to go too. I can use my vacation time," Armin said quietly. "After all, Hu Knows employees are always ready so that we can go anywhere at a moment's notice. Both of our overnight carry-ons are already in my van."

"You've saved up your vacation, but you sure you want to do this on your own time?" Deshon asked.

Armin nodded. "Personally, I don't want Kelsey to travel by herself. The Steward is still at large, remember? I know Ruby prefers to work alone, but she might be happy to see familiar faces."

"Good point." Deshon thought quickly. "Let's do this. Both of you can go on company time, but only for four days."

"Thank you." Armin would've paid his own way, but if Deshon offered a free ticket and a hotel room, he'd take them.

"I guess I'll be alone in the office the rest of the week, all by myself."

"Oh cue the violin, why don't you?" Armin laughed.

"If Armin and I are both going to Tokyo tonight, who will pick you up from the airport tomorrow afternoon?" Kelsey asked.

"Good question," Deshon replied before Armin did. "Just drive my Humvee tonight and park at the overnight parking. Let me know the exact spot so that I can find it when I arrive. I have the spare key, and I can drive myself home tomorrow."

"That works," Armin and Kelsey said together.

Armin was amused that they were in sync.

"Listen, I have to run. I haven't had dinner yet, and it's lunchtime for you." Deshon said a quick goodbye.

Armin was silent after he hung up. He didn't want to show his worry about Kelsey's safety. Ruby Tanaka could be a maverick, and he didn't want Kelsey near her. In their last project together, Kelsey had gone through a lot.

"Don't worry." Kelsey rubbed his shoulders. "I'll be fine. I know how to handle weapons—even though I don't expect I'll need to overseas—and I know Krav Maga. Remember that Nicholas taught me to protect myself for three years in my past profession."

Nicholas Bay.

She'd mentioned his name so casually. Armin studied her face. What was this woman thinking right now?

"What's on my mind, you wonder?" Kelsey patted his shoulders and then stepped away.

Armin was convinced that they should take personality tests soon because they seemed to think alike a lot of times. "Tell me."

"Lunch, for one. I didn't eat in the campus cafeteria because we'd made plans to go out to lunch at the Indian place. Now we have to wait a bit until after I book our plane tickets."

"And?" Armin pried. He didn't want to say

Nicholas's name, but she had brought it up. "What else crossed your mind?"

"Nothing escapes you, does it?" Kelsey smiled.

*I don't want you to escape me.*

"On the way here, I heard on the news that Nicholas still refuses to say who The Steward is." Kelsey walked back to her desk, and Armin followed—with the velvet box in a hand behind his back.

"He took responsibility for a lot of things, including your carjacking, the fake traffic stop, our abductions."

Kelsey sat down in her office chair and logged into her computer. "I think he's protecting somebody."

"My thoughts exactly." Armin remained standing, watching Kelsey access their default online travel agency to book two round trip tickets to Tokyo. "Is he protecting The Steward?"

"Or someone closer." Kelsey scrolled through the search results. "The Steward may not even be a real person."

Armin nodded. "With deep fake AI nowadays, that might be true. Or The Steward could be a team of unknown entities."

"That too. Regardless, Tanaka's—I mean Ruby's—work in Japan might be in vain." Kelsey sighed. "She still believes that The Steward is one real person."

"Do you?"

"I don't know."

"I don't either."

"Knowing Nicholas as long as I have, I suspect that he's exchanging his own life and freedom to keep someone else out of jail," Kelsey said.

"That's for the FBI and police to find out."

"Hmm... The next flight out to Tokyo is midnight." Kelsey scrolled through a list.

She didn't turn to see what Armin was doing. He was getting nervous standing behind Kelsey.

"Midnight is fine," he said.

"Since it's an international flight, I'd like to be at the airport three hours early."

"Fine. That gives us enough time to run up to Alpharetta to pick up the USB drive." Armin wondered whether he should volunteer to drive to the Binary Systems office.

"That shouldn't take long. One of us can go see Cayson."

"We need to give ourselves enough time to drive through rush hour traffic back and forth. The same goes for the airport drive. Plus, we have to find an overnight parking spot, and then wait for a shuttle to take us to the terminal."

"There goes the rest of today." Kelsey nodded. "All that work, and we'll be back in four days. No time to sightsee."

"Then our work is done and we can move on to the next project," Armin said.

"And what project might that be?" Kelsey finished typing and turned around in her chair. She crossed her legs.

She looked feminine, and Armin's heart fluttered a bit. He couldn't speak. All he could do was go down on one knee.

Kelsey gasped. She reached for Armin. "Are you okay? Is your knee giving out?"

Armin laughed as he loosened his grip on the red box he'd been holding behind his back, and brought it around to show to Kelsey. He opened the box, revealing the sparkling diamond ring.

"Kelsey..." He couldn't continue because she started to cry. "No, no. Please don't cry."

"Tears of happiness, Armin."

"Oh. Then please make me the happiest man in the world by marrying me, Kelsey Murphy." He had forgotten all the rest of what he had rehearsed over the months.

"Have you prayed about it and sought God's counsel?" Kelsey asked quietly.

"Yes, ma'am." Armin couldn't recall how many times he'd prayed. "I want us to love each other as Christ loves the church. You heard what Pastor Kim preached at church about biblical marriages. I want that for us. Our holy matrimony and marriage will be undefiled. You are the only woman for me for the rest of my life. God will hold me accountable for how I treat you. I want to be the biblical husband that Jesus talked about in Ephesians 5:21."

*Husbands, love your wives, just as Christ also loved the church and gave Himself for her.*

"But your parents might still..." Kelsey's voice cracked.

"They might still what?" Armin held her hand. "You're not marrying them. Ephesians 5:31 says that only you and I would be married to each other."

*For this reason a man shall leave his father and mother and be joined to his wife, and the two shall become one flesh.*

"I talked to them last month," Armin added.

Kelsey nodded. "Yes, you told me. That was when you flew Arun's ashes back to Mumbai."

It was Armin's turn to have teary eyes. He wished that Arun's grave would still be in Atlanta, but their parents wanted him to be buried in the land of his birth. So Armin flew his brother's ashes home in an urn.

On the entire flight from Atlanta to Mumbai, with a couple of layovers along the way, Armin regretted heavily not spending more time with Arun to talk about matters pertaining to life and death, to salvation, to eternity. It was all too late now as Arun had repeatedly rejected Christ while he'd been alive.

Armin wasn't sure how it would go when he arrived in Mumbai, especially as he couldn't participate in any non-Christian burial ceremony or rituals. He was the only Christian in the entire family.

However, the trip was not all negative. Armin's sister-in-law was still grieving, but also focusing on raising Arun's daughter as a single mother. Everyone was grateful that the videos of her with a "boyfriend" were all fake.

The length that The Steward had gone to mess with the Dhillon family made Armin suspect that they hadn't seen the last of the crypto king yet.

Still, Armin's trip to India had a positive outcome in the end.

"Remember that Mother has agreed to let me make my own life choice," Armin said. "She gave me her blanket approval. She said it would be what Arun would've advised her to do. Father goes along with everything Mother says."

Tears puddled in Kelsey's eyes. "If I marry, I marry for life, you know."

"I know." Armin knew that once he married her, he wouldn't want to be separated from her either.

*Until death do us part.*

"This is my first and last marriage," Armin said.

"Mine too." Kelsey wiped her tears. "You know my past."

"Jesus Christ has washed away all your sins and mine too," Armin reminded her.

"Yes, I'm saved in Christ." Kelsey paused.

Armin waited.

"However, I'd rather not wear pure white at the wedding." Kelsey seemed to be reminding Armin of her past. "I think I would like ivory or cream or blush."

"Whatever color you prefer is fine with me. As long as we marry, you can wear anything you want."

She nodded slowly.

Armin didn't want to hurry her along. He gave her time to think. She had to be sure she wanted to be with him for the rest of her life—or his, if she lived longer than he did.

But he wanted her to think fast so that he could take her out to lunch to celebrate. One good thing about working at Hu Knows was that lunch was one hour at any hour. If they ended up going to lunch at one o'clock, then they had until two o'clock to get back to the office to resume work.

However, Armin realized he was taking up their lunch time with this proposal.

"I've prayed about us too," Kelsey finally said. "God has delivered me through many sufferings in my life. He brought different people to help me along the way. And then He brought you to walk with me though the valleys of the shadow of death."

"And in the sunshine too. God is good to us."

"All the time." Kelsey smiled. "I think you're the one."

"The only one you'll ever marry?" Armin's eyes brightened.

Kelsey nodded, and extended her left hand.

"For the record, just so we're clear on this and have no doubt... Will you marry me and only me, Kelsey Anna Murphy?" Armin asked.

"Yes, I will marry you and only you, Armin Dhillon." Kelsey smiled so sweetly that Armin's heart melted in the air-conditioned office.

Armin put the engagement ring on Kelsey's finger, drew her to her feet, ignored all office protocols, and kissed his future wife.

Dear Reader:

Thank you for reading *Never a Fugitive* (Defender Sweethearts Book 3). I hope you've enjoyed this Christian Romantic Suspense novel. It was hard for me to write about Kelsey Murphy because she had a messy past prior to salvation. I had no reference point to write about her, no experiences in my life that came close to her situation, and no one I know to ask research questions. However, I do know what the Bible says about sin of any kind, and I also know that God can heal anyone from any sin—past, present, and future. Praise the Lord that the blood of Christ has cleansed Kelsey. She has a new life going forward.

Toward the end of *Never a Fugitive*, I established that former FBI Special Agent Ruby Tanaka has some unfinished business with a mysterious cryptocurrency trader named The Steward. The next novel, *Always a Maverick* (Defender Sweethearts Book 4), is Ruby's story. Sign up for my newsletter to be notified when *Always a Maverick* is published.

*Always a Maverick*
JanThompson.com/maverick

Ruby has also appeared as a guest character in *Look for Me* (Vacation Sweethearts Book 4).

*Look for Me*
JanThompson.com/look

Private Investigator Deshon Kernaghan will also have his own story in *Always a Champion* (Defender Sweethearts Book 5). He has previously appeared in *Never a Traitor* (Defender Sweethearts Book 1), in which he provided assistance for Earl and Sienna in Atlanta. That was before Helen Hu, their boss, decided to build a new branch office in Atlanta with Deshon in charge.

*Always a Champion*
JanThompson.com/champion

In *Never a Fugitive,* we met Private Investigator Earl Young briefly before he left for the hospital to be with his wife in labor. Earl and Sienna met in *Never a Traitor* (Defender Sweethearts Book 1). What began as a white collar crime turned deadly for people around whistleblower Sienna Halstead.

*Never a Traitor*
JanThompson.com/traitor

Helen Hu, the co-owner of Hu Knows, had her own European adventure with a reformed art thief (was he really?) in *Once a Thief* (Protector Sweethearts Book 1).

*Once a Thief*
JanThompson.com/thief

Hacker Cayson Yang, who helped to recover the cryptocurrencies in *Never a Fugitive*, was in a near-death experience in *Zero Sum* (Binary Hackers Book 1). This series is a near-future Christian suspense series.

*Zero Sum*
JanThompson.com/sum

To be notified when new books are published or when book sales happen, sign up for my mailing list. I send out newsletters nearly every week.

Join Jan Thompson's Mailing List
JanThompson.com/newsletter

# HAVE YOU READ NEVER A TRAITOR?
## DEFENDER SWEETHEARTS BOOK 1

A paranoid whistleblower on her last task. A private investigator posing as her fake boyfriend. An international conglomerate that eliminates its enemies.

Calling for help...

Administrative Assistant Sienna Halstead has one last task to do for the FBI Criminal Investigative Division before she can quit her corporate job and disappear. Scared that the evidence against the international conglomerate she works for is not sufficient, paranoid Sienna starts to make mistakes. When she calls Hu Knows, Inc., for help, Helen Hu sends the no-nonsense Earl into her chaotic world.

Cashing in on overtime pay...

The last thing Private Investigator Earl Young expects to do on his week off is to pose as a fake boyfriend to one of two whistleblowers at a business convention, although the former Special Ops soldier is confident he can handle any task his employer assigns to him. Besides, he gets to stay at a five-star hotel and eat for free.

Crossing the line...

Earl's driving need to solve problems forces him to work alongside Sienna as she draws him deeper into her corporate world of secrets and subterfuge. The more time they spend time together, the more Earl feels attracted to Sienna, and forgets that he is only her bodyguard. When Sienna's life is endangered, how far will Earl go to protect her?

*Never a Traitor* is book 1 in *USA Today* bestselling author Jan Thompson's Defender Sweethearts Christian romantic suspense collection, a sister series to Protector Sweethearts. While the heroes in Protector Sweethearts search for lost treasures and lost people, the Defender Sweethearts novels focus on protecting the helpless and hopeless. The main characters in Defender Sweethearts come from the supporting cast in Protector Sweethearts.

*Never a Traitor* (Defender Sweethearts Book 1)
JanThompson.com/traitor

Defender Sweethearts
JanThompson.com/defender

For Book News from Jan Thompson:
JanThompson.com/newsletter

# NEVER A TRAITOR SNEAK PEEK (CHAPTER 1)

## DEFENDER SWEETHEARTS BOOK 1

Sienna Halstead regretted letting Private Investigator Earl Young tag along with her to visit a former coworker. Earl's presence caused Dana Nesbitt to be extra nervous, and now Sienna couldn't get her to talk in detail about what she had overheard their CEO say, anything that could be useful to FBI investigations.

"I was only the accountant," Dana said, in between deep puffs of smoke. "He didn't have to fire me. I wouldn't have talked."

Sitting in a worn armchair across from the shabby couch, Sienna held her breath and prayed that her lungs would survive the conversation. Where was her mask when she needed it?

She could see the headlines now.

*Administrative assistant died from smoke inhalation. Buried in an unmarked grave. Case unsolved.*

Earl was fortunate, then. Sienna had sent him outside to wait in the great outdoors so that Dana could speak freely inside her own home.

Sienna felt bad that she had to lie to Dana about her relationship with Earl. No, he wasn't really her boyfriend, but the ruse was necessary to prevent Dana or Sienna or anyone else from getting killed. Technically, neither Sienna nor Earl had said they were an item. They simply let Dana put two and two together without correcting her.

Dissimulation was a form of lying, nonetheless.

Sienna closed her eyes. She wanted this entire project to be over as soon as possible so she could leave the company and disappear. She was no longer impressed by the size and scope of Gavard Owens Oppenheimer Properties or by the quiet and studious Finnegan Ford, the CEO and half brother of Zachary Gavard, the smooth-talking front man of GOOP.

Dana lit another cigarette and shrugged. "Why am I so worried? Everyone sleeps with him."

Sienna prayed for the right words to say. Mom's words came to mind.

*When in doubt, speak the truth.*

"I didn't," Sienna said.

"You're different." Dana laughed nervously. "You're religious. Finnegan is scared of you."

"He told you that?"

"I could tell. He would never touch you like he touched everyone else..." Dana started to cry. "I wish I never..."

"Oh, Dana." Sienna sprung up from her armchair to get to Dana, and heard a rip. She looked down to find her linen pants torn on one side, part of the fabric stuck at the end of a giant spring that had somehow shot out of the threadbare armchair. "Whoa."

She checked her thigh to see if there was a cut—and whether she needed a tetanus shot.

Thank God there was no cut.

She tugged her pants away from the spring, and hobbled around the chipped coffee table, her arms waving away the smoke until she found the petite and helpless Dana on the couch, weeping.

"Should I keep the baby?" Dana's voice was tinged

with regret and anger and probably a million other emotions.

Sienna wondered how a pastor's kid such as Dana could turn out this way. Sienna prayed for the right words to say to her friend.

"Shhh." That was all that came out of her mouth as she sat there, holding smoky Dana in her arms—

*Wait a minute.*

"You shouldn't smoke if you're carrying a baby." Okay, wrong words. She should be more diplomatic.

"Don't tell me what to do!" Dana pulled away from Sienna's arms.

Sienna blinked in the smoke, her eyes stinging. She was still partly holding her breath, and now she felt dizzy.

*I have to get out of here.*

However, she could not ask Dana to take a walk with her. It was too dangerous for Dana to be outdoors. In fact, she had to leave town and go somewhere safe.

"Can you get out of town for a few days until we figure out what's going on?" Sienna coughed. She had read somewhere that secondary smoke was really bad.

"Where do I go?"

"Somewhere nobody would find you." Sienna lifted the collar of her blouse over her nose.

Dana's eyebrows shot up. "You mean like Alaska or Hawaii? Or maybe the Amalfi Coast?"

"I was thinking someplace more affordable."

"Like where?"

"I don't know, but you can't stay here."

"Here is all I can afford." Dana jammed the rest of her cigarette in the tray, bending it out of shape. "He won't give me any more money."

"You asked him?" As in blackmail?

Dana barely nodded.

"Did you tell him about the child?" Sienna asked.

"Before I left the company."

"What did he say?"

"That's a perk for employees only." Dana made a face. "He was trying to rub it in. Told me in no uncertain terms that I shouldn't have quit."

It had been sudden. Even Sienna didn't know about it until the next day when she went to work and saw Dana's desk cleaned out. It took Sienna a week to find Dana hiding away in this rat hole.

She had to give Earl credit for tracking down Dana.

"I can't believe he moved on to Genevieve." Dana reached for her cigarettes.

Sienna pushed the lighter away. "Genevieve in the mailroom?"

"Is there another woman with repeated wardrobe malfunctions in front of every senior staffer?"

"Well..." Sienna prayed for mercy. She had made

up her mind that as soon as this final project was over, she would leave the company. It was a cesspool of sin, as Uncle Tabbebo had called GOOP. He wanted her to leave the company and put her college degree to better use.

However, the FBI Special Agent had told her that if she did this one thing for them, it would shut down GOOP forever. And they would put her in the Federal Witness Security Program, in which she would never have to worry about looking over her shoulder for the rest of her life.

Unfortunately, it also meant she would not see Mom and Uncle Tabbebo again. They would be devastated.

Unless she could take down GOOP anonymously.

Which was where Dana came in.

Sienna's only hope shook her head. "I should've known. Why didn't you tell me he was no good?"

"I did. Countless times."

"I guess I wasn't listening."

"No." Sienna wanted to ask Dana how Mr. Ford had seduced her, but this wasn't the right time.

Well, she didn't have to ask.

"I loved his offers. Nights in five-star hotels. Private jets. Weekends on his yacht. Dining with his friends. I loved it all."

"What friends did he have dinner with?" Sienna asked.

"High rollers, investors, and in one case, even his brother showed up."

"You mean Mr. Gavard?" Bingo.

"I know, right? His brother never showed up at any of Finnegan's events. But that one time two months ago..." Dana straightened up. "He was staring at me the whole time. You know how we hate each other?"

"Yeah, even though you're his accountant too."

"Well, I don't do more than I have to." Dana sighed.

"You were saying that Mr. Gavard showed up on the yacht. Did he get into an argument with his brother?"

"It wasn't like that. Although it was strange that he disappeared with Finnegan into our stateroom for what seemed like hours."

"Stateroom?" Sienna asked. "So this was on his superyacht?"

"Actually, let me correct myself. They were in our suite. Finnegan had to remind me a lot that staterooms are smaller. Our suite took up the entire upper floor of the yacht."

"Wow."

"I know, right? I mean what do you expect? The yacht is worth a hundred million dollars."

"No way." Sienna couldn't imagine. "Must be souped up."

Dana nodded. "It even has a helipad. That's how Zachary flew in on a chopper. Can you believe it? Landed right on top of the yacht. That was how he left too. Didn't stay for dinner."

"What did they talk about?" Sienna asked.

Dana gave her a look. "I really like his wife."

"His wife?"

Why had Dana brought up Gavard's wife at all? Celestia Gavard had nothing to do with the day-to-day operations at her husband's company, as far as Sienna knew. She was a silent partner—she poured her inheritance money into it—but that was all.

Dana pursed her lips.

"So you do know more about what's happening than you're letting on," Sienna said.

"Probably why I got fired." Dana sniffled.

"You said the brothers talked privately." Sienna wondered if she should record this conversation, but this was Dana, her friend, who had gone through so much in the last two months that she deserved some privacy.

Perhaps Sienna could gain Dana's trust and then have her repeat whatever it was she was about to say.

Instead, Dana reached below her collar and pulled out her necklace. At the end of the necklace was a pendant that looked like a silver whistle. She took the necklace off and handed it to Sienna.

"What is this?" Sienna looked at the whistle.

"I'm giving it to you."

"Me?"

"Happy belated birthday, Sienna."

"That's thoughtful of you." Sienna had no idea what was swirling in Dana's head. She wondered if she could go around wearing a whistle on her neck.

"It's sterling silver. Sorry it's not gold."

"I don't care." Sienna put it around her own neck.

Dana expelled a breath. "That felt better."

"What felt better?"

"It was so heavy around my neck. Like a noose, you know?"

"This whistle?" Sienna asked.

Dana nodded. "Please keep it for me?"

"I thought it was a gift."

"Yes. It's yours now. But it's also my insurance."

"What are you talking about?" The last thing Sienna wanted was to be responsible for something that wasn't her own. "What is this? Does it even work?"

"It works."

And another last thing Sienna wanted was someone else's used whistle.

"I'll explain later." Dana touched her stomach. She

got up, drew a deep breath. "I'm thirsty again. Do pregnant people get thirsty all the time?"

"I have no idea." Still staring at the whistle, Sienna had second thoughts about the gift.

Dana opened an old refrigerator in her studio kitchen. Behind her, a farmhouse sink backed up against a wall with a small window. Outside the window, there was a fence that seemed to be too close to the ramshackle house. The sun was setting and the fence looked dark and weary.

"Would you like some water?" Dana asked.

"Yes." But she almost said no, when she saw Dana pour unfiltered water from the sink faucet into a plastic cup she had picked up from the countertop.

Was that cup even washed?

Sienna was going to put the necklace into her crossbody bag when she realized she didn't have it with her. She must have left it in Earl's SUV, together with her phone and pepper spray inside.

She was about to put the necklace into the pocket of her ripped pants when she heard shattering glass.

Her eyes snapped up just as Dana collapsed to the ground, the plastic cup bouncing off the old linoleum floor. The kitchen faucet was still running. The window above the sink looked broken.

"Dana!" Sienna gasped as the house went silent.

Sienna threw herself on the ugly green rug

between the coffee table and the couch, and held her breath. She wished she had her phone with her.

She could not call Earl. Could not call 911.

The only Person she could call was God.

*Help me, Jesus!*

From the corner of her eye, she saw someone move in the hallway between the kitchen and the bedroom. She looked up to see the figure moving toward her, dressed in black from head to toe, with a ski mask and goggles.

Sienna froze when she saw the silencer pointed in her direction.

"Give it to me." It was a low male voice.

He sounded like he could hurt her.

"Give what?" Sienna bravely asked.

"What she gave to you."

"She was getting me water."

Ninja grunted. "You're not stupid."

"Thank you for the vote of confidence."

He inched closer. "Now."

"I don't know what you're—"

A blast blew Ninja back, his weapon flying out of his hand. He landed on the green carpet, blood seeping out of his ski mask. He went still.

Sienna screamed.

~

JAN THOMPSON

*Never a Traitor* (Defender Sweethearts Book 1)
JanThompson.com/traitor

Defender Sweethearts
JanThompson.com/defender

For Book News from Jan Thompson:
JanThompson.com/newsletter

# ACKNOWLEDGMENTS

Many thanks to my Georgia Press publishing team for keeping up with my writing schedule.

Thank you to editor Kim Kemery for editing and proofreading this novel.

A special thank you to my loyal readers who have been with me from the beginning of my publishing career. You've waited patiently for me to write my books, and you never let up over the years. May God bless you!

Thank you to these first responders for answering my many questions about real life scenarios. All mistakes are mine.

- Firefighter Captain Ken Shoemaker, about vehicle extrications, rescue protocols and tools.
- Police detective and thriller novelist Dony

Jay and retired police officer and author Wesley Harris, about police procedurals.

- ER nurse Jerrid Edgington, about EMT and paramedic at crime scenes.

For IT fact checking, thank you to my husband, who was also my classmate back in the Computer Science department at the University of Georgia last century. Yes, we do speak the same love language: computer code!

I am grateful to God for my husband and son for their support and encouragement. I also thank God for my parents and my three brothers for my happy and memorable childhood. I'll always remember my beloved mother and my late father for having instilled in me the love of reading and writing from a very early age. I miss my father here on earth, but I will see him again in heaven someday.

Most of all, I am eternally thankful to my Lord and Savior, Jesus Christ, who died on the cross to save me from my sins and rose again from the grave to give me eternal life. Without Him, I can write nothing (John 15:5).

Joyfully in Jesus,
Jan Thompson
John 3:16

# BOOKS BY JAN THOMPSON

Contemporary Christian City, Coastal, and Beach Romance

**Seaside Chapel (7 Books)**
JanThompson.com/seaside
**Savannah Sweethearts (12 Books)**
JanThompson.com/savannah
**Vacation Sweethearts (8 Books)**
JanThompson.com/vacation
**Midtown Christmas (4 Books)**
JanThompson.com/christmas

Christian Romantic Suspense and Near-Future Technothrillers

**Protector Sweethearts (6 Books)**
JanThompson.com/protector
**Defender Sweethearts (6 Books)**
JanThompson.com/defender
**Binary Hackers (4 Books)**
JanThompson.com/binary

Subscribe to Jan Thompson's mailing list:
JanThompson.com/newsletter

# PROTECTOR SWEETHEARTS

Private investigator Helen Hu and her associates specialize in searching for missing persons and hunting for lost treasures. Join them in their adventure suspense around the world in *USA Today* bestselling author Jan Thompson's Protector Sweethearts, a series of Christian Romantic Suspense with a side of mystery.

Protector Sweethearts is a spin-off of Savannah Sweethearts and Vacation Sweethearts.

JanThompson.com/protector

- Book 1: *Once a Thief*

- Book 2: *Once a Hero*
- Book 3: *Once a Spy*
- Book 4: *Twice a Fighter*
- Book 5: *Twice a Convict*
- Book 6: *Twice a Soldier*

## DEFENDER SWEETHEARTS

Defender Sweethearts is a sister series to the Protector Sweethearts Christian romantic suspense collection. While the heroes in Protector Sweethearts search for lost treasures and lost people, the Defender Sweethearts novels focus on protecting the helpless and hopeless. The main characters in Defender Sweethearts come from the supporting cast in Protector Sweethearts.

JanThompson.com/defender

- Book 1: *Never a Traitor*

- Book 2: *Never a Hostage*
- Book 3: *Never a Fugitive*
- Book 4: *Always a Maverick*
- Book 5: *Always a Champion*
- Book 6: *Always a Guardian*

# BINARY HACKERS

Like more suspense with your Christian romance? Like to read suspense thrillers? If you're looking for clean near-future romantic suspense without compromising the Christian faith, these books are for you.

From *USA Today* bestselling author Jan Thompson come these inspirational near-future cyberthrillers combining technothriller and romance, starting with Binary Hackers that feature computer specialists living at the edge of cyberspace, where they have to juggle being law-abiding truth-telling Christians while carrying out their assignments by any and all means possible.

The Binary Hackers series is set in the same story world as Jan's other books, and characters from the other series may make cameo appearances in this series and vice versa.

JanThompson.com/binary

- Book 1: *Zero Sum*
- Book 2: *Zero Day*
- Book 3: *Zero Base*
- Book 4: *Zero Trust*

# SEASIDE CHAPEL

Welcome to *USA Today* bestselling author Jan Thompson's Seaside Chapel Christian beach romance series. These novels are set on real-life St. Simon's Island, Georgia—a beach town where history is all around and the future is a moment away—and the neighboring fictitious Seaside Island, where the rich and famous live.

Savor the small-town atmosphere and the warm southern beaches of St. Simon's Island and the idyllic Golden Isles along the Atlantic Ocean. Enjoy the music of the orchestra and hymns of the church, and hang out with our Christian friends who attend Seaside Chapel, a little church by the sea known for its beach weddings and fair share of love and life.

As these Christians grow in their knowledge and

understanding of God, they are tested in their spiritual maturity, their love lives, and their relationships with others. Share their heartaches and healing, and cheer them on as they celebrate faith, family, and friends.

JanThompson.com/seaside

- Book 0 (Prequel): *His Surprise Proposal*
- Book 1: *His Longing Heart*
- Book 2: *His Wake-Up Call*
- Book 3: *His Morning Kiss*
- Book 4: *His Quiet Serenade*
- Book 5: *His Waiting Love*
- Book 6: *His Beach Retreat*

## SAVANNAH SWEETHEARTS

Welcome to the new south! From *USA Today* bestselling author Jan Thompson come these clean and wholesome, sweet and inspirational Christian romances set on the romantic beaches of Tybee Island and in the coastal town of Savannah, Georgia. Meet a group of multiracial and multiethnic churchgoing Christians who love the Lord, work hard in their careers, and seek God's will for their love lives. Against a backdrop of ocean, sand, and sun, these inspirational romances showcase aspects of the human need for God and for one another. Have some tea, settle in a comfortable reading chair, and enjoy these sweet celebrations of faith, hope, and love in Jesus Christ.

JanThompson.com/savannah

- Book 1: *Ask You Later* (Artist Romance)
- Book 2: *Know You More* (Multiracial Romance)
- Book 3: *Tell You Soon* (Asian-American Romance with Suspense)
- Book 4: *Draw You Near* (International Romance)
- Book 5: *Cherish You So* (Wheelchair Billionaire Romance)
- Book 6: *Walk You There* (Old-Meets-New Tour Guide Romance)
- Book 7: *Love You Always* (Romance with Suspense)
- Book 8: *Kiss You Now* (Multiracial Romance)
- Book 9: *Find You Again* (Multiracial Romance)
- Book 10: *Wish You Joy* (Christmas-Themed Romance)
- Book 11: *Call You Home* (Deaf Chef Romance)
- Book 12: *Let You Go* (Asian-American Romance with Suspense)

Read *Ask You Later* (Book 1) for free:
JanThompson.com/ask-free

# VACATION SWEETHEARTS

Travel with our friends from Savannah, Georgia, to the coast and to the mountains. Cheer them on as they celebrate the immeasurable grace and undeserved mercy of God through Jesus Christ.

The Vacation Sweethearts novels are a spin-off of Jan's Savannah Sweethearts series, and fans will recognize familiar faces from Riverside Chapel, a church in the coastal city of Savannah, Georgia. In fact, we might even visit the beach town of Tybee Island from time to time to visit old friends and beloved families...

JanThompson.com/vacation

- Book 0 (Prequel): *Time for Me*
- Book 1: *Smile for Me* (International Romance)
- Book 2: *Reach for Me* (Romance with Suspense)
- Book 3: *Wait for Me* (Romance with Suspense)
- Book 4: *Look for Me* (Romance with Suspense)
- Book 5: *Pray for Me* (International Romance)
- Book 6: *Care for Me* (Small Mountain Town Romance)
- Book 7: *Cheer for Me* (International Romance)

Read *Time for Me* (Prequel) for free:
JanThompson.com/time-free

# MIDTOWN CHRISTMAS

Big city romance, small town feel. Four Christian couples minister at Midtown Chapel in metro Atlanta, and Midtown Village, the community of tiny homes for needy families. From November to January every year, this place turns into a Christmas Village for a small-town feel right there in the metropolis of Atlanta, Georgia.

- Book 1: *Let Me Hold You* (Levi Theroux and Maggie Jacobs from *Pray for Me*)
- Book 2: *Let Me Want You* (Erika Song from *Look for Me* and Hiroki Yamada from *Walk You There*)
- Book 3: *Let Me Need You* (Forsythia

McDevitt from *Call You Home* and Owen Grayson from *Find You Again*)

- Book 4: *Let Me Love You* (Leila Patel from *Find You Again*)

# ABOUT JAN THOMPSON

*USA Today* bestselling author Jan Thompson writes clean and wholesome contemporary Christian romance with elements of women's fiction, Christian romantic suspense with an air of mystery, and inspirational international thrillers with threads of sweet Christian romance. Jan's books are for readers who love inspiring stories of faith, hope, and love in Jesus Christ.

Raised on a tropical island in the eastern hemisphere, Jan now lives and writes in the western hemisphere. Her international background gives her a unique multicultural and multiracial perspective to her novels and books. The island has never left her, and she reminisces about beach life in her beach romance novels.

When Jan is not busy writing small-town stories, she writes big-city romantic suspense and international technothrillers, a nod to her previous career in computer science. She weaves technology with human interests, reflecting the current and future digital world. And romance. There's always romance.

Beyond the printed page, Jan is a wife, mother, family scribe, avid reader, occasional artist, erstwhile pianist, and chief of staff to the family cat.

Find out more about Jan Thompson:
JanThompson.com

Subscribe to Jan's book news mailing list:
JanThompson.com/newsletter

For God so loved the world,
that He gave His only begotten Son,
that whosoever believeth in Him should not perish,
but have everlasting life.
—John 3:16